Henry Sutton

Henry Sutton was born in 1963 in Hopton, a small town on the Norfolk and Suffolk border. He worked for an auction house in London and sold shoes in New York before embarking on a career in journalism. He has written for *The Times*, *The Daily Telegraph* and *GQ* and was Travel Editor of *The European* from 1993 to 1996, when he opted to work freelance. His first novel, *Gorleston*, was published in 1995. He is married to a painter and lives in London.

SCEPTRE

Also by Henry Sutton

Gorleston

Bank Holiday Monday

HENRY SUTTON

SCEPTRE

First published in 1996 by Hodder and Stoughton
A division of Hodder Headline PLC
A Sceptre Paperback

British Library Cataloguing in Publication Data

Sutton, Henry, 1963–
  Bank holiday Monday
  1. English fiction – 20th century
  I. Title
  823.9'14 [F]

  ISBN 0 340 64989 5

Typeset by Palimpsest Book Production Limited,
Polmont, Stirlingshire
Printed and bound in Great Britain by
Cox & Wyman Ltd, Reading, Berkshire

Hodder and Stoughton
A division of Hodder Headline PLC
338 Euston Road
London NW1 3BH

To my brother and my father, and to James

'I want to go back to the sea' – 1793
'Tell Hardy to carry me home' – 1805
Horatio Nelson

Alice could imagine the ice squeezing and scraping over the land. A great weight flattening everything. She often thought of how things were shaped. She saw it now, how it was, a repressed land. A land still struggling for breath. The air was thick with fading light and remarkably everyone was quiet. It was as if they had entered a wide but sacred place. A place they knew should not be disturbed. The car was warm and smooth, but Alice had had enough. She wanted to get out into this ancient land, this soft flatness and light. She wanted to tell Henderson to stop. Though she knew they were not quite there, she couldn't see the sea.

'Are we there yet?' Tristram asked.

'Nearly, darling,' Laura replied for the twentieth time, 'nearly.'

'I want to be there now. I feel sick.'

'It's not long.' She wiped his forehead. It was hot and clammy and she thought he might indeed be sick.

There was silence again, apart from the car's low rumble and the wheeze of air passing through a window that wouldn't completely close. Tristram screamed, 'The sea, the sea. I can see the sea.' He wriggled on his seat, the seat-belt cutting into his stomach.

Alice turned to look at Tristram and his mother both strapped to the back seat. She smiled at them. My relatives, how strange, she thought. She turned back to face a great marshland, darkening. Beyond were the browning tops of dunes and the thin strip of shadowy sea that Tristram had caught sight of first.

'It was once called the German Ocean,' said Henderson, who just knew things.

To Alice it was the North Sea, which stretched to the Arctic, a vast whiteness. In the twilight she could make out silvery creeks and channels snaking through the marshes. She thought of the creeks as the last tendrils of the North Sea, stopped finally by solid land, or at least boulder clay left by the last retreating glacier. Alice had been good at geology at school. Geology and art.

The steering wheel was slimy with sweat. Henderson was nervous. He didn't know what, if anything, he would recognise of this place. And for a moment it even occurred to him that he might have confused it with somewhere else, or imagined it all. But when he saw the vast dune that was known as Gun Hill he knew he had been here before. He looked at Alice beside him with relief, his eyes falling on her dark brown hair and eyes. He might have sighed, suddenly realising she was meant to be here too. He wiped his hands on his trousers one at a time so he always had a hand on the wheel. 'Alice, could you check the directions?' He felt strange calling her by her name, asking her for help. He hardly knew her. 'I think we turn right here.' They had reached the coast road. There was no further way forward by car, the marshes quite impassable.

'Yes, right. It's definitely right.' She repeated herself because she wanted to make sure she had been heard. She was unsure of her voice, her accent; she had said little on the way. She held the scrap of paper and map tightly in her hand.

The coast road was narrow and largely enclosed by high hedges. It was suddenly night. Still there were flashes of luminous openness on their left as they passed gates and gaps in the shrubs and brambles. Laura pressed her face against the window and waited for these flashes. Her breath began to cloud a small part of the window and the sudden light on this cloud made it look like frost, she thought. Her son was asleep. She could hear his snuffly sleep breath. It reminded her of how tired she was. She had felt tired for years. She didn't know whether she was looking forward to the long weekend or not, she didn't think it would be much of a rest. Still she was pleased Alice was with them. And she was pleased Carey and Francis were coming. Of course she was. Laura pulled her head away from the window. She looked ahead, at her husband's thinning hair, then Alice next to him with hair so thick that it mocked his. Beyond she saw only the dark blue of the early night in the windscreen. She wanted to see the windmill. She wanted to be there too. Her head ached.

When Henderson had come across the windmill in the brochure he knew it wasn't just by chance. That it was what he had been waiting for. And he knew instantly they had to stay there. For so long whenever he had tried to picture the windmill all he had seen was something small and dark and toy-like, something far, far away, from childhood. Now it was real and glossy and vacant on the August bank holiday weekend. Once he had made the booking he tore the page from the brochure and kept it folded in his wallet, taking it out, staring at the photograph of the windmill continually, trying to see beyond it. He had never been in the windmill as a child and he tried to imagine what it would be like looking out from it, rather than to it: the views that would tumble over the marshes that he used to think went on for ever. As a child, as a teenager, he had stayed in a caravan nearby with his mother and father and sister. The windmill forever on the horizon.

Alice saw the windmill first. While Tristram slept and Laura thought of supper with her eyes closed and Henderson stared blinkered through the headlights' beam, Alice glimpsed the dark shape against the early night sky, not sure what it was at first. She had been wondering how full the moon was and whether the clouds were going to completely clear, when it appeared beyond a coppice on the brow of a slight hill running up from the marshes. She didn't say anything when she realised what it was. Instead she shut her eyes and tried to picture it in daylight, its sails billowing against a blue sky, puffy clouds scudding past, the rumble of the stone crushing and grinding, and flattening. She had come a long way and her mind was shaky with jet lag. She knew the directions were of no more use, but still she held tightly the map and scrap of paper that Henderson had scrawled on. She couldn't let them go, even though she knew the journey was coming to an end. She felt quite unsure of where she really was. Why she was here. She didn't think she was ready to stop just yet.

Henderson slowed in the coppice, which housed a mill and a humped-back bridge. After the bridge he didn't accelerate and the car crawled out of the trees and into the proper night again, burnt brown by the headlights. The windmill was suddenly huge and still and looming in front of them. 'We're here,' he said, turning to look at his wife and child in the back, catching the whites of Alice's eyes on the way round. 'The windmill. Isn't it fantastic?'

Moonlight was seeping through the clouds catching the cap and the sails, and the sails made Alice think of skeletons, not windmills under drifting blue skies. 'It's a bit sombre,' she said, sitting forward. 'Scary.' She shivered as if to emphasise her point. But she was also excited.

'Shsssh.' Laura didn't want Tristram frightened. And suddenly she didn't want them to be here. The windmill was dark and sinister and horrible. Typical of Henderson to have found somewhere like this for us to stay, she thought,

still wondering quite why he had been so keen on it. She
wanted to be in a cosy hotel with friendly staff and hot food
waiting.

There was a gate and Henderson stopped the car so Alice
could get out and open it. Sea air tickled her face and
she felt momentarily light-headed, the sudden change in
atmosphere. She pushed the gate towards the black tower,
which looked sticky in the headlights. The ground was wet.
She thought it must have rained recently. The car swung
in so Alice was blinded by the headlights for a while. After
some time she found she could see to shut the gate and see
the vastness of the marshes spreading out in front of her.
The clouds thinning and the moonlight getting stronger all
the time. The water, weaving and pooling throughout the
marshes, reflecting this. She could smell the sea, hear its
murmur. Though she couldn't see it now. And it occurred
to her then that perhaps the sea wasn't what Henderson
had brought them all this way to see, but this repressed,
difficult land that sank slowly into it.

'It's scary,' Tristram whined, peering through the windscreen. The car headlights had been left on. 'I don't like it,'
he continued. Laura helped him out of the car. He stood on
the wet ground, wobbling, looking up. He yawned, walked
over to the windmill and kicked the tarred brick. Backing off
and looking up again, the sail frames white and motionless
in the night, he said, 'It doesn't work.'

Alice laughed, 'There's no wind.' She thought Tristram
looked sweet, tired-out and obviously confused. She moved
towards him, then hesitated. She wasn't used to children.

'It hasn't worked for years,' said Henderson, wondering
whether Alice really thought it wasn't working because
there was hardly any wind. 'Most windmills don't work
anymore.'

'Why not? Why not?' Tristram demanded, moving forward and kicking the round wall again. 'I want it to work.'

'There's no need for them. Other than to turn them into homes, like this one,' Henderson replied, matter-of-factly.

'Shame,' said Laura quietly. She started to get the bags out of the car, setting them down on the damp grass beside the short dirt drive. Some things shouldn't be changed, she thought. She saw the tiny white-framed windows that ran up the tower, like square portholes. The thin stage that clung around the tower just above head height. Some things are better left alone.

'Wait, Laura,' Henderson shouted, walking away from the car, 'let's open up first.' He disappeared behind the windmill.

Alice looked at Laura standing stiffly by the car, and thought she didn't look very happy. Laura was listening to the sea and a car somewhere, way away, too tired to relax. She took a deep breath, trying to taste the salt in the air. She always felt tense after a long journey and not much to eat. And she knew that if she didn't eat shortly her headache might develop into a migraine. She heard a latch lifting, creaking. Then something scraping over the ground, over stone. Alice thought of a glacier. Tristram felt brave.

Henderson came out of the darkness carrying a large iron key. He held it in both hands, as if to emphasise its weight. 'It was where they said it would be. Tristram, come and look at this,' he said. But Tristram ran to his mother instead, burying his head between her legs. Henderson held the key up anyway, turning it in the insect-thick light of the headlights. It was worn smooth. He went to the low door set square in the wall, and sunk the key into the huge lock. He knew Alice and Laura were staring at him. And he felt shy, stupidly. It took some wiggling before the key engaged and two hands to turn it. There was something familiar about the smell which hit him as he opened the door. A stale sweetness. Though he couldn't place it as he entered the darkness.

*　　*　　*

Francis was throwing thick socks into a bag. 'Will it be cold? I expect it will. That part of the country always is. It'll probably rain as well. Non-stop,' he said, quickly, distractedly. He tucked in two jumpers. Then took one out. He also took out a pair of socks, held them for a while feeling their thickness, then put them back, pushing them into a corner. He was incredibly indecisive. It drove Carey mad.

'What are you doing?' She stopped by the bedroom door on her way out. 'Why don't you bring everything? Go on, stuff it all in.' She knew he hated taking a lot of luggage.

Francis laughed. 'Really, are you taking shorts? Do you think I should take my shorts?' He wasn't sure whether he had really pissed her off or not.

'It's August, Christ. It's still fucking summer.' She went downstairs. She had packed ages ago. It never took her long. She always knew exactly what she needed. She filled the kettle, knowing he would be some time yet, packing, unpacking. They were always late. She was always waiting for Francis. Fucking Francis. Ignoring the rattling kettle she poured herself a glass of white wine from a half empty bottle she had opened the night before. It tasted sharp. She lit a cigarette.

'I'm driving, I suppose?' Francis asked, appearing at the kitchen door with his unzipped bag in one hand and a pile of clothes under an arm. He always drove.

For all her efficiency and competence Carey hated driving. It frightened her. For years she had tried to forget how. 'Would you mind?' She was calm now, resigned to being late, knowing she couldn't get too angry with Francis as he was going to drive. She exhaled slowly.

'Where exactly are we going?' Hell, he said to himself. He liked Laura. Laura was Carey's oldest friend. He had grown fond of her, loyal even. But he couldn't bear Henderson, the way he was so miserable, so stifling. He didn't know what

Laura saw in him. He didn't understand their marriage at all. And then there was Tristram, their child, Carey's godson. He just made Francis glad he and Carey didn't have children.

'You know damn well. It'll be wonderful.' Carey had not been to that part of Norfolk before, but she knew enough about it. She could imagine the vast beaches and marshes. How she could.

'No, the directions. You have got the directions?'

'Of course. It would've taken a little over two hours had we missed the traffic. I've no idea now.'

Francis thought of bank holiday traffic, decrepit drivers, caravans on the motorway. God how he hated caravans.

Going east they passed through Docklands on a new road, wet from rain earlier in the afternoon. Lights were appearing in Canary Wharf, faint in the twilight like early stars. The car windows were wound down but the air was warm and sticky, the rain having done little to clear the heaviness. It had been a hot summer.

The traffic was thinner than Carey had anticipated. Maybe everyone's left already, she thought, left ages ago. She had been dying to leave London for weeks. She felt she couldn't breathe properly. She looked at the office blocks, the see-through structures of steel and glass, and those of stone made to look old. The Light Railway like some toy train threading its way through all this, this bloody grime, she thought. What she really needed was space, openness. Somewhere natural.

She knew there was never much space around Henderson. But she wasn't going to let that spoil her weekend. Norfolk was large enough, and she loved Laura. When they were children they liked to think they were sisters, neither had real sisters. It didn't matter that they looked quite different, or that they had different parents. They were inseparable. And much later, after Laura had married Henderson, they still occasionally called each other sister on the telephone.

'Hello sister,' Carey would say. Laura would whisper 'sister' into the mouthpiece. She didn't want Henderson to hear. He had once shouted at her for calling Carey her sister, 'Why can't you grow up? She's not your bloody sister. If you had a proper sister you'd know why. It's quite different. You'd probably hate her.' Laura had told Carey about this and ever since then Carey thought he was probably jealous of her. But she knew Laura was more than a sister.

London soon levelled out and fields emerged beside the motorway and the yellowness in the dim air turned blue. Francis couldn't leave London without feeling sad, missing the noise and the dirt and the possibility. Now he was going to the country, which he knew would be wet and windy and uncomfortable. Why? he asked himself, without answering. Why? He supposed the others would be there by now, Laura and Henderson and bloody Tristram. And Alice, who he had to admit at least sounded interesting. He had heard she was an artist, a painter. And that she was a relative of Laura's who had recently returned from Australia. He wondered about Australia as he flicked in and out of the traffic, driving too close to cars that got in his way, flashing his headlights. He didn't think he would like it. The empty spaces. The heat and the hole in the ozone. Nature. All those snakes and every other imaginable poisonous creature. It wasn't his thing at all.

Henderson ran his hand down the cold wall feeling for the light switch. It was an old metal switch, stiff as anything, salted up. Then it struck him, the roundness of the room. He knew it was going to be round, of course, but still he found it odd. 'Look how round it is,' he shouted, laughing. Laura and Tristram and Alice were just behind him, trying to look past him. He moved into the room. There was a large, round dining table in the middle surrounded by old wooden chairs. Side tables, chests of drawers and cupboards, all chipped and scratched, lined the walls awkwardly jutting out. A faded map was pinned above a desk. The ceiling was low and crossed with heavy beams. A lantern hung from a beam to the edge of the ceiling. Tristram set off round the table skipping. There was a small door across the room and some stairs just by the door they had come in. Henderson didn't know which way to go, where to explore first. He felt as if he were in a dream, the others not really there. Yet he felt in control. He felt if he concentrated hard enough on his dream he would be able to drift wherever he wanted. Through the door or up the stairs, through time even. He decided he had to go up. Up the tower. See what he could see. But he hesitated, not quite ready to set off on his own, not trusting his imagination, not trusting himself.

It was better than Alice had imagined. More real. More solid: the thickness of the beams, the stone floor, the worn, heavy furniture. She felt for a moment, oddly, that time was slipping backwards, and that she could feel the history of the place, the presence of past inhabitants. She shut her eyes, trying to see these others, inhaling the strange sweet, stale air. But no one came to mind. At least no one unexpected. Tristram skipping and sliding around the room putting her off.

The main light was dim and Laura could discern Henderson's car's headlights coming into the room through one of the square portholes, brightening a patch of wall. Of course, there are no dark corners, Laura thought. She felt better about the windmill now she was inside. She felt safer, more secure than she had imagined she would. She watched her son, glad he no longer seemed scared. He was excited and it was late but she didn't mind he wasn't in bed. He had never been in a windmill before. She had tried to describe a windmill to him before they had left. She had told him that windmills were found in wide open spaces where the wind was strong. They are all over Holland, she had told him, and Norfolk where we're going to this weekend. That windmills had sails that went round and round, like the hands of a big clock. She had tried to impersonate this, windmilling her arms, thinking time would be going very quickly. He had asked why windmills do this, and she had had to think for a minute before telling him to grind corn for flour. Then she had told him that windmills were like great sailing ships of the land that didn't go anywhere. She had read that description somewhere. But she hadn't thought to tell him that windmills didn't work anymore.

Tristram was becoming dizzy and slowing down, bumping into the chairs and cupboards. 'Tristram, Tristram, stop,' Laura said, grabbing hold of him, his jumper. He looked at his mother, somehow knowing he was the most important thing in her life. She ruffled his curly fair hair, suddenly feeling self-conscious. Sensing Henderson and Alice wanted to look around, Laura said they should get the stuff in from the car first. She needed to cook Tristram's supper, and her own at least. Her headache was like waves breaking.

'Of course,' said Alice, shaking her head, realising she had been day-dreaming. She wanted to be helpful, and for Laura to like her. She had thought time would not have been such an obstacle, and that the memories they had of each other and the fact that they were cousins would overcome the years. Though in reality Alice had very few memories of Laura. But one was overriding. It was from a party, a birthday, a Christmas? Christmas probably. She wasn't sure. It didn't matter. Laura was wearing a brown smock and red tights. They were playing a game with other children, and they were running round in a circle wildly, and laughing. They were all holding hands and Alice was holding Laura's hand very tightly. It was slippery and she was terrified Laura would let go and fall because they were going so fast. After the game Laura rushed outside to be sick. It had been snowing and she was sick in the snow.

Alice watched her from a window inside. As the years passed Laura grew taller in her brown smock and red tights, her laugh louder, more uncontrollable. The snow became whiter and purer and Alice felt more and more responsible. She felt she could have stopped her from being sick, at least have comforted her. She knew she had harmed her in some way. And when she realised she had to leave Australia, she kept thinking of Laura and that she could come back and make everything all right, at least go back to a time when games were played by children, even if they did make you sick. And she ran towards her, because there was no one else, hoping, and escaping.

On her way to England another recollection came to her. Laura falling off a swing and cutting her head, blood trickling down her face and smudging on her summer dress. She went with Laura and Laura's mother to the doctor's. She wasn't allowed to watch but she heard Laura scream as the wound was stitched. Then Laura came out from behind a screen bandaged and pale. The doctor said the scar would not be bad and when she was grown up nobody would notice it. But the flight was long and Alice was sleeping on and off. So she thought it might have been just a dream. She told herself to look carefully at Laura's forehead to see if there was a scar, however tiny. Then she fell asleep again forgetting to remember to look at Laura's forehead.

It was cool outside, the car already covered in a film of dew. Henderson had forgotten how cold it could get here in the summer at night. He breathed deeply, expecting to remember the smell of sea air. He opened his mouth, wanting to taste it. But his mouth was dry and there was just this bitter taste. He had drunk too much black coffee earlier, waiting for Alice to return from the West End so they could leave. He was used to waiting, it always took a long time getting Tristram ready, for Laura to worry about everything. Though today as he waited he felt increasingly anxious. As if they were going to miss a train or a plane. He kept thinking, hurry up, hurry up or we'll miss it. On the motorway he thought it must have been the coffee that had made him so anxious, that he should watch how much he drank. Not that he couldn't leave without Alice.

Alice had noticed that Henderson was agitated in the car, his neck red. She had admitted that she had got lost, finding London bafflingly large and loud. She had felt more disorientated than she could ever remember, more even than the first time she had stepped into the outback. She said she would need much more time to get used to the people and the traffic. The geography. She had brought maps with her and she kept looking at these maps, street maps, tube maps, maps of Britain. But they didn't make things much clearer. She couldn't focus on them properly. Her eyes watering in the thick summer smog. Still she bought another map from Stanfords.

Alice and Henderson carried in the bags and the box of food, Henderson returning to switch the headlights off and lock the car. And he stood for a moment looking at the windmill. Light from the ground floor window seeped up the black tower catching the useless sails. How peaceful it all looks, he thought. How calm the evening is.

By the end of the motorway it was dark. 'We're about half-way,' Carey announced. She wound the window down a short way and breathed in heavily. 'God, you can smell the difference already.' She didn't light a cigarette for some time, until the car was quite engulfed in the night, made even thicker by tall trees either side of the narrow road. She was excited, the weekend getting under way. She had never stayed in a windmill before. She was looking forward to the views, all the way round. And at night-time too, when surely it would be like an observatory, the domed top, closer to the stars, just the telescope to imagine.

Carey only smoked because she lived in London, at least that's what she told herself and Francis. But she couldn't help smoking now, now they were rushing through the countryside. It felt so good to be out of the city she needed to celebrate.

The trees ended and they were moving across open land. The sky had largely cleared and Carey could see stars and the moon which was nearly full. She could tell it would be full by Sunday night, or Monday. She loved the night sky and missed not seeing it in London.

Francis didn't know why Carey always had to smoke in the car. It drove him mad. He wound his window down, right down to make a point. The air was cool and the smoke dispersed quickly. The air was very cool. He now regretted leaving his other jumper behind. And he couldn't imagine it would be hot enough to wear shorts. 'Why do you have to smoke so much?' he said, but he wasn't expecting an answer and he didn't get one. Still he couldn't understand her smoking now, having gone on and on about wanting to be in the countryside for the fresh air. 'I don't understand you,' he said.

They didn't talk much and Francis felt increasingly lonely on the rough road. They hadn't come across another car for some time now. He wondered whether they might have taken a wrong turning and that they were lost. But Carey was directing and she never made a mistake. Sometimes he wished she would. 'Maybe we're on the wrong road?' he said. 'Perhaps we're lost?'

'We're not. I know exactly where we are.'

'Where?'

'Here.' She turned on the map light and stuck her finger on the map which was spread across her knees and fluttering in the draught. He knew he wouldn't be able to see what she was pointing at so he didn't bother to look. 'Here. It's not far now. Please shut that bloody window.'

Francis knew the windmill would be draughty. He couldn't imagine it not being. 'You might as well get used to the draught,' he said. And he wondered why they weren't staying in a hotel, a small hotel which served large breakfasts. He hated the idea of self-catering. He imagined Carey organising the washing-up rota. He'd probably have to wash-up with Henderson. Fuck it.

Laura found the kitchen through the small door at the far side of the sitting-room. It was in the cottage attached to the tower, and it was cold and damp. She put the box of food on a counter and opened the cupboard below the sink, as if by habit. Inside was a blue bucket, turning white with bleach and calcium. She picked up a dried cloth, crunched it, and threw it in the sink. She smelt her hands afterwards and smelt the staleness of the cloth, a sick smell. Tristram had rushed past her in the cottage and she went to find him, not wanting to cook now.

Next to the kitchen was a room with a large wooden cot and a table. On the table was a stained leaflet. It was a guide to local birds and Laura flicked through it, the careful drawings, trying to spot the differences between common terns and sandwich terns, marsh harriers and oyster-catchers. She read about the terns, how they are sometimes referred to as sea swallows. How they feed on the flood and ebb tides in the creeks and lagoons, diving many feet for young herring and sand eels. That they come in April and nest in the dunes and on the shingle ridges of Scolt Head Island. She read that sandwich terns pair for life, though the pair bond is broken outside the breeding season when they leave Scolt Head by the end of August for Africa. Laura found herself wondering if they ever couldn't remember who they were meant to be with when they returned here. She thought she would look out for the terns, see if she could spot any wandering across the shingle ridges that looked like they had been forgotten or forgotten who they should be with.

Tristram was in the bathroom. He had found a dry, cracked piece of soap and he was trying to push it down the plug-hole. He looked guiltily at his mother. But Laura didn't take in what he was doing, she was still thinking of the terns, how to identify them. Black legs and shaggy crest, short tail, yellow tip to black bill, she repeated to herself. 'What else have you found?' she asked Tristram, finally.

'There's a room with old tins in it and there's a toilet. I'm hungry.'

'Let's just see what's up the stairs, shall we?'

'I'm hungry, Mummy.'

There were some narrow stairs by the bathroom and Laura wanted to have a look, thinking she might as well see all the cottage now as she'd probably be spending much of her time in it, cooking, washing up. 'Come on Tristram, let's look upstairs. You never know what we might find.' But there was nothing to find. The upstairs room was empty except for an old single bed that sank in the middle and was covered with a rough, thin blanket. There were no cupboards and no curtains. And Laura couldn't see anything outside, the bare bulb reflecting on the black glass.

'I'm not sleeping here,' said Tristram. 'Urrgh, it's horrible.'

'It's all right, you won't have to. No one will be sleeping here. There are enough bedrooms in the windmill.' She and Henderson had worked out where everybody was sleeping with the brochure beforehand.

'Laura?' Alice shouted. She was in the kitchen below and could hear Laura and Tristram. 'Can I help?' she shouted.

'I don't know,' Laura shouted back. 'Come on Tristram let's go down. Let's cook supper.'

Henderson felt he could wait no longer, knowing he had to

be brave, face whatever there might be there, and he rushed up the steep stairs that curled round the tower two at a time, feeling for light switches, flicking them instinctively. On the fourth or fifth floor, he didn't know how many floors he had climbed, the stairs ended and there was a ladder leading to a trap-door in the ceiling above. He clambered up the ladder, praying the trap-door would open. He hated the thought of not being able to get to the very top, having got this far. He pushed and the heavy wooden slab opened. He didn't move further up the ladder for a few moments, waiting for his eyes to grow accustomed to the dimness. He then eased his way into the room. He found a light switch. The room was quite bare, the walls covered with whitewash that had gone green with damp in places. In other places it had flaked off leaving red brick and piles of dirty white shavings and dust on the floor. There was a large stone four-pointed star in the centre of the floor. The stone was smooth, glinting directly under the electric light. There were four windows, evenly spaced around the room, the points of the star pointing to the windows. Henderson moved to one and looked out. He didn't know which way he was facing at first, inland, or out across the marshes. After some time he could tell he was looking inland, through the white struts of a sail. He could see the lights of a few distant houses, the glow of a village. The moonlight was strong now and hedges and trees lining fields cast shadows. He walked across the room to the opposite window, his pulse quickening. He pressed his face against the window, feeling the cold glass and the draught curling through gaps in the rotten frame. Slowly channels and creeks appeared, moonlight on the water. Nearer the windmill, the thick, dark line of a flood bank.

I'm really here, Henderson said to himself, his breath moistening the window. I've come back to Norfolk. He felt alone at the top of the windmill. Quite alone. Which is what he wanted this moment, not wanting to be observed.

He stepped back from the window and saw himself, like a shadow, in the wet glass. He supposed he had known for a long while that he would have to come back one day. He wiped the wet his breath had made on the window, smudging himself. He didn't know whether it was too late. Above him an iron cogwheel appeared to have spliced through the beams, like a giant circular saw. There were other cogwheels and pieces of machinery suspended somehow with it. And there was another ladder leading up to a small platform set amid these workings of the windmill, that no longer worked. He started to climb the last ladder.

'No, I just see nothing,' Francis said. He couldn't make out much that wasn't within the headlights' beam. He didn't want to either.

Carey could see the faint ridge of the sand dunes and she wanted Francis to see it too. 'But, you must see it,' she said. She reached across and stroked the back of his neck, feeling the downy hair. 'Never mind.' She could sense he was fed up with the journey. 'We're nearly there.' She stopped stroking his neck with a pat and ruffled his hair, the way she would ruffle Tristram's. 'Isn't it a beautiful night? I have a feeling we're in for a great weekend.' All summers should end like this, she thought.

'Please,' Francis said, shaking his head, 'do you have to?'

Tristram played on the floor with his truck that lit up. The floor was sandy but Tristram didn't mind because it was a tough truck and he imagined the truck was travelling across Australia, which was mostly desert. And kangaroos. He didn't want to run over any kangaroos, so he pushed the truck across the lino carefully, watching out for kangaroos, and other Australian animals which he couldn't remember the names of. He loved animals and he loved to draw them at school. He was looking forward to playing on the beach. He wished he had a friend to play with though. Maybe Alice will play with me, he thought. She's nice.

Alice walked across the kitchen floor, feeling the grains of sand on it, minding out for Tristram and his truck, remembering for some reason stepping off the aeroplane. God she'd felt awful, her skin stretched and dehydrated, yet her nose runny. She hadn't taken her clothes off for two days and they were filthy and a part of her. And there had been the strange sensation of standing on solid ground, ground she had been born on which hadn't felt solid at all. She could feel movement even now, as if she were still being propelled forward, unable to stop, which in a way she was. She remembered standing in the airport concourse trying not to wobble, waiting for Laura, a gangly girl in a brown smock and red tights. And then Laura had appeared at last not looking like Laura. She was someone else completely and Alice had suddenly felt very young and small. Laura looked like a mother. Laura's mother. And Alice knew then she had to keep travelling, and she nearly ran off wanting to be invisible, stronger than anything.

Alice helped Laura unpack the box of food and cook. Neither liked cooking much. They each found the easiest things to prepare, mostly in silence. Steam rose from a saucepan of boiling water and they both went to pick up the packet of spaghetti on the counter, their hands touching. Alice let go first leaving Laura to open the packet and bend the spaghetti into the boiling water. Laura flinched each time a drop of water splashed onto her hand. 'Cooking's not my forte,' she said.

'Neither mine,' said Alice. 'I didn't cook much at home.' She looked away, at Tristram on the floor. She couldn't think of anything else to say, so hard was she trying to think of something to say, wondering who was the most shy, thinking Laura's cloudy blue eyes were sad, dull even. Her fair hair thin and lifeless. Wondering if this is what happens to you when you marry, when you have children. Or whether it's because you've just had enough.

Laura was still unnerved by how different Alice was to whom she had been expecting. She had thought she'd be much larger and louder, more determined, more decisive. She had imagined being whisked off by Alice, an Alice who was full of energy and bursting to see everything. How everything had changed. Because Laura could remember being pulled around by Alice before, at parties, on the beach, everywhere. And she could remember not being able to keep up, Alice being so much bigger and stronger. Alice had made her sick once, Laura remembered now. She had been flinging her round and round a room, she wouldn't let go, hurting her wrist badly, and when she'd finally struggled free she'd had to rush outside to be sick. It had been snowing and she remembered looking up from the pool of sick that had melted the snow and seeing Alice watching her from a window inside. She didn't know why she remembered being sick now. The smell of cooking? Food sometimes made her sick.

At the airport Laura had initially been shocked by how old, how grown-up Alice looked, then how beautiful, a graceful, slightly withdrawn, pale beauty. Her eyes were much darker than she had remembered, deeper, and over the next few days she couldn't help looking into those eyes to see if she really was the same person, the same fat, boisterous little girl. Laura thought she seemed so quiet and gentle now, so disorientated. And Laura felt mildly guilty that she hadn't thought more about Alice over the years, their families having drifted apart. She had been surprised that Alice had chosen to come and stay with her.

There was nothing more to be done in the kitchen for a while, the sauce simmering. Alice urgently wanted to look around the windmill. She felt she was missing out, not wanting Henderson to discover everything first. 'I think I'll go and have a look round, if that's OK?' she asked Laura.

'Yellow tip to black bill,' Laura said softly as she stirred the pasta with a fork.

'What?'

'Oh, sorry. Yes. What did you say?'

'I thought I would go and have a look round, if there's nothing more I can do for the moment?'

'Oh, of course. But don't be too long. If you find Henderson tell him supper will be ready soon.'

Alice waved at Tristram still pushing his truck on the floor, then she stepped back into the windmill, pausing by the faded map pinned above the desk. It was a large-scale map of the area. The land had gone a dirty cream colour, the odd contour a faint orange. Someone had circled the windmill in red biro. It stood just in the cream, an area of muddy green spreading out from it. The dull green was fanned with thin, turquoise lines, and in places there were dots of turquoise too, like small birds. Beyond this were soft shapes of sandy orange stretching far into the rest of the map which was all turquoise, all sea. The light was bad, the map faded and Alice didn't pause by it for long, believing she had a better example.

On the first floor she found two large bedrooms, one bedroom with two bunk beds in it. In the other bedroom there was a side table in between the two single beds. She opened the drawer. Faded newspaper lined the bottom. She felt to the end, but found nothing but dust and grit and sand. There were two smaller bedrooms on the next floor, both with two single beds in each and no cupboards. She looked under one of the beds and found an old sock. It was a child's sock, a girl's sock. It had once been white, but seemed to have developed rust in patches. She flung the sock back under the bed and left the room. The stairs seemed to get

narrower and steeper, though Alice thought that that might
be because her legs were tiring. There was just one bedroom
on the next floor and a small landing. The room had three
bare black windows, the fourth window on the floor being
outside the door by the stairway. The room didn't feel as if
it had been used for some time. It looked quite undisturbed,
still, the air heavy with dust and something indescribable.
It was where she wanted to sleep. She sat on one of the
single beds, there were two separated by a small cupboard,
and lay back gazing at the wooden beams dappled with
damp and wood worm. The bed creaked and sagged as she
tried to get comfortable, her eyes falling on the light bulb
dangling from a beam. She shut her eyes and saw nothing
but orange. Sand.

She heard someone moving above and sprang upright,
her hand brushing the film of dust on the cupboard as
she balanced herself. The footsteps were directly above her
now. She knew it was Henderson, but she still thought it
might not be, that it could be someone from the past or
an intruder. She stood up and went out of the room. She
climbed the stairs, compelled, not nervous.

Henderson was leaning against a bookcase, flicking
through a book.

'Hello,' Alice said. It was a large book and she could make
out drawings, engravings, from where she was.

'Sea holly grows here,' he said, without looking up.
'It's quite blue. I remember it, sharp as anything. We
must look out for it.' He turned some more pages. 'And
there's sea kale, sea bindweed and horned poppy. I don't
remember those.' He continued turning the pages, but
slowly. 'Oh, yes,' he said excitedly, suddenly reminded
of more things he had seen before, 'there'll be plenty
of flowering sea lavenders, swathes of mauve across the
marshes. And samphire.' He looked at her. 'Do you know
what samphire is?'

'No.' Alice edged into the room.

'It's like this seaweed, well not really seaweed, some people call it sea asparagus. It grows all over the saltmarshes here, best on the land that's only covered by spring tides.' He wasn't looking at the book now. He was looking at Alice and beyond Alice, the whitewashed walls that he thought could do with another coat. 'You can eat it.' He could recall the stalks of samphire he would pull from between his teeth. His mouth and face covered in butter and bits of samphire, butter dribbling down his chin. He put the book on the table. 'I can taste it now.' Butter and salt. He wiped his mouth without realising. Butter and salt.

'We must pick some,' Alice said.

'Yes. There's Nelson.' Suddenly not wanting to share his recollection, he pointed to a bad print of Nelson, white hair, epaulettes, medals, two eyes. It wasn't possible to tell whether he had two complete arms. 'He was born near here.' Samphire, he said to himself. What a beautiful word.

They were in a sitting-room at the top of the windmill, and Alice realised how lovely and homely it was. There was an old rug on the floor, sagging armchairs, battered wooden chairs, a small round table, and faded and dusty hardback books in bookcases around the room. Some books having spilt onto the floor. 'What's up there?' Alice pointed to the ladder leading to the trap-door.

'Nothing. Just an empty, damp room and another ladder leading to old bits of windmill machinery and a small door in the roof. I couldn't open it. It doesn't look safe.' He didn't want anyone else going into the room. It was his place, a place where he felt he could be on his own, removed from everything, and think. Besides he had found it first.

'Supper's nearly ready,' Alice said.

'Yes, I must go down and help.' Henderson left the room, a taste of salt still in his mouth. 'Coming?' he shouted.

'In a minute.' Alice had to go to the top before supper. She couldn't stop having got this near. She climbed the ladder and pushed open the heavy trap-door. Henderson wasn't going to put her off. She pulled herself into the room, running her back against the wall. She found the light switch, and found her arms and bottom were covered with white dust. She tried to brush it off, then gave up, suddenly feeling very calm. She walked around the edge a couple of times as quietly as possible, not wanting to disturb anything, wondering why there was a stone star in the centre of the floor. She stood on it and swivelled, her arms outstretched, feeling the old air for substance, something she could hold on to. She stopped and the room seemed to sigh, and she was dizzy.

She saw the cogwheel and other bits of corroding machinery falling through the beams above, and the final ladder leading to a small platform and the door. She had to duck on the platform, the roof shaped like a bell. She wondered when these wheels had last turned and who would have been up here doing what. She touched the main cogwheel, running her hand along the rim and then across the cogs, her fingers flipping. The cogs were cold and rough, not sharp but rusty. She took her hand away, as if she had touched something she shouldn't have, and wiped it on her jeans leaving a dark stain along her right thigh. The door rattled as she shook the small handle. Wind blew through the cracks. She shook harder but it still didn't open. There was a lock, but she didn't think the door was locked, it seemed stuck at the bottom. She turned round on the platform and kicked backwards with her right foot. The door moved slightly. She kicked again and it flung open, a gust of air rushing in. Holding onto the frame she turned and saw there was a small platform outside. It was vaguely luminous. She got down on her knees because she thought it would be safer and crawled out onto the fanstage, wind seemingly blowing from every direction, but not strong. Above her was the fantail. She could have stood up had she moved further out and to the side, but she remained on her knees near the entrance.

Looking down through the gaps in the platform she could see the windmill's tower, dark and slippery, descend to the ground far below. In front of her were the marshes, reflective and wavering. To her right she saw the lights of the staithe cottages. And she thought of oil lamps and people from a different time. She wondered how much the land had changed since they were built. She knew she was in a transient, shifting place. And she thought she'd have to get working on her map as soon as it was daylight, so she would have her own record of how it was one August weekend. Then she would at least be able to place herself there, somewhere. She began to picture her map, shades of green, and yellow and blue. Shadows perhaps of other times. She saw car headlights travelling along the coast road, coming towards the windmill. A flickering.

Laura hated it when Henderson tried to help. He was always wanting to add more salt or butter, or wanting to know why she hadn't yet drained the pasta. Sometimes she just hated to stand so close to him in a warm kitchen. She said he could help best if he played with Tristram. That was better than helping her cook, but not much. Henderson wasn't very good at playing with Tristram. And Tristram didn't like playing with his father, she sensed. Henderson had always been awkward with Tristram, expecting him to perform or behave like a child who was much older. And there was a distance, Laura believed, that he deliberately kept between himself and his son, as if that were the only way in which his son would be able to respect him. He told her as much. Henderson's father had been distant and strict with his children, Henderson was no different, she often thought.

Henderson pushed the truck to Tristram, fast. Tristram missed the truck and it crashed into the wall, the lights dimming and then going out. Henderson couldn't understand why Tristram was so unco-ordinated. Where he got it from, this lack of balance. Henderson went over and picked up the truck and fiddled with the undercarriage until the lights came back on. He smiled at Tristram who had been staring at him. He pushed the truck to his son once more, this time slowly. Henderson loved Tristram, of course he did, he was his son. But he believed he shouldn't get too close, that distance was sometimes better, more appropriate perhaps, than closeness. 'I'll open some wine,' Henderson said, turning away from Tristram.

'Can you call Alice?' Laura asked.

He walked to the door, but before he got there it opened and Alice stepped out of the windmill and into the kitchen covered in dust and rust and dirty whitewash. 'I've just been to the very top,' she said, smiling broadly. 'I managed to open the door and there is this little platform that juts right out. I crawled onto it. There's an incredible view, even in this light. I can't wait until tomorrow.' She couldn't help telling them about it. She felt quite elated, the fresh air, the danger. Daylight looming in her mind, forcing back the shadows.

Henderson was annoyed he hadn't managed to open the door. 'I should think that platform's rotten. I'm sure it's incredibly unsafe. I'd better have a look at it in the morning. It's called the fanstage anyway.'

'I don't think we should talk about it now,' Laura said, looking at Tristram, a wave of pain sloshing across her mind.

They sat down to eat. Laura wasn't hungry now, she was past that, but she knew she had to eat. She helped Tristram with his food then toyed with hers. Alice helped herself to a huge plateful, she was hungry. Henderson thought of samphire as he filled his mouth with buttery pasta, samphire and his sister and father and mother. Family holidays. What held families together, what split them apart. The caravan. The bloody caravan. He laughed, nervously to himself.

Carey tried to imagine they had a child and that it was sleeping in the back, wondering really whether she and Francis would have children. She often thought about it. She couldn't decide whether she wanted them with him or not. It was the only thing she was indecisive about, children and Francis.

Francis pulled onto the grass behind Henderson's car and stopped with an unnecessary jerk, the wheels instantly turning the grass to mud. 'Thank God,' he said. An uneasy feeling about the whole weekend had been growing inside him on the way down, and as he got out of the car and looked up at the windmill he didn't feel any happier about it. 'Typical Henderson,' he said. 'Just look at this place.' The tower seemed to drip with blackness and bad omens.

Carey was looking up at the sky. Now the headlights were off she thought she could see craters on the moon and the Milky Way. The air was thick and proper, the sea audibly present. 'It's lovely,' she said. 'You just don't appreciate nature. The great outdoors. Ha, well we're here.'

They banged on the door and no one heard them. They've probably been murdered, thought Francis. He turned the thick handle and they stepped into the sitting-room which didn't smell so stale now, Francis immediately finding, like Laura, the roundness comforting. This is not a place to be leapt upon, he thought. There are no dark corners. No intruders here. He instantly felt happier about the windmill.

Carey liked the old furniture. Things need to be used, worn, she thought. What a great place for children. 'Hello,' she shouted. 'Hello.'

Henderson suddenly appeared through the kitchen door, a glass of wine slopping in his hand. 'You've made it. Well done. Come in.'

We're already in, thought Francis.

'I'm afraid we've started supper. We couldn't wait, Laura was getting a headache and we've got to get Tristram off to bed, otherwise he'll be hell tomorrow.'

He'll be hell anyway, thought Francis.

'Yes, of course you have,' said Carey.

'Funny old place isn't it? Come through, we've kept some food warm for you.'

They followed Henderson through the kitchen and into the room with the cot and the small table, which the others were squashed around. The room was hot and steamy, condensation dripping down the windows, drops clinging to the ceiling, then falling. Francis saw Alice first, struck by her, her thick brown hair and eyebrows, her shiny deep eyes. She got up and so did Laura and Tristram, Tristram rushing to Carey, grabbing hold of her legs, pulling her down to him. Carey tried to reach Laura, but she couldn't walk, anchored by Tristram. Laura went over to her instead, and kissed her on the cheek, whispering in her ear how pleased she was she was here. Francis introduced himself to Alice, holding out his hand. He could detect a hint of an Australian accent when she said, 'I'm Alice.' Softer than he had imagined though, realising he had imagined her speaking.

'I don't know why we're all crowded round this table,' said Laura, returning to her seat. She did, she found it cosy. 'We should be in the sitting-room.'

'It doesn't matter for tonight,' said Carey, 'we'll fit.'

They rearranged themselves, knees and shoulders rubbing, elbows getting in the way. Tristram, over-excited and not at all tired, fidgeted next to Carey. Carey thought Alice, who was sitting opposite, looked familiar. She reminded her of someone. It wasn't the eyes or the hair, perhaps the mouth. But she couldn't recall who. Francis couldn't decide whether he wanted a beer or wine. He was thirsty but he had drunk a lot of beer that week. Alice was drinking wine so he settled for the same, reaching across her for the bottle. 'Sorry,' he said, realising, too late, he might have been rude.

'How's business?' Henderson asked Francis, pleased that grown-up male company had arrived, even if it were Francis.

Francis hated being asked this question, and Henderson always asked it, as if he knew what really bothered him. Francis looked at Carey, wearily. 'It's much the same.' He knew he wasn't very successful, he'd been in the same job for too long, not managing to find anything more rewarding in his field. 'Secure, I suppose,' he added, as usual. He didn't know why Henderson couldn't ask Carey, Carey was much more successful and interested in business than he was. He often thought he might do something completely different, not that he had told Carey. She wouldn't have understood. 'How are you enjoying this country?' he asked Alice, wishing to change the subject.

Alice thought for a while. 'I'm still trying to get my feet. London's very confusing. It's not much how I remember it.' She looked at Francis, his thick curly brown hair, brown eyes. He could be my brother, she thought. 'Though it's all very exciting, particularly the countryside, being here.' She looked away, wondering whether she had sounded enthusiastic enough. She had eaten all the food she had mounded on her plate and now felt like lying down. 'But tiring.' She felt heavy, her limbs ached, as if she had wandered a long way over sand.

Laura waited until everybody had finished eating before she took Tristram to bed. Carey offered to help, though Laura said that that would only hinder things. 'Tristram will never go to sleep if you're there.' She left the warmth of the cottage and entered the windmill, dim and cool, and not half as friendly as her first impressions on entering it had led her to believe. She held Tristram's hand as they rounded the sitting-room, not letting go as they climbed the stairs.

But he wasn't scared. 'Can we go to the top, to the fanstage?' he asked.

'No.'

'Why not?'

'It's dangerous. Maybe tomorrow. Come and look at your bunk bed.' She found his bedroom, just as the brochure had described, next to Henderson's and hers on the first floor. There were two bunk beds and Tristram climbed to the top of one of them. 'Not up there darling.'

'Yes, yes.' Tristram screamed and jumped up and down on the flimsy mattress.

She said he could sleep on the top if he went straight to sleep and promised not to get out of bed until the morning. Though she couldn't just leave him in the cold tower on his own so she read him a story about a Mr Business who took an extraordinary plane ride. It was a long story, but with a happy ending. Tristram loved it and she had to finish it before tucking him in with a couple of other books and his rabbit that had gone floppy and moulted over the years. My lovely little boy, I'll not be far away. I'll always protect you, she said to herself, leaving Tristram with the light on. She then went into her bedroom, pleased that there were two single beds, tired of being woken by Henderson's restlessness and nightmares. She pushed down on one of the beds. It creaked loudly.

The conversation had slowed by the time Laura returned, tiredness having crept over them all like the mist that would finally drift over the marshes and absorb the fading moonlight. They were all eager to get to bed, eager for tomorrow when the weekend would properly start, in this place where so much of the land was under the sea for so much of the time.

Walking up the curling stairs woke Alice slightly, and she climbed into her sagging bed at the top of the windmill with her stomach full, but still feeling somehow empty inside. There were no curtains and she could see the moon through one of the windows. She lay on her back and shut her eyes soon forgetting the moon, and the wind whispering round the tower through the naked sails. She thought of a man she once knew, but knew she would never see again. She curled into a ball, stuffing her hands between her legs.

2

Carey woke suddenly. She was a light sleeper. She slept waiting to be disturbed. She heard a strange scraping, grinding sound. As if something heavy were being dragged across the floor above her, but she didn't hear footsteps. 'What's that Francis?' And then she heard a sigh, inhuman. Like air being squeezed out of armbands. 'Francis?'

Francis could not sleep enough. He loved sleep, the density of it.

'Francis.'

'What now?'

'What's that noise?'

The scraping ceased and Francis heard light wind. He felt cool air drift across his face. I am on a beach, he thought. I am lying on a beach covered in towels. He dug his fingers into the mattress, expecting sand. 'What?'

'Never mind.' Carey shut her eyes, trying to forget about the noise, the light pouring through the useless curtains, Francis breathing in the other bed. But she couldn't sleep anymore. Then she heard something shudder above, felt it, the windmill moving. She got out of bed and walked around the room looking up at the ceiling. Her nightdress was translucent. 'It's been light for hours,' she said, annoyed. Bloody annoyed Francis hadn't moved, his eyes still closed. 'I'm getting up.' She reached under her bed for her socks and pulled out a small dirty white sock she didn't recognise. There was a dark brown stain by the heel. Similar, smaller stains spotted the toe. She suddenly knew what it was. Dried blood. She dropped the sock on the floor, then picked it up between the nails of her thumb and forefinger and looked for somewhere to put it. She couldn't see a bin. She moved over to the window, squinting at first. Through the gap in the curtains she could see the sun catching the bottom of the sail, giving the filthy struts a vividness they didn't deserve. She parted the curtains further and fields became clear, billowing almost in the brightness. The land was patched, light green where the fields were fallow, and sandy yellow where the fields had been harvested. Red roofs of a village crowded a small dip. A church tower stood solemnly above a brow. And she thought for a moment about opening the window and dropping the sock outside. She didn't want it in the room. But she turned and threw the sock behind the door as she opened it and walked out barefoot headed for the toilet, thinking, Francis can deal with it.

Alice lay as still as she could for as long as she could in her thin, creaky bed. She heard light wind outside, as though the marshes were breathing. Or was it the sea, waves breaking beyond the dunes? The harder she tried to listen the more unsure she became. She watched the sun rise on her bedroom wall, the whitewash turn from grey to amber. She felt the room warming, but she felt quite alone, removed from the others. She could hear no human sound. Just the marshes breathing or waves breaking. Whatever it was. Then she wondered what sound glaciers made advancing over land. A terrible, shuddering earthquake sound, she thought. But it would be so slow no one would hear it. Waves of frozen sound.

She turned onto her stomach. She could see there was nothing under the other bed, and nothing in any of the corners of the room because there were no corners. Then she saw something had been wedged under the cupboard separating the two beds. A folded piece of paper. She got out of bed and stretched. She always stretched when she got up, imagining some weight lifting, her bones expanding like a sponge. She bent down and tried to pull the paper from under the cupboard. But her bed was in the way and she couldn't get a good enough hold. She pushed the bed back, trying to silence the noise of wood scraping on wood with a grimace. She then pulled much harder, the paper suddenly released and the cupboard shifted sideways with a shudder.

The paper was yellowing and soft with age. She unfolded it carefully in the sunlight. It quickly became clear it was a hand-drawn map of the area. She then knelt on the floor, spreading it out on her bed. She found it hard to follow at first, a mass of black lines, some dotted, some dashed, small handwritten words and marks she hadn't seen used on maps before. Some code? But slowly she began to decipher the lines and was able to follow the footpaths and old cart tracks through the marshes, across creeks and cockle beds and mud-flats to the harbour mouth and the banks of dunes stretching either side, Scolt Head Island to the west. And she noticed the marshes had been split up and given names: Plantago Marsh, Plover Marsh, Overy Marsh, Little Ramsey and The Nod. The dunes had been charted as well, as if they were more than just sand and grass: Norton Hills, Long Hills, Privet Hill and Gun Hill. And beyond the dunes were grey areas spreading into the sea, sandbanks uncovered at low tide. Sunk Sand, Stubborn Sand, Tom Baxter's Sand, which had a mark in the middle of it. She went to the small index at the top left corner and saw the sign represented a wreck. She also saw the map was created by a John Baxter. Tom's son, grandson, father even? She liked the name Baxter, John

Baxter, finding it honest, simple. And memorable for some reason.

She stood up and crossed to the window. Looking out she saw the marshes she now knew the names of. But from where she was they were indistinguishable from one another. There was just a shimmering, mauve-tinged flatness laced with silver channels and mud-flats. 'Which path?' she said softly. 'Whichever path?' She looked up, thrilled. The sky was vast, a few clouds stretching to nothing.

'Do you have to fidget quite so much?' Henderson shouted.

'I can't help it. I'm just trying to get comfortable.' Laura's neck ached. The bed sagged so badly she felt as if she were sleeping on a hammock. 'You can have this bed tonight, it's hell.'

Henderson looked at the sunlight flooding round the edges of the curtains, felt it pooling on the blanket by his feet. And he realised he had slept through the night without having a nightmare, undisturbed. He closed his eyes, felt his body relax. But not completely, not quite believing it would be as easy as this. 'I'm sorry. I'm sorry Laura, forgive me.'

Francis could see that Carey's bed was empty. He was not surprised, used to her leaping out of bed as if it were the last place she wanted to be. His dream then came back to him, that he had been lying on a beach, a breeze brushing his face. He had fallen asleep in his dream while the tide came in. He finally woke on a sandbank a long way out to sea. He stood up and could see the others on the distant shore, tiny and waving to him. Water started to cover the sandbank, advanced by light brown foam like the head of a beer. He paced the thin strip of soggy sand until the water came up to his knees, then he plunged in and started to swim back to land. The water was warm and he was carried by the current. Except he didn't reach the others and was swept into a channel, then smaller and smaller channels cut out of a soft green sponge. Pushing himself up, Francis could see the marshes from his bed. 'Henderson, you have excelled yourself,' he said, aloud. 'What a bog.' He got out of bed. The floor was firm and reassuring. He blew his nose on an old tissue and searched for a bin, finding the bloodied sock by the door. Using the tissue he picked up the sock so he wouldn't have to touch it with his fingers. He moved to the window, shoved it open with his shoulder, and dropped the tissue and sock outside. 'Yuk,' he said, watching the tissue hover then float up into the sky, the sock falling to the ground unnoticed.

'What are you doing in here?' Tristram asked.

'I'm smoking.'

Tristram had found Carey in the upstairs room of the cottage, the kettle boiling away in the kitchen below. 'It's cold,' Tristram said, walking over to Carey. Carey put her arm around him and he pressed against her, feeling her warmth through the thin cotton. 'What's out there?' He was too short to see out of the window.

'Sky, mainly.' Carey watched as her smoke curled out of the window, dissipating into the sea air. 'Here, stand on the bed.' She helped him up, careful to keep her cigarette away from his face.

'It's flat. That's why the windmill's here, isn't it? Because nothing gets in the wind's way. Like in Holland.'

'Yes.' Carey was often struck by Tristram's understanding of things, not knowing how much a five-year-old should know. 'What's a windmill for?'

'It used to be to grind corn to make bread. Now windmills don't work anymore, except they are used for holidays.'

'Where's your mother?'

'She's getting up. I don't like this room.'

Carey stubbed her cigarette out on the window-sill and flicked the butt off the edge, not seeing anywhere else to put it. 'Come on, I'll make you a drink.'

'Windmills are like sailing ships that don't go anywhere,' Tristram said, as he walked down the stairs ahead of Carey, one step at a time.

Clever boy, thought Carey.

'Tristram, where have you been? Come here, I've made you a drink.' Henderson was by the kitchen counter pouring water from the kettle into cups, feeling unusually serene. He had pulled an old jumper over his pyjamas. He moved slowly, stirring the cups, not bothering to wipe up the spilled water immediately. 'Carey, how did you sleep? I slept like a log. So peaceful here, isn't it?'

Carey didn't want to be trapped by Henderson now, it was too early in the morning for him. 'OK.'

Henderson edged round the kitchen trying to get the light right, figuring out just how see-through Carey's nightdress was. He thought it a naïve, young girl's sort of nightdress, somehow familiar. He spilt some of Tristram's hot apple drink on the floor, feeling a sudden rush of heat move up from his chest, losing his breath. He took a deep breath. 'Blast,' he said, exhaling. He handed Tristram the mug, then went for the cloth by the sink. 'These cloths always stink,' he said, crossly. Tristram backed away leaving his mug on the floor as Henderson began wiping. Short, angry strokes. 'Don't leave that there.'

'It's hot.'

'It's all right.' Carey picked it up and led the small boy into the windmill. 'You can drink it in here.' She sat him at the table.

'No,' Henderson shouted. 'He's fine in here. I've finished. Tristram.' God, I'm trying at least, he thought.

Carey headed for the stairs thinking she didn't like the way that Henderson sometimes looked at her. Poor Laura.

Poor bloody Laura. 'Hello, darling,' she said, walking into Laura and Henderson's bedroom.

Laura was belting her shorts, looking out of the window. She turned to Carey and smiled, an uncomplicated, simple smile. 'It's still summer. And look, the land seems to go on for ever.'

'I've heard someone else say that about here.' But Carey wasn't sure who or when. The sun caught Laura's face, and she glowed. 'You look lovely,' Carey said.

'I don't feel it,' Laura said. 'The first peaceful night I've had in ages and my bed was appalling.'

Alice took another look at John Baxter's map, then her own which she had spread out on the other bed. Hers was a large-scale Ordnance Survey map which she had bought from Stanfords: the symbols regulation, the information clear. Though after comparing both maps for some time, crossing from one bed to the other, she found John Baxter's chart, in its difficult, squiggly monotone way, to be more detailed. Different even in places, channels and lagoons elsewhere. Particularly the area around the harbour mouth. Here Baxter had drawn many more channels and a large creek, which was absent from the Ordnance Survey map. This creek ran in from the main harbour channel and across Overy Marsh then through Little Ramsey, seemingly cutting off the Cockle Strand from the mainland. Above it in tiny black letters was written Trowland Creek, Creek smudged and stretching into Norton Hills. But it was possible, she could see, to walk inland from the Cockle Strand missing Trowland Creek completely by keeping north and going as far west as Plover Marsh then skirting Plantago Marsh and onto Norton Marsh, then over an embankment and onto the pasture eventually leading up to the windmill. This path was marked by dots, not dashes. A minor path unsuitable for ramblers according to the index, which also warned that anyone venturing onto the marshes should carefully note their timing and whereabouts or they may be trapped by the tide.

Alice searched all over the felty paper for a date, but there was none. She had no idea whether the map was still accurate, how the shingle ridges and sandbanks might have shifted. Where new channels might have cut. But she had a better feeling about Baxter's map than the Ordnance Survey. She folded it carefully and put it into a canvas day bag, empty except for a small tin of watercolours, hardened into tiny bricks.

She bumped into Francis on the stairs, her head still full of paths criss-crossing the marshes, paths leading this way and that. She didn't know who he was at first, just recognising herself in him. Smiling to herself. She didn't hear him say good morning, or Laura talking to Carey as she passed Laura's open bedroom door on the floor below. She just continued winding down, to the ground floor sitting-room. Here she found Tristram sitting at a large table drawing. I used to do that, she thought. 'Can I have a look?'

'It's a land ship,' he said, proudly.

'Yes, I can see. It's lovely.'

'We're going to the village to get some food for a picnic,' Carey announced, holding Laura by the arm so she had to go with her. The others looked up from what they were doing. 'Tristram, are you coming with your mother and me?'

Tristram was still drawing, Alice helping him now. 'No,' he said.

'Be good and do as Alice says then.' Carey hurried Laura outside, Laura quite helpless, but loving it.

The unkempt lawn was drying in the sun and the salty air was already warm. And they both realised how much cooler the windmill was, and how dark. 'We could be somewhere else completely,' said Laura. 'A different country.' She got into the car and found the steering wheel hot from the sun.

Carey went to undo the gate, noticing the fields on either side of the windmill had been harvested and were a fawn, almost a skin colour which looked like it could get sunburnt. Over the coast road was greener, tussocky pasture, which sloped gently and with no animals in sight to a small embankment, protecting it from the marshes. The dunes lay beyond all this, seemingly miles away, and a thin strip of dark blue sea was wedged between the dunes and the horizon. Carey shut the gate and got in the car.

'It looks like a long walk to the beach,' Laura said, just noticing the sea as they set off. Air began to tussle her fine hair, tickling her nose.

Carey laughed. 'Francis is not going to like it. You know how he hates walking.'

'Neither's Tristram.'

'Well it'll be good for them. We'll cope,' said Carey.

Of course we will, thought Laura, you're here. You always cope.

Carey knew where to go, guiding Laura from a card showing the local shops and pubs, which she had found with other papers and pamphlets for guests in the windmill. They soon turned off the coast road and sunk into a lane shaded by high hedges and fat, overhanging trees. Laura suddenly thought she was driving back to childhood, the lane so childishly simple, so comforting, she felt it could lead nowhere else. After a few miles she had to pull onto the verge to let a van pass. The driver waved and hooted his thanks, the horn playing Colonel Bogey, which shook Laura back to the present.

'Where the hell are we?' said Carey, metaphorically.

'I don't know.' Laura didn't want to be in the present. She didn't want to know where she was, wanting to drift further down the lane. But the spell had been broken and the lane was not straight and Laura couldn't see far ahead. Then she was driving into the village, past rows of small cottages, toy cottages, dolls' houses. Shops started to appear, some with hanging signs waiting to swing in the wind that would not arrive this morning. They reached the village square and parked in the shade of an oak, not far from a flint church with a square tower. It was all neat and perfect and radiating warmth.

'Is this real?' asked Carey.

'I don't know,' replied Laura, dazed.

Francis could see Henderson was watching Alice play with Tristram. It was the way he pursed his lips and then looked away, sheepishly, as if he hadn't been looking at her, that Francis found so distasteful. That and the way he chewed slowly so his whole face snarled and wrinkled making him look thick and aggressive. Francis was often drawn to what he found most disturbing. The sitting-room was quiet except for Henderson's chewing, which made it worse, and Tristram's crayons scratching on paper. Francis sat in an armchair not being able to think of anything nice. Occasionally Alice spoke, encouraging Tristram, or expressing delight at what he had done. Her strange, soft accent. It wasn't normal Australian, he thought, or an English Australian cross. There was something else there, some other derivation. I must find out, he said to himself. I can't sit here. 'Have you finished?' he asked her. He could see she had, but waited nevertheless for her to speak again. She nodded. He picked up her empty breakfast plate and Tristram's. 'Henderson, here, I'll clear up.' He added Henderson's smudged dish to his small stack and went through to the kitchen, the counter already cluttered with many other dirty plates, cutlery and cooking utensils. He couldn't understand how so few people could make such a mess.

Henderson followed. 'I thought I would leave them to it. I've never been any good at art. I don't understand it. He must get it from his mother.'

'Probably,' said Francis. Hot water splashed on him as he washed the plates leaving the hot tap running. The windows quickly steamed up and Francis was relieved when he could no longer see the great bog. Art, now I know about art, he said to himself. The language of interpretation. Francis had always believed he was more sensitive and perceptive than he was, which was why he thought he was wholly unsuited to his job.

'Looks as if we're in for a splendid day,' said Henderson, rubbing a patch clear in the window, so from where Francis was it looked like someone had painted a blue streak on a glass of milk. 'It was like this when I used to come here as a child. Clear skies, sun. Great weather.' Henderson didn't know why he had said that; it was a lie, and the heavy patter of rain on the caravan roof came immediately to mind. An endless, torturing sound he would never be able to forget. It still woke him up at night. And there would be other sounds that would rise in volume and drown out the rain, always. Henderson grabbed the kitchen counter, feeling unsteady, feeling the caravan begin to rock. Shaking his head, trying to shake the noise away.

'I can imagine the weather could be bloody awful here,' said Francis. 'What with there being no shelter anywhere. Absolutely bloody awful.' He at last found there was nothing left to wash up and stood by the sink awkwardly, not knowing what else to say to Henderson.

The room was becoming still again, but Henderson knew he couldn't remain in it, fearing what else might catch up with him now, knowing the nightmares weren't really over. But he knew he wasn't running away any longer and that he had to get a grip. Struggling hopelessly with himself. He pictured the photograph of the windmill from the brochure in his mind, and felt better. 'There's a small platform on the roof. The fanstage it's called. I'm going to have a look. Do you want to come?'

'No. Thanks. I'll wait down here for the others.' Turning away from Henderson Francis went to the sink, as if he had missed something. The condensation on the window was easing from an even film into droplets that were beginning to trickle down the window, the sun catching these rivulets, turning them into gold streams.

Many of the shops, Laura and Carey found, were named after children's stories. Treasure Island for gifts, The Silver Chair for antiques, The Horned Man, oddly, but then perhaps not, thought Carey, for wine. The food stores had honest, country names, Laura decided: Bowers, Gurneys, Stubbings, even simply Fishes. The while cars, like playthings, shifted slowly into unmarked parking spaces around the green, and out again, as if they were on a track. Laura and Carey marvelled at the orderliness, the gentleness, their arms growing heavy with smoked fish and pulpy fruit. Thinking they had stepped into an old film, that wasn't totally fictional.

They returned by a different route, because Carey couldn't bear doubling back. They left the village by a pub called The Hero. The road was more open this way, and soon they could see the windmill over the fields on the horizon.

'It could almost be a tree,' said Laura.

'You've been spending too much time with Tristram.'

'I can't help it.' But she didn't mind. Time with Tristram was more than special. 'I suppose, though, I wouldn't know what to do without him. I'll miss him when term starts.'

Momentarily the windmill was lost behind a coppice, then it came back into view, unmoving in the sun-drenched air.

*   *   *

God, it's going to be hot, Henderson said to himself on the fanstage, wiping sweat from his brow, with relief. There was no breeze, just a stillness that was hazing. He had managed to kick the door open, determined not to be defeated this time, and he was watching the tide coming in, lagoons spreading like ink stains. We'll be able to swim if we hurry, he thought. He looked for the embankment that led out from the staithe to the east of Harbour Creek, finding and following it, then losing it just before the dunes and Gun Hill. But knowing it led all the way. In an instant he could remember everything about Gun Hill, so fantastical had it been. The way it was volcano-shaped, and rose out of a mossy moonscape of rabbit warrens far higher than any dune nearby. He remembered having to grab hold of clumps of marram grass as he scaled the sand like snow. Then he saw in his mind's eye the thin lip at the top and the vast crater that the dune hid so well. He hadn't forgotten tumbling into this hollow centre, head over heels. Or launching himself from the edge, the seemingly endless flight, and the leg-buckling landing that would leave him half-buried in sand, sometimes winded as well. It was a secret place. Warm and windless and safe. And it was where he went to hide, sneaking away from his father. Sometimes he took his sister, if he could. And they would invent games.

We have to go there, he said to himself. And he watched his car negotiate the coast road below, coming towards him. He left the fanstage and hurried downstairs, eager to get moving as quickly as possible. Feeling his stomach rising, his pulse quickening. Knowing he had come so far he owed it to himself to go on retracing, the momentum gathering and unstoppable. Ho, hum, he skipped two steps at a time, nearly knocking Alice over on her way up.

'Well, look at this.' Carey walked up to Francis and tickled his neck, the way she did. 'What are you doing?' He pretended to ignore her. She peered over his shoulder. He was drawing a windmill for Tristram, Tristram looking on as well. 'It's not bad,' she said, not sure what surprised her more, Francis's picture or Francis entertaining Tristram.

Francis was pleased with his effort, he thought it quite original the way the sails billowed like spinnakers and the sky looked like the sea in a storm. 'What do you mean not bad? It's bloody good. Better than anything you could do.' He looked at Tristram for support. But Tristram only smiled shyly and Francis suddenly felt embarrassed. 'The others left me with him,' he said, hurriedly. 'Alice went to fetch something and Henderson's gone to the roof. The fanstage or somewhere.' He winked at Tristram, hoping for a more enthusiastic response. 'There, finished.' He had enjoyed drawing the picture. He handed it to Tristram, suddenly feeling sorry for him. 'You're not so bad, are you?'

'Let's go,' shouted Henderson, appearing from nowhere. 'Chop, chop.' He clapped his hands, panting.

'Where?' asked Laura, putting down a bag of picnic stuff.

'The beach. Come on, the tide's nearly in and we'll be able to swim if we hurry. We can have the picnic in the dunes, by Gun Hill. I've worked it all out.' He moved over to the map pinned above the desk. 'Here,' he pointed, 'we walk along here and come out here.' His finger traced the route. But no one could see clearly where his finger was going. And Henderson didn't need the map to remind himself of the way. He thought he could visualise every bend, the ruts in the path even.

'Well, I suppose that's what we're doing then,' said Carey.

'Which beach?' Francis walked over to the map and Henderson pointed to an area of sandy orange. It didn't mean much, but he could see where the windmill was and it looked a very long way, nearly the width of the map. 'There. How on earth are we going to get there?'

'Walk. It's not too far.'

'No,' said Francis, 'it doesn't look it at all.'

'I want to go to the beach,' said Tristram. He dropped his crayons and Francis's picture on the floor and jumped up. He clapped his hands, imitating his father. Laura flinched, having seen him do that before. 'I want to go swimming.' Tristram couldn't swim but that never stopped him from wanting to. He was not afraid of water.

'Chop, chop,' Henderson said again, a great smile spreading across his face.

'Chop, chop,' Tristram giggled.

'Where is everyone. Where's Alice? Where the hell is Alice?' shouted Henderson. He was waiting outside with Tristram and Carey for the others. Tristram had found something on the ground and Carey was looking at the sky. Francis was inside still deciding what to bring, it seemed quite hot to him now but he couldn't be sure what would happen later. The wind might get up, it could even rain, he thought. Laura was checking she had packed enough towels, and an extra jumper for Tristram. She was repacking her bag, thinking Tristram's jumper was nearly two years old, suddenly anxious about how quickly Tristram was growing up. She sat on her bed for a moment and thought of him two years ago.

'I don't think she's inside, I checked,' said Carey. 'I went as far as the top sitting-room.'

'Alice,' Henderson shouted, 'Alice.' His voice carrying over the fields and across the marshes, unhindered by obstacles or wind. Anger and consternation in it, and again he had a feeling that she was meant to be here too, stronger now, and that they couldn't leave without her.

Laura heard Henderson shouting, his voice penetrating

the thick black wall, wishing he wouldn't shout. Worried because he seemed so over-excited, childish in a way.

'Yes, I'm here,' Alice shouted. She saw Henderson and Carey and Tristram look up, and she laughed to herself because they looked so small from where she was and they hadn't noticed her before. She was standing on the fanstage, hanging onto the fan with one hand, waving with the other. She felt like she was waving to the world. 'I'm here,' she repeated too quietly for the others to hear, still giggling to herself. 'I can see everything from here.' She looked wildly around, jerking her head, pointing her nose as if it were the needle of a compass, swinging back to north every few seconds, at least what she thought was north, which was directly out to sea and not far off true north. She believed then she was magnetic. And that she could find her way to wherever she wanted to go, the way she thought Aborigines could. Except she didn't know where she wanted to go, just away. Away from home, away from Australia, travelling on.

'She's going to kill herself,' Carey said, calmly.

'Alice, come down. We're off to the beach now. You have to come.' Henderson thought about adding be careful, but he didn't, annoyed she was delaying him, that they might not get to the beach in time to swim, or have time to see everything. Careful, he muttered to himself, knowing they had a long way to go.

'Coming.' She took a last look, dying to immerse herself in the marshes, dying to lose herself.

It was mid-morning before they set off, a trail of five people and a small child, all carrying many bags. The sun was high, having burnt away any trace of cloud. They crossed the coast road and soon found the track leading through the cow-less grazing land towards the embankment, or the sea wall, and the staithe. Birds chirped and Tristram was sure he heard a frog. But there was no one else about. Just this trail of people.

'Is there not somewhere nearer, somewhere we can drive to?' asked Francis, not long after they started out, half joking. All he could see was land, land stretching to the horizon. He wanted to see beach.

Carey looked at him. 'Really, Tristram can manage. You're more than twice his size.' She walked ahead quickly, catching up with Laura and Alice.

'We'll see,' he said loudly, lagging behind with his new little friend. 'What have you got there?' he asked Tristram.

Tristram had the bloodied sock Francis had thrown out of the window scrunched up in his hand. 'Nothing,' he said, pushing the sock into the shallow front pocket of his shorts. He had found it at the back of the windmill. He didn't know why, but he thought it might be important. 'Just a thing.' He liked to collect lost things. He had a box full of them under his bed at home. He believed no one knew about this box and its contents. Not even his mother or father. It was his secret. Sometimes he would get the things out, a pair of glasses, a camera case, an earring, a letter in an envelope, and imagine who they had belonged to. He imagined people looking for these things, how much they would miss them. He knew how people could miss things. But he knew he couldn't give them back, that they had been lost for good. So he had to look after them for the people who had lost them.

Francis smiled at the boy, what he thought was more of a friendly, brotherly smile than a paternal smile. He didn't want the boy to think he was in any way similar to Henderson. Did Tristram think that, he worried?

Henderson was leading the party, marching across the thick grass, breathing heavily, missing the piping calls of a curlew, a pair of oyster-catchers bleeping to one another, and gulls darting overhead. Instead he was watching the track, which was overtaken by pasture in places, remembering walking across this land as a boy. He kept turning round to see if everyone was keeping up, catching sight of the shrinking windmill. Often he would have a feeling someone was missing and have to slow and look back, counting carefully. And even then he still thought someone, or something was missing. There was a sense of emptiness. He couldn't work it out, so he shook his head and tutted to himself and walked on, eyes scanning.

Soon they reached the embankment, over which they climbed, leaving the reclaimed land and curlew behind. A creek ran close by the other side and they followed it on a muddy path towards the staithe. The creek was full and brown scum floated and circled like leaves by the banks. A small jetty protruded precariously into this fast-flowing murk by a fine house that was at the beginning of the staithe. A wooden rowing boat was tied to the end of the jetty and half-submerged, green slime creeping over the badly weathered paintwork. It was all marvellous, and decayed, thought Alice, loving the way water seemed to rot everything here. Even the marshes. She had been to places in Australia that were as hard and dusty as this land was as soft and wet. Places far from the sea where it never rained, and where nothing grew. She thought of the Nullarbor Plain, another flat and treeless land, but how different. And how glad she was for that.

The sun was hot on Alice's face. She took her sun hat out of her canvas bag. The hat was canvas too, and had a large rim that drooped unevenly, but shaded her brow and eyes and most of her face. Her skin was smooth and fair. She had been careful under the much harsher sun that fell on South Australia like lead.

And then, magically, the balmy air was filled with the voices of people and children and laughter. They passed the fine house and a row of fishermen's cottages rounding a bend, the path widening into a track for cars. In front of an old granary on a mud and shingle quay people were rigging sailing boats. Holidays, thought Laura immediately, admiring how some crowds simply had an air of joviality about them. Mothers and fathers were helping children with their boats, wooden and ancient with thick, crumpled sails the colour of clotted cream. Everybody was wearing smocks and faded shorts and worn-out plimsolls. Faces and legs were brown and weathered, and in places caked white with salt like peeling skin. They stopped for a moment by the quay and watched. We must make an odd sight, thought Laura, so unused to this part of the country, or holidays. They were in clothes that had barely been worn, shorts and T-shirts still creased from the shelves that they were sold from. Except Alice, Laura noticed. She almost fitted in, her frayed shorts and dull pink T-shirt that might once have been dark red. Her hat the colour of the sails, and as lifeless in the windless morning. Yet Alice appeared so unweathered, as if she'd rarely been outside. Laura marvelled at the smoothness of her skin, blanched in the dense light. It was like a child's, quite unaged. And Laura saw Henderson staring at Alice, his eyes fixed upon her, but not focused, she thought. He seemed to be peering beyond her. Laura often didn't know what Henderson was really looking at.

Some of the boats were being pushed into the water and Francis and Tristram went down to the water's edge, Tristram looking keenly about him. Francis sensed how much Tristram wanted to be mucking about in the water with a boat and possibly a dad, and he felt oddly impotent. 'Never mind,' he said, almost involuntarily. Children with sodden plimsolls clambered into the boats while the grown-ups held onto them in the current. A few set off, but the sails hung limply and the boats started to drift not out to sea, but inland down the creek, and round the bend the way they had just walked. Paddles were brought out and the boats reappeared, slowly pushing against the tide. 'It doesn't look much fun,' Francis said, watching the sailors, of all sizes, fraught with effort in the middle of the creek. Some gave up and hauled their boats out of the water on trolleys. 'There's just not enough wind,' he said echoing somebody nearby. He looked back up the quay and saw the others at the top by an old granary. He saw Alice's hair falling from her hat and the redness glinting in the brown.

'I thought it was meant to be windy here,' Tristram said. 'What did they bother to build the windmill for?'

Francis couldn't think of an answer, he was distracted by a feeling that he had witnessed this scene before.

Laura felt a sudden pang of regret watching Tristram with the other children by the water's edge. Regret for a way of life she didn't know. She wanted to be one of the mothers on the quay with loads of children and a dilapidated sailing boat that was worn with joy. It all seemed so natural and happy. Large families. And she wondered where Tristram's brothers and sisters were. How mad Henderson must be not to want any more children. She heard other people's children laughing and fighting with one another, their small voices floating out across the waterlogged marshes.

Carey emerged from the granary with ice-creams. The granary was now a shop called the Boathouse and heaped with all manner of boating gear and crab-lines and a fridge stuffed with drinks and a freezer with ice-creams. 'I know it's early, but we're on holiday aren't we?' Carey wasn't keen on ice-cream but thought that ice-cream and holidays and hot summer days were inseparable. And she liked to hand things out, acting as if she were in charge. Alice and Henderson took theirs and moved away in the same direction, but not intentionally together. Carey then gave Laura the biggest ice-cream because she seemed unusually quiet and Tristram wasn't looking. They stood together watching the quay, waiting for Tristram and Francis to spot them eating, and almost instantly Carey felt as if she were looking at an old cine film of a family holiday, the sun so bright the picture slightly over-exposed and yellow and everyone smiling and moving quicker than normal. She could almost hear the homely projector in a dark room and sense everyone's delight at watching themselves falling into the water, forgetting the days of bad weather and arguments and tantrums. Things that were never filmed. How cine films make everything silently perfect, she thought. But it wasn't her family she was watching, and she wasn't in the film, and she could tell Laura was thinking something similar. 'God, I sometimes wonder where my childhood went to,' she said. She licked her ice-cream that was melting madly now and tasted sweet and stale.

'Don't say that,' said Laura. 'That's what Henderson says.' Laura believed childhood was sacred. She held onto her past like life, sometimes remembering instances that had never happened to compensate for the times when she had been lonely or unhappy. Though she knew people could never really forget all the unpleasant times, the feelings they left in your mind to be stumbled upon or rediscovered so much later, any more than they could forget the times of great happiness.

'I'm sure Tristram won't forget today,' said Carey, as if drawing on Laura's thoughts.

'How do you know?'

'Look at him, he seems so happy.'

'Do you think so?' said Laura. Tristram had at last noticed they were eating ice-creams and was smiling and running towards them up the mud and shingle quay, Francis following. And she tried to imagine what Tristram would remember when he was grown up if he were to look back on this day, this scene. Hoping he wouldn't feel as left out as she felt. 'God, this ice-cream's disgusting. I'm sure it's stale, is that possible?'

Tristram grabbed his ice-cream from Carey, and so did Francis. Both were already hungry, and they charged back to the water's edge balancing their melting cones. Carey laughed at Francis.

Henderson told Alice that the staithe had once been a small port, busy with schooners and brigs. He explained the sail configurations of the vessels, like a boy detailing the finer points of his model yachts, the while slurping his ice-cream between sentences as if he were catching his breath. He remembered the differences exactly, obsessively, pleased someone was listening. Sorry his father couldn't have heard him now, heard him get it right. Henderson finished his ice-cream and stopped talking, suddenly aware he was addressing the wrong person. And he had a sick taste in his mouth that began to sink to his stomach.

Alice tried to picture the boats with their masts and gaffs and booms, fore and aft, or wherever they were. But she found it hard and she gave up, wondering whether the harbour really used to be that much busier. And she watched a sail in the distance glide across the marshes, away from the turmoil and the present.

Henderson caught sight of the solitary sail too. 'Eventually the railways came, and the staithe lost much of its purpose,' he said rapidly, and he felt oddly pleased, pleased that the schooners and brigs had no place here anymore. Holding down the sick feeling.

'I would say there's plenty of purpose left,' she said. Everything has a purpose, she thought. It must have. But she knew deep inside her how places could quickly become somewhere else and mean quite different things. Their images ruined.

'I don't know,' Henderson said. He saw the children with

their boats and parents in the near distance. But he didn't see himself as a boy amid a flurry like this. He watched Alice finish her ice-cream and suddenly thought of his sister while studying Alice's mouth, seeing her quite clearly. He gagged, melted ice-cream and bile coming to his own mouth. He swallowed. 'We should be getting on, there's a long way to go yet,' he said, swallowing again. He went to grab Alice's hand, then realised what he was doing and moved away from her, towards the others.

3

They walked out of the staithe and onto the embankment that followed Harbour Creek to the sea, Henderson taking the lead again. Soon the shouting and laughter and life of the staithe sunk behind them and they were on their own once more. They fell into a steady pace. Reeds and bulrushes, lining a drainage dyke on the other side of the embankment to the creek, rustled gently in a sea breeze that had rolled in with the end of the tide. Though it could just as well have been the air squeezed out of the marshes by the last rush of sea. Oozey air that smelt of clay and ancient forests, waves of it, sweeping over the marshes.

Now with the tide turned the odd sailing boat slid past on its way to sea or Scolt Head Island, packed low with people and provisions. Tristram might wave and someone might wave back. But no one shouted a greeting and there was little noise, just birds and the rustling reeds and the rippling water falling seaward. Laura walked with Tristram now. She held her hand down to him, opening and closing her fingers, urging him to reach up and grab hold of it. But he didn't, preferring to keep his hands in his pockets, one hand, sticky with ice-cream clenching the bloodied sock. Tristram normally held her hand when she did this on walks, when they went shopping, and she wondered why he wouldn't now. She stopped opening and closing her fingers and tried to forget about her empty hand.

Francis had picked a reed and was thrashing the tired yellow grass and wild wheat that lined the path. Tristram, too, picked a reed and copied Francis, but his reed was much thinner and soon snapped. He waved the dangling end in the air, shaking it until it dropped off. Then he found a much thicker stalk and started to whip Carey on the legs with it. Carey didn't notice for a few moments. But Francis saw what Tristram was doing and he joined in too, and they both started to whack Carey, laughing to themselves. Carey turned suddenly with her hand raised, as if she were going to swipe them. Francis being so much taller recoiled, but Tristram being so much shorter and younger continued his beating. 'Stop it,' she yelled at Francis. It hadn't hurt but it was pissing Carey off, the way they were being so bloody boyish. If she had children she hoped, more than ever, that they would be girls. She couldn't imagine any woman not wanting to have girls. 'Grow up,' she shouted.

They came to a sharp corner and the embankment curved round to the east enclosing another pasture. Harbour Creek swept northward and in front of them were the marshes proper. A plank of wet wood lay across a small creek and they could see a path cutting across the marshes to the distant dunes and marram-tufted bluffs. Creeks and gullies spread out, and made Alice think of lungs. Henderson went down to the plank and hopped along it as if he did this sort of thing all the time. The water underneath was fast-moving, the banks dark and slimy. Tristram ran down the embankment to join Henderson, but Laura rushed to grab him before he got too far, pulling him back by the back of his shorts, losing her breath. 'We don't go across here do we?' Laura shouted to Henderson, who was jumping up and down on the plank, testing its elasticity. 'There must be an easier way, surely?'

Not answering, Henderson moved across the plank and started to walk out on to the marshes. Bindweed and sea lavender were matted together and the surface was soft and springy. He took off his shoes and the heads of the wild marsh plants stuck between his toes. It is like walking over nothing else, he thought, remembering the sensation from long ago. But soon he came to a steep-sided gully; the path continued the other side, but there was no plank across the drop. He clung to some shrub and edged himself down, his feet sinking deep into the fine mud. He could feel sharp shells in the mud, he was soon in it up to his knees, water curling round. He pulled himself out, the mud slurping and slapping loudly, and walked back to the others by the embankment. 'The tide's still too high to cross here. We'll have to go around the outside.'

Laura let go of Tristram, seeing a flash of him in her mind floating head down in a creek. Tristram laughed at his father covered in mud, wanting to be muddy too, rushing to him.

But Alice wanted to move onto the spongy mass, feel what it was really like, get it between her toes. She had never seen anything like it. As Henderson came closer she could smell the mud on him, a salty, peaty smell. 'Are you sure?' she asked him, the gullies like paths beckoning. 'There must be a way across.' She was about to get out John Baxter's map, but Laura looked at her in such a way she knew she shouldn't pursue it.

'Which way now, then?' Francis asked Henderson.

Henderson pointed further along the embankment that they had come along, then swept his arm round and out to the dunes. 'If we carry on this embankment we'll finally come to a wooden path. Look, there.' He spotted two tiny figures.

'How do you know that's the way?' Francis asked, suddenly sure Henderson had no idea where he was leading them. Panic rising in him. 'It looks all the same to me.'

'I've been here before. Of course I know the way.' Henderson could feel the mud drying on his legs, itching, and he felt angry with Francis. Of course he knew the way. I've brought you all this far, haven't I? He questioned himself.

Francis caught Alice looking straight at him, and he turned away abruptly, embarrassed because he was sure she could tell he had sounded panicked, and still embarrassed from having been told earlier by Carey to grow up.

'Come on,' said Carey, eager to keep moving, realising they had a long way to go yet. The picnic stuff was getting heavy and she could imagine everyone tiring well before they got anywhere near where they were meant to be going, and having to stop somewhere which was far from perfect. She hated that idea.

So after much jostling they fell into a new line with Carey now leading the group. They moved quickly, urgently along the rutted embankment. Laura grabbed Tristram's hand and didn't let go. His hand was still sticky, but it usually was and she didn't mind. She felt his small fingers wriggling. It charmed her. She needed to keep hold of him, she needed him near. She asked him whether he felt tired yet, too tired to walk, but Tristram knew that grown-ups didn't feel tired, not men like his father and Francis anyway, so he said he still wanted to walk. Inside he felt like an adult today. Like everyone else. He was no different. He certainly didn't want to be carried. He wished his mother wouldn't hold his hand, though.

Francis watched Alice immediately ahead of him almost skip along. She had a rhythmical step, entrancing. He could tell she was used to walking far over flat land. He found himself admiring her legs, their shapeliness, their smoothness. His shoulder ached from the heavy bag and he kept looking up and into the distance, but the dunes didn't seem to be getting any nearer. He knew he shouldn't complain, that Alice might think him pathetic, but he couldn't imagine that everyone would be enjoying themselves for much longer. How could they? He swapped the bag onto his other shoulder, fumbling with the strap, trying to untwist it. He looked into the distance again half expecting to see a mirage. The sea, aquamarine, whales tooting offshore. He knew he had a wild imagination, that he was artistic.

The purple shimmer of the marshes was making Alice dizzy, and making her long for something, but she wasn't sure what, and then she heard the sea. There was no mistaking it, the murmur of small waves lapping sand. She felt the rhythm soak into her. It excited her much more than she could have imagined, tingling her back, which was damp with perspiration. And all she wanted to do was take off her clothes and plunge in. She tried to dismiss the marshes and kept her eyes to the path and her feet as she increased her pace. Thinking of the cooling sea, happy memories of it and childhood.

The others, too, heard the sea and they all began to walk a little faster. Henderson licked his lips. The two tiny figures he had pointed to earlier were suddenly just in front of them. They were an old couple with small rucksacks and walking boots. The man had a white beard and a thin piece of driftwood, as white as his beard, which he was using as a walking stick. Carey walked straight ahead seemingly not noticing them, and the old couple had to step into the overgrowth at the edge of the path as the others followed Carey as if they were in a trance, no one saying excuse me, or nodding hello, all just concentrating on the sea murmuring ahead. Tristram powering along as if he were an adult, pulling Laura behind him.

In this state of concentration time went double-quickly

and it wasn't long before they left the embankment, taking a path of hard marsh mud and heading directly out to the dunes and the sea beyond, Henderson having overtaken Carey because he had to. It was his place. He knew the way. Ho, hum, he said to himself, feeling light-headed. Ho, hum, he liked that. Gun Hill was becoming more defined, the fringe of marram circling its perimeter discernible, and so, he thought, was his past here. He hesitated for a moment, getting out of step, losing his rhythm. Get a grip, he said to himself. Stay with it. Carey levelled with him and he strode ahead again, feeling the others pushing him forward to where he knew only he could go back.

Sand appeared, at first in small drifts to the sides of the path. Then a belt of moss and lichens, and finally marram, all trying to control the sand. But there was too much sand and the path had to be stabilised with short wooden planks, grass sprouting between the gaps. And Francis, walking on the man-made path, knew at least they weren't lost, amazed Henderson seemed to have found the right way. They walked through rising dunes, the sea getting louder and gulls multiplying. Tristram pulled free from his mother and started to run, his feet patting the planks. Laura didn't chase after him, knowing no harm could come to him here. And then the beach opened out in front of them, so vast and flat it took Alice's breath away. Tristram had already gone beyond the dry sand and was walking onto the hard sand left rippled and wet by the tide. The sea was fast retreating and sandbanks were emerging, streaking the sea under the sun, leaving shallow lagoons of trapped water glittering.

'Let's leave the stuff here,' said Henderson dropping his bags and pulling at his T-shirt.

'Thank God,' said Francis rubbing his shoulder. 'Thank God.' He sat on the sand and crushed shells with the heels of his feet, hot and deflated.

Alice smiled at Laura nervously, shocked that she had

seen a place just like this before. For an instant she believed she was in that other place. The warmth and the sand engulfing her in nostalgia. She must have shut her eyes without thinking for she opened them expecting to see footprints trailing off, and the wistfulness was gone. He would disappear in the briefest of moments, silently. She shuddered because the footprints weren't there, because she knew she couldn't follow him. How odd games people play with each other are, she thought. How odd.

The water was cool and murky, heavy with sand. Carey waded in up to her waist, until she couldn't see her feet, the wetness shockingly real. She fell forward pushing her arms apart. She swam straight out not looking back, suddenly wanting to swim into a new holiday, a new beginning, thinking she would soon be out of her depth. Small waves splashed in her face and she heard Henderson thrashing about behind her. She tried to swim as fast as she could, thinking she was in a race, then thinking something awful was swimming after her, a shark, some unimaginable monster. She always had irrational thoughts in the sea. Water got into her mouth and she tried to spit it out as she swam. Her knees then brushed something solid, she pushed on frantically, shivering, and pushed into a sandbank. She stood up and found the sea came to below her knees. She then felt foolish, dripping, a gentle breeze cold against her. She looked back and saw Henderson calm now, floating in the middle of a new lagoon, the others still on the beach not noticing her. She walked further out through shallow water, her feet sinking deep into soft sand, until she came to the proper sea once more, soon finding herself up to her waist in water. She plunged ahead again and built up a steady, powerful stroke. She had to prove to herself that there was nothing nasty lurking nearby, nothing coming after her. She wanted the others to see her swimming so far out, strong and unafraid. She dived and swam underwater, pulling herself through the water blind, her eyes tightly shut. How devious, how crafty the sea is, she thought.

Alice helped Laura with Tristram's armbands, blowing up one herself until it was red and tight on his thin arm. They both then held a hand and led the small boy into the sea. Laura could see the emerging sandbank in the middle distance, waves breaking there, and thought the lagoon would be ideal for him.

Tristram was eager for his mother and Alice to let go, shaking his arms angrily. 'I can manage,' he said. 'Let me go.' Once free he walked in up to his waist and peed, the warm liquid lingering in his tight trunks. He walked further until his arms in their armbands started to rise. He wasn't afraid of the water.

Laura walked a few yards beyond him and held her arms out. 'Now Tristram, push towards me and kick.' She remembered learning to swim like that herself. Struggling towards her mother. Tristram launched himself forward, kicking and paddling madly. Laura looked at her son trying so hard, thinking how difficult growing up really is. And how much further he had to go. She caught him and pulled him towards her, hugging him in the water, his armbands scratching her. She wanted to protect him.

Alice clapped. 'He's nearly there,' she shouted to Laura. 'Again,' Tristram screamed joyfully, pushing his mother away, feeling proud and grown-up. Feeling he didn't need her anymore.

Francis followed Alice into the water, finding the temperature outrageously cold. 'Christ,' he shouted. He wasn't keen on swimming in the sea, especially if he couldn't see the bottom clearly. Though on occasions he preferred it when he couldn't see the bottom. It was seldom right.

'Come on, it's fantastic,' Alice shouted charging further into the water. She dived forward and started to crawl, effortlessly passing Henderson who was still floating in the middle. She loved to swim. She loved the way she felt free of the land, free of any ties. And she loved the power of the sea, the way it shaped the land. She had seen waves higher than houses and felt rip-currents like torrents. She had known people who had been swept away and lost. But she thought not of them now, but icebergs melting into the sea thousands of miles north of where she was. How they would slowly dissolve. Groaning now and then like floundering sea mammals. Surely.

Francis shut his eyes and tried the crawl after her, not bothering to lift his head out of the water and breathe until he had run aground on the sandbank. He stood up, bewildered, panting, blinking the salt water from his eyes. He was always losing sight of where he was going, what he was meant to be doing. How unlike Carey I am, he thought.

Still dripping, Henderson led them back up the beach, onto the sand and crushed shells that had missed the last tide, almost too hot to walk on and too white under the noon glare. Sand stuck to their feet and legs. Tristram popped a drying skate egg with his big toe. 'We can play games here after lunch,' Henderson shouted. 'I've brought a ball and a frisbee.' But other games came to mind, games played without balls and frisbees. Before frisbees had been invented even. Games he'd make up and play on his own. With his sister if he could make her play with him. And in the seclusion of Gun Hill if he could get her there. That was best. He felt the damp and sand caught in his shorts and tugged at the bottoms, while increasing his pace because he didn't want to think about those times just yet, not too hard anyway. Or he might turn round.

They started to climb into the dunes and Henderson led them along a narrow path. Marram was pressing into it, the leaves pricking their legs leaving red spots almost instantly. Tristram started to complain, the grass attacking his arms and head. But he still felt brave and grown-up and he tried not to cry. Then he saw a lizard, green as the grass, dart across the path. 'Look,' he cried, 'a lizard.' Even though it had gone. He stopped, watching the direction it had disappeared in, watching for it to reappear. But no one else seemed interested in the lizard and he felt his mother gently push him from behind. Grass spiked his face again and he felt angry and left out. Not wanting to go along with the others. Wanting to do what he wanted to do. He was always being told what to do. Soon, he thought, I'm going to walk away and do what I like, before anybody can stop me.

The long marram eventually shrunk back to a mossy, dry, brittle stuff, spotted here and there by sandy mounds and tunnel mouths. Here's my moonscape, Henderson said to himself, almost expecting to see his footprints undisturbed from years ago. There's no going back now.

'Help,' Francis suddenly shouted. He was floundering on the ground, one leg having disappeared down a rabbit burrow. 'Tristram, help.' Tristram ran over to him. 'Oh, ow, something's biting my foot.' The small boy grabbed an arm, starting to pull Francis clear. Francis struggled and rolled on the ground. Then his leg came free. It was sandy and earthy, and he rubbed his foot as if it had indeed been bitten. But he couldn't help smiling and Tristram began to realise Francis had been joking. Tristram looked at his feet, suddenly shy and embarrassed with everybody looking at him, laughing at him.

Henderson thought everybody should be quiet. He nearly told Francis to shut up. This is a special place, he said to himself. Sacred. And he then regretted bringing them all here. He wanted to be on his own, to scale the towering side of Gun Hill, almost within his reach now, and peer over the edge, just in case he saw more than he could cope with. Maybe I have left something behind, he thought, something recognisable, like a spade or a T-shirt, part of my past. Maybe there'd be something belonging to Victoria. He'd bury whatever he found before any of the others had any idea what it could mean, before he had any idea what it could mean himself. He looked behind him, at the others struggling over land that belonged to a different world, pushing him on, pushing him forward. As much as he wanted to be on his own he knew he wouldn't have been able to go any further without them. He wanted to see what they saw. See it all for the first time. Children tumbling head over heels. Giggling.

The sand gave way as Henderson climbed, falling back in mini-avalanches. He had to grab hold of clumps of grass to pull himself up. He was quickly out of breath, panting, the bag on his back heavy. The others followed him, like an advancing army. Finally Henderson neared the thin lip at the top. Leaning into the side, he straightened his body and could at last see into the cream crater. It was how he remembered and not. It appeared the same shape, the same depth. But there was nothing to show he'd been here before, nothing he couldn't cope with. It was undisturbed. He felt momentarily blank. Then he felt relieved, dazed. Successfully over the first obstacle, he said to himself, in a military voice. Though he shook his head, not trusting his feelings. He couldn't do that. He climbed further and stood up on the precarious edge. He felt tall and thin, but stable. Then something caught his eye, a blue bag or piece of plastic, half-way up the far side of the crater. His heart started to thump. He took a deep breath and leapt off the edge. He flew in the air, seemingly for ages, then landed with a jolt, sinking into the sand-side and falling backwards, squashing the bag on his back. He pushed himself forward and ran and slid down the rest of the crater, across the bottom, dropping his bag there, and then up the far side, stumbling. As he came closer he saw it was a piece of cloth, not plastic. He kicked it with his foot and it turned over and unravelled. It was a small T-shirt. And he had a vision of Victoria wearing one just like it. That's ridiculous, he said to himself. It can't be hers. How could it be? Still he covered it with sand, desperately, using his foot, the while picturing himself and his sister clambering around the inside of the crater losing shoes and shirts. The stillness, the warmth. The secrecy. He felt unbearably claustrophobic, in need of air. There was no sign of the T-shirt now and he left the scuffed sand and climbed the rest of the far side. He reached the top and pulled himself out of the crater onto the edge, almost gasping by now. He sat there looking out, calming himself. The moonscape stretched unearthly, the marshes beyond unearthly too. On the horizon, above the happy staithe, was the windmill, just how he had seen it before. Small and out of reach. The sails like helpless arms, the arms of someone drowning.

'Shit,' said Carey breathlessly. 'What a bloody great hole.'

'Shit,' said Francis, thinking the same.

'Careful,' Laura said, to Tristram. She was still holding his arm, having helped him up.

'What now?' said Francis.

'I don't know?' Carey shrugged. 'Why don't you jump in?'

Francis, feeling strangely irreverent, dropped his bag, and flew off the edge screaming, his arms waving above his head. He landed on his feet, sliding some way in a cloud of sand, then he somersaulted the rest of the way down.

'Wow,' Tristram exclaimed. 'I want a go.'

'No,' said Laura, 'it's too steep.'

'Let me, let me,' he screamed.

'It's pretty soft,' Francis shouted from the bottom. 'It's quite safe.'

Laura let go of her son, realising it probably wasn't dangerous, and that she couldn't keep control of him all the time. She knew she had to let him do what he wanted to do sometimes, however hard it was. She knew it would only get worse the older he got. She watched him standing on the edge and she could tell he was scared. He stood there for a while, quite still, looking down. Finally he looked at his mother for support. Then he jumped, his arms straight above him. He didn't drop far onto the steep side, and instantly turned and looked up at his mother triumphantly. He climbed the short way back to the top and told everyone to watch as he jumped again. This time he flew further out and fell over as he landed. He pretended he had meant to fall and continued to roll down trying to somersault.

'It's funny how children never seem able to somersault properly,' Laura said. 'They always go off at odd angles.'

Carey didn't answer. She hadn't been watching.

'Come on you two,' Francis shouted, wanting Laura and Carey to join him and Tristram at the bottom. Wanting to get lunch started, wondering where Alice was.

Carey was awestruck by the enormity of the view. 'I'm staying up here for a while,' she shouted.

'I'll sit with you,' said Laura. 'The air's so wonderful, isn't it?' She took a deep breath.

Carey didn't hear Laura, or at least what she had said didn't register. She lit a cigarette and pulled the smoke in as if her life depended on it. The view and the temperature and Henderson were unsettling her. Alice also, she reluctantly admitted to herself. She was used to Henderson being difficult, even though he was being particularly disturbing this weekend, but she couldn't understand Alice at all. She hated it when she couldn't work someone out. And she had a bad feeling about Alice. She didn't trust her. 'Laura, what's up with Alice?'

'What do you mean?' Laura realised she hadn't seen Alice for a while. She scanned the beach. A few people like stick figures were moving in the distance.

'Well, what do you make of her?' Carey liked to know exactly where she was, be on top of things, feel in control. But she didn't feel in control now, or feel she had any power to do anything about it. God, it's only Saturday, she thought.

Alice had watched the others climb the big dune and had hung back. She wasn't used to groups of people. And the beach had shocked her. She hadn't realised quite how a place, a landscape, could bring back somewhere else, someone else, so completely. She kicked at the mouth of a rabbit burrow knowing that that was all in the past, but wishing it wouldn't keep creeping up on her, not here. She tried to fill the hole in with sand and loose dirt, pressing the dirt hard into the hole. She left the filled-in hole behind with a tap of her foot and moved silently away, pretending she wasn't really here at all. Pretending she had moved on to somewhere else already.

'I like Alice,' said Laura. 'She's sweet. And she means well.' Laura was always looking for the best in people and saying things like she means well, she has a good heart. 'She's quite changed though,' Laura added, then told Carey what she remembered of Alice when she was a young, boisterous girl. How she used to push everyone around, how she had once made her sick. When Alice had pushed her off a swing and then refused to speak to anyone for a day. 'I suppose I feel a bit guilty about having lost touch with her for so long. I really forgot about her, or I wanted to, ha, and she obviously never forgot about me. She's come all this way to see me, hasn't she?' Laura looked at Carey. She didn't think she would be able to cope without Carey, Carey and Tristram. How they made her feel balanced. 'It's funny, isn't it, how relationships can be so unequal, without either person realising at the time. How some people think so much more about other people, than they think about them.'

Carey lit another cigarette. She rarely smoked two so closely together. She didn't think it was necessarily a bad thing for a relationship to be unequal. She couldn't imagine being on an equal footing with anyone. She just knew that some relationships should never happen in the first place. How some people should be left alone, or leave other people alone. 'You just have to be careful who you become close to,' Carey said, as if it were easy.

'Hi.' Alice was suddenly behind them.

Carey jumped, dropping her cigarette in the sand. She looked at Alice, not knowing how she could look so pale and unpuffed. Wondering how long she had been there, listening surreptitiously. She picked the cigarette out of the sand. It was still alight and she blew the sand off.

'What a wonderful view.' Alice remained standing, turning on the spot, slowly. 'It goes on for ever.'

'Yes,' said Laura, eager to sound friendly, encouraging. 'It's a view you'll never forget. Quite unlike anywhere else I'm sure.'

Henderson had jumped and rolled back into the crater, feeling calmer and that he couldn't sit on the edge all day. He was unpacking his bag, Tristram and Francis looking on longingly. 'Lunch, you lot,' he shouted up. 'Come on, it's lunchtime.'

Carey stared at the two men and the little boy who thought he was a man, taking out the lunch things in the centre of the crater. 'I suppose we've got no say in the matter,' she said, quietly. 'Why don't you come up here?' she shouted, but knew the men wouldn't pay any attention to her. She knew lunch was now out of her control. Like everything else. Damn it.

'It'll be out of the wind,' said Laura, helpfully, not remembering that there was hardly any wind anywhere.

Once they were at the bottom Alice felt the weight of the heat fall on her. They spread out rugs and crawled onto them, piling the food in the middle. Laura and Carey started to go through the plastic bags, opening lids and unravelling parcels of damp newspaper, taking over from the men. Quickly the smell of smoked fish and rancid butter filled the air. Francis opened a bottle of white wine that had warmed and smelt of cheap perfume. He poured the wine into plastic cups, but he was unable to avoid sand getting into them, grains drifting to the bottom. He handed the cups out and everyone tried to balance them in between their legs or in the sand while they filled rolls with soggy bits of fish and pâté. It reminded Francis just how much he hated picnics, the smell of plastic and fetid food. Eating on his lap and sand getting everywhere. He drank most of his wine in one swallow, then threw the remaining mixture of wine and sand behind him. He poured himself another cup, still seeing sand drifting at the bottom. He thought he would try to get drunk.

Laura made Tristram's rolls, hiding the fish underneath tomatoes and lettuce. But they still didn't look very appetising, so she gave him a can of Coke. She wondered why picnics always seemed such a good idea, but never worked out very well. She felt sweat on her forehead.

Aware of the strong sun Alice tried to tuck her legs under her. Henderson watched her struggling to keep everything balanced, admiring the smoothness, the childishness of her skin. The while avoiding her face, her mouth.

Carey caught him staring at Alice's legs. 'Henderson, it's like a fucking furnace in here,' she said. 'It's far too hot and airless. What on earth made you bring us here?'

'Memories,' he said automatically, turning away from Alice's legs. 'Childhood memories,' he added, more softly. 'Don't you like it? It's very private at least.'

But there's no one else about anywhere near here anyway.'

'Well we're here now aren't we,' his voice was rising. He felt Carey picked arguments with him just for the sake of it. 'I'm not moving until I've finished lunch.' He knew nobody else would be moving until they had finished lunch either. It would be too much effort. He felt sweat drop from his armpits and trickle down his sides inside his T-shirt. But he didn't mind the heat, he thought it made everything seem more unreal. Hazy. He saw moisture on the creases of skin by the side of Alice's left knee. He couldn't help looking.

'The fish is excellent,' Alice said, feeling that everyone might be getting a little irritable, not wanting there to be an argument. No one said anything. 'We are very out of the way here,' she added, implying that was a good thing. But she didn't like the crater much. She found it oppressive, felt trapped. She would rather have picnicked on the top. She wanted a view, wanted to look into the distance. See just how far she could see into the future. She untucked her legs, helped herself to more food, and shifted a little closer to Laura.

Laura hated it when Carey and Henderson argued. She didn't think that they loathed each other, at least she hoped they didn't, but that they couldn't accept what each other meant to her. She used to feel flattered, though over the years she had become exhausted by their bickering. Her parents had tirelessly argued, each trying to control her in their own, peculiar way, much like Carey and Henderson now. She needed balance, that was all she had ever craved. Balance and commitment. But she had long realised neither came easily. 'Well we don't have to stay here all afternoon,' she said, looking around hopefully.

'It is like a sauna in here,' Francis chirped. He was opening another bottle of wine, feeling the first few cups and sun penetrating his hot head. He had taken his top off and his torso was slowly burning.

'You do have a scar on your forehead,' Alice suddenly said to Laura, louder than she intended. 'So it's true. You did fall off a swing. I remembered about it on the plane, only I thought it might have been a dream.' Carey looked at Alice quizzically, then Laura. Alice could hear Laura screaming in her mind. She could picture clearly Laura's mother and the doctor's surgery. Laura's mother, how Laura looked like her now: thin and tired, her light-blue eyes sinking into her face, her cheek bones protruding through skin, which was starting to sag and wrinkle. Her hair, always fine and fair, but without bounce. Yet Laura was not frail. Alice could detect there was much strength left, and, she decided, an unusual beauty. A sensuousness, probably never realised or appreciated properly. Then Alice suddenly remembered that the doctor had examined her also. And how she had said nothing to him except, I didn't do anything, over and over. I didn't do anything. She could hear herself now. And she realised it was somehow her fault that Laura had fallen off the swing and cut her head. That it was no accident. That she had forgotten what had really happened. Then she heard someone else saying, I didn't do anything, I didn't do anything. Thumping in her mind, stunning it. Then another doctor's surgery, another face. And she hadn't been able to say anything at all to this doctor. She was suddenly very sure of that.

Laura was embarrassed. She was not vain, but the scar was so tiny she knew Alice must have been looking at her very closely. She was not used to people studying her, except perhaps Tristram who would probe her face with his fingers. Or he used to anyway. She didn't even know whether Henderson knew about it. He had never commented on it. She took a sip of wine. 'Yes,' she said swallowing, feeling the flush on her cheeks. She couldn't tell Alice that in fact it was she who had pushed her off the swing. That it was her fault. Not now, so many years later. It doesn't matter, she said to herself. But she was bemused, not being able to understand how Alice couldn't remember exactly what had happened. I would have remembered, she said to herself. I can remember everything important that happened when I was a child. Perhaps she has deliberately forgotten, she thought. 'I had completely forgotten about it, actually,' Laura lied, looking at Carey, hoping Carey wouldn't say anything to the contrary. 'You came with me to the doctor's.'

'Yes,' said Alice, 'I remember that bit clearly now.' She found a peach, her fingers breaking the skin as she lifted it to her mouth.

Henderson was not listening to them. He was watching Tristram burying himself in the sand. After some time Tristram gave up and crawled along the crater and half-way up a side, finding another spot. Henderson watched intently as his son began to cover his legs with sand again, then his shorts and half his tiny chest, flinging the blue T-shirt onto his body before realising what he had done.

Tristram sat up. He examined the T-shirt carefully, even looking inside it. 'Hey, look what I've found,' he shouted, his voice shrill. He stood up, sand showering about him, and ran across to the others. He felt remarkably lucky, it was the second lost thing he had found in the day already. How his collection would grow. 'Look.' He presented the T-shirt to his father because his father was the nearest, and sort of reaching for him.

'Tristram, throw it in the rubbish bag, you don't know where it's been.'

Tristram pulled the T-shirt into his chest. 'No.'

'Tristram, throw it away,' Henderson exploded.

'I found it. It's mine.' Tristram stood in front of his father defiantly, but shaking slightly. 'It's mine. It's mine. I need it.'

Henderson reached over without standing up and grabbed Tristram. He pulled the T-shirt from him. Tristram burst into tears.

'Henderson,' Laura shouted. 'It's only a rag. It doesn't matter. Let him have it.' She got up and walked over to Tristram. Kneeling she put her arms around him, drawing him to her.

'It does matter,' shouted Henderson, quite red in the face now. 'It matters a lot. You don't know where it's been. You don't know who it belonged to.'

'Really,' Carey said, loudly. 'You're impossible.'

'It's all right, darling,' Laura whispered into Tristram's ear, his face wet with tears. 'I'll find you something else.' She knew about the box under his bed, his box of special things. 'There'll be plenty of other things we can find.'

Henderson suddenly felt foolish clasping the T-shirt, the others looking at him. 'Look, I'm sorry Tristram.' Tristram wouldn't look at him. 'I didn't mean to shout at you. Have it.' He threw the T-shirt to him, feeling he was throwing all sense away with it.

But Tristram didn't pick it up. It wasn't special any more. It was ruined.

'This is great,' said Carey. 'Henderson brings us to this hell-hole and then he goes berserk.'

Laura didn't look at Carey. Neither did Alice, wishing to keep out of it.

'Come here, Tristram. Come here, darling.' Carey held her arms out, wanting to protect him too.

Francis covered his top with a towel, put another behind his head and lay back on the sand, his body moulding it. He was too hot and sleepy to get involved. Children, parents, it was always the same, he thought. No one ever gets it right.

And soon there was near-silence, no one knowing what to say. The sea, having retreated miles, was barely audible, just a soft tinkle, more a sort of swishing. Francis fell asleep, shockingly quickly. Alice watched him for a while, the towel on his chest rising and falling gently, his left hand twitching slightly. She loved to watch people sleeping, thinking how secure they looked, feeling secure herself.

4

Laura opened her eyes. She saw nothing for a while, blinded by the sand glare. She thought she might still be in a dream, looking out onto an unreal landscape. But she didn't think she had slept. She could never just fall asleep. She blinked, rapidly. She blinked and her heart began to race as she tried to focus, but the glare was so harsh things only became clear very slowly, and she knew she wouldn't be able to relax and breathe calmly until she saw Tristram, not just shadows. She crawled onto her knees and stood, catching her breath. Her legs felt as if they hadn't been used for a long time. And she could feel the blood throbbing in her head and she lifted her right hand to her forehead to shield the brightness, people distinct now. But her heartbeat didn't slow, nor the throbbing, and she instantly felt faint and sick. 'Tristram,' she called, softly because she didn't want to sound too alarmed, because she didn't want to admit to herself the full horror of what she really thought, that he had disappeared. 'Tristram?'

The others were strewn about the bottom of the crater as if they had fallen from the sky, or at least from the top of the dune and their rolling and somersaulting had ended in an inglorious heap, after smashing into someone else's picnic. They began to stir, perhaps aware of Laura, her calling, or just aware subconsciously that something wasn't quite right.

Carey sprang up, as though she were oblivious to the sun and the heat pushing down on her. She couldn't believe she had slept. Not out here, with so much to disturb her. Then perhaps there was nothing to disturb her. She remembered she had just been been playing with Tristram. She looked about her. 'Laura,' she said, 'is something the matter?' She suddenly knew what the matter was. She knew. 'Laura?' But like Laura she couldn't submit so easily to the fact that Tristram had disappeared.

'Oh, God,' Laura, sighed. 'Where's Tristram?' She looked around the crater once again, scanning the steep bright sides, the bodies in the middle, but not spotting his anywhere. She saw the blue rag, still where Henderson had thrown it. She walked over to Henderson and kicked him gently in the side. She thought about kicking him much harder, as hard as she could. But she realised she was not angry with him yet, and too weak with fear. 'Tristram's disappeared. Get up.' He immediately leapt up, and she could see he was worried, which worried her more. 'Oh, God,' she sighed. 'Oh, God.'

'I'm sure he hasn't gone far,' Carey said, putting on a pair of sunglasses, setting off. 'We'll find him,' she shouted, breathlessly. She knew she had to find him. She had been playing with him last. It was her fault. She had fallen asleep. Fuck it, she said to herself. Fuck it. This is all we need. She struggled up the inside of the dune, clawing at the sand.

Henderson raced to the opposite side from Carey and ran up it as if it were flat, leaving Laura not knowing in which direction to turn, and Francis and Alice not sure what was happening. 'Tristram's gone,' Laura said, looking at them wildly, her voice strained with panic. And then she took off too, running and stumbling, desperate to get out of the sand dune.

Francis turned to Alice. 'Children can really be a pain in the arse sometimes.' But Alice didn't smile, and he quickly realised he had been insensitive. And it began to dawn on him that if anything serious had happened to Tristram it would be the end of the weekend already. He might never see Alice again. 'We'd better go and help look,' he said, trying to sound grave and important. They set off together, but separated once they reached the top: Francis heading over the rabbit warrens and lichened folds towards the marshes the way they had come. Alice heading straight for the beach because it seemed so vast and obvious, and she couldn't shake it out of her mind.

Henderson hurried through thick marram towards the distant pine woods, because it was the way he would have gone if he had been a child. Indeed, that was the way he had gone before, the woods too dark and appealing. The grass irritated his legs and he had to watch out for sharp blue sea holly. 'Tristram,' he shouted, then thought he shouldn't shout again, because if Tristram heard him shouting he would probably hide. He soon started to sweat. He broke into a trot, ran in a large circle, before carrying on towards the woods. He knew he had to find Tristram, that it was his fault he had run off because he had shouted at him about the blasted T-shirt. He felt a great anger sweep through him, but he didn't know what exactly he was angry about, who he was angry with. He'd just lost himself. Was losing it far too often, losing track. He had to keep it together. He had to find Tristram. 'Tristram,' he called desperately, not being able to keep quiet. And he had a feeling that something so strong and powerful, something so vital, was pulling away from him. He felt his heart sink as its beat quickened so that his stomach felt as if it were vibrating, and he dropped to his knees catching his breath for a few moments, forcing his heart back into his chest, before charging on.

He can't have gone far, he can't have gone far, Carey kept
repeating to herself. She was walking along the last bank
of dunes by the beach. They were low and she followed
a path that wound its way across the top, dropping into
silent hollows every so often. Each time she expected to
see Tristram, but the dips were empty. A few, however, had
signs that they had been occupied before: piles of stones,
charred remains of driftwood fires, the odd item of clothing.
She paused on the peak of a small dune and listened. But
she didn't hear a human sound. And she carried on, walking
and trotting, trying to think rationally.

Alice reached the wet sand and looked for footprints,
thinking she could track him. But she couldn't find a set
small enough, and on their own. Just groups of people's,
probably theirs earlier. She squinted, looking into the distance, not able to make any people out, the sea almost as far
as the horizon. Still she went forward, wondering just how
far a small boy would venture out here on his own. She
saw a figure, a small black silhouette. She started to run,
and more figures came into view, all standing some distance
from each other, all still and sinister. She stopped, looking,
puzzled. She realised they were birds, cormorants.

Francis kept looking over his shoulder at the big dune,
expecting someone to be standing on the top waving for
him to come back, signalling the search was over. But no
one was, and he found himself going further and further
back the way they had come, except he managed to miss out
the wooden path, cutting across the hardened mossed-over
dunes straight to the embankment. He was walking slowly
now, high up with a good view over the marshes, thinking
there was no way a small boy could have got this far. He
paused for a moment then turned back.

Laura tripped on a rabbit burrow. And she felt tears
welling up as she scrambled back to her feet, not bothering
to brush the loose dirt off her knees. She reached the

wooden path Tristram had run ahead on earlier. 'Tristram,' she called. She couldn't decide which way to go, out to the beach or back towards the marshes and the embankment. She couldn't see clearly either way because of the tears misting her eyes. She listened and she remembered hearing Tristram running along the path towards the sea earlier. The patter of his hurried footfalls. So she turned towards the sea. But she didn't hurry now, the path widening and the beach ahead brightening and enlarging. She reached the edge of the path, suddenly, inexplicably not wanting to go any further. Not wanting to step onto the sand. The beach shimmered, but she saw no one. Then she heard a voice, someone talking, muttering, and a clanking sound. She cupped her ears with her hands, but it didn't help, hearing now only the sea, so she dropped her hands to her sides. She felt movement behind her, a shiver, and she looked over her shoulder to see a man stepping out from behind a small dune to her left. Her mind went blank. She gulped for air.

The man hesitated. He was broad, with a large head, his face made of pulpy red skin. He opened his mouth, as startled as she was, but he didn't say anything. Binoculars hung from his neck, along with a camera with a large zoom lens. He was also carrying a telescope with a tripod, and this equipment seemed to swing about him, even though he wasn't moving.

Laura couldn't move. Or speak, only gasp. The man muttered something, but she didn't understand. What? she mouthed.

'Are, are you lost?' he said, quietly.

She looked at him, not sure whether she had heard him correctly. Not able to focus on him at all clearly. 'Lost,' she said. 'Am I lost?'

'Can I help?' he said. 'I've got a map somewhere.' He started to go through his pockets.

'Oh, no. I've, I've lost my little boy. My son. Have, have you seen a small boy?'

'A small boy,' he said, scratching the side of his over-sized head, his brow furrowed. 'No, no I haven't, I'm afraid.' He paused for a moment longer then started to walk away slowly on the path, inland. 'Sorry,' he shouted. He had a lot of ground to cover that afternoon. He couldn't hang about.

Laura watched him go, his shoulders drooping and his equipment swaying. She thought of the staithe where he appeared to be headed, full of children, laughter. She didn't know where to go next. She didn't think she could head out across the beach alone. She wiped her eyes.

'Laura.'

She heard her name, faintly, she was sure.

'Laura.'

She turned in the direction of the big dune and saw someone standing on the top waving, beckoning to her. It looked like Carey.

'Laura.'

She started to run.

Tristram tried not to cry. It was hard because the grass hurt and he had sand in one eye. And he knew he was lost. He left the beach, carefully carrying his shells, and headed back into the dunes, too small to get a clear view of the highest dune. But he saw the tops of the pine trees in the distance and decided to go in that direction, using various paths and areas of just sand, avoiding the thick grass. Then he saw a man carrying a long pole and other hard objects around him. The man was huge and lumbered along making chuffing and clanking sounds, and Tristram didn't want him to see him, so he quickly sat down in a dip and spread his things about in front of him. He lined them up in order of importance. This took a long time because although the biggest shell should have been the most important, it wasn't the prettiest. He quite forgot where he was, moving the shells about and the odd bit of twig, until he heard a chuffing sound again, and realised someone was very close.

Laura's mouth was suddenly full of sick, and she had to stop to spit it out, clutching the stitch at her side.

Henderson found Tristram, in a small dip obscured by grass and a bramble bush, still a long way from the woods, but far from Gun Hill. He was quite still, and didn't look up until Henderson was almost beside him. When Tristram saw that it was his father he looked straight back at the ground, where there was a pile of shells, a skate egg and a piece of horn wrack. 'I'm sorry, Tristram. Really I am,' Henderson said. Tristram proceeded to pick up various objects and pretended to study them closely, running a finger along the edge of a razor shell. Henderson crouched down and picked up the horn wrack. 'Do you know what this is?' Tristram didn't answer, but continued to fiddle with the razor shell. 'Oh, Tristram, I'm sorry. Please?' He put his other hand on his son's shoulder and squeezed gently. 'Did you know that this is an animal, not a plant?'
'It looks like a twig.'
'Yes, but it's an animal.'
'How does it eat?'
Henderson laughed. 'I don't know. I don't think I was ever told that.'
They continued sifting through the stuff Tristram had just collected, Henderson telling Tristram what he could remember, Tristram not understanding very much; Henderson forgetting he was only five and becoming quite excited himself with all that he was so impressively recollecting. Then Henderson had an idea. 'Would you like to see

the Queen's beach hut, in the woods? I can take you there.'

Tristram looked at his father and smiled. 'Yes, Daddy. Yes.' Tristram knew about the Queen, he knew more about the Queen than shells and dead animals washed up on the seashore. He had forgiven his father, for the moment, and was no longer interested in the pile that was in front of him.

'Great, but we'll have to tell the others first.' Henderson helped Tristram to his feet, and he held his son's hand as they returned to Gun Hill, on the way telling him a few things about the Queen's beach hut. Not everything. Remembering how sticky, just how sticky children's hands got.

Carey was moving across the last bank of dunes by the beach when she saw Henderson and Tristram walking towards Gun Hill. She waved, but they didn't see her, so she raced to the big dune herself because she was nearer it than them. She reached the top and started to shout and wave. She felt a great release. She felt as if she hadn't let go for a long while. She could see Alice on the hard sand, her slight figure hopelessly swamped. And she could see Laura by the edge of the wooden path leading onto the beach. 'Laura,' Carey shouted. 'Laura.' Something had suddenly changed inside her. 'Laura.' She didn't know what, but she didn't feel quite like herself. She felt lighter, freer. She wanted to take her clothes off.

Laura held Tristram to her chest, despite Tristram trying to push her away. using his arms as a barrier. She felt ridiculous and happy. And Tristram felt shy because his mother was smothering him, smelling strongly of herself. He struggled to get free, wanting to get going, seeing his father in the corner of his eye. He wanted to be at the Queen's beach hut more than anywhere else he could think of. He didn't need his mother to protect him. He knew he could look after himself, suddenly realising he could always just run away if his father or anyone else shouted at him. 'Mummy,' he protested. 'Mummy, I'm going to the Queen's beach hut in the woods.'

'What? I'm not letting you out of my sight. You're staying with me.' Tristram struggled harder, but Laura wouldn't let go of him.

'Daddy's taking me. I'm going with Daddy.'

Laura looked at Henderson. 'Really?' She was shocked that Tristram wanted to go anywhere with his father. 'What the hell is this, Henderson?'

'I thought I could take him,' Henderson said, quietly, hurt. 'I thought it would be a good idea. I should spend more time with him, you know. You're always telling me to do so.' He found himself wanting to please Laura as much as he wanted to please Tristram.

Laura felt too exhausted to argue. She could see Tristram was desperate to go. And she knew Henderson had a point, Tristram was his son as well, she couldn't keep control of him all the time. 'Why don't you take Alice also?' Laura found herself saying, thinking Alice was responsible. Alice was at the bottom of the crater packing up the picnic stuff with Francis. 'I'm sure she'd like to see it. The Queen's beach hut, or whatever it is.' She didn't want Henderson going off with Tristram alone at the moment. Anything would be better than that. She could imagine him upsetting Tristram again, and Tristram really disappearing. Or Henderson not paying attention and Tristram having some awful accident. The more she thought about it, the more she could imagine happening to Tristram. Henderson's negligence.

'Oh, OK,' said Henderson. 'That's a good idea.' He was suddenly excited about the prospect, sort of wishing Tristram wasn't coming now.

'You can take Francis, too,' Carey said. She had overheard them and was eager to spend some time away from Francis, finding him maddeningly childish and quite unapproachable today. Feeling a strange sense of freedom surge through her again. A need to escape. 'We can go for a walk on our own, Laura,' she said.

So they gathered their things together and put on more suntan lotion and sun hats and sunglasses, stuffing their shoes into their bags, and filling one bag with rubbish. Tristram tried to carry the rug like a man, giggling because of the size of it, but he gave up before he had even climbed out of the crater. They were all pleased to be leaving Gun Hill and the heavy heat behind.

Laura felt anxious, but not as anxious as when they had set off from the windmill that morning. Maybe, she thought, she was too drained to feel anything much. She surveyed the area from the high-point. To the east beyond the light, tufted grass she could see the pine woods, dark and velvety and mysterious. In front of her the sand seemed to be stirring, alive, naked. She was sure the breeze had picked up. At least she could feel something on her cheeks, a soothing.

Carey still felt like taking her clothes off. 'We'll see you by the sea, directly out from here in an hour or so,' she told the others, taking Laura's arm, as was her habit, and leading her away on a path worn through the marram.

'Just don't let Tristram out of your sight,' Laura shouted back. 'Don't you dare, any of you. You're all responsible for him.'

Alice felt surer of herself heading for the woods, moving on to something new, pleased to be leaving the aching sand behind. There was a spring to her step, a sashay. Francis was tired from the wine, but eager to make it to the woods. Walking isn't so bad, he thought to himself, following in Alice's footsteps. I could quite get into it.

Henderson was calm and clearer headed. He was happy to be moving away from Gun Hill, away from a moment that he had not been able to control. Nevertheless he felt that he had somehow shaken something out of himself. And he felt stronger for that, surer about continuing, still recognising that he had a lot more to come to terms with. In fact he felt quite in control now, when not even Carey was around to get in his way. 'Follow me,' he shouted, lifting his right arm above his head like a tour guide. Then he wondered whether he would remember the way. He could remember the woods, the ferns and moss and smoky green light. The mushrooms, shocking and ominous. His sister had called them fairy woods. 'Let's play in the fairy woods,' she'd say. 'Let's play by the Queen's house.' They both knew the way then, taking it in turns to lead, charging through the trees, over the needle beds and pine cones. One perhaps hiding from the other, Henderson really hiding from his father, pulling his sister further away from him too. Then he could have found it in the dark. But he didn't know whether he would be able to lead them straight to the Queen's beach hut now. Whether their paths had become overgrown, those memories obscured by time or just confused by later events, like so much else.

Henderson looked behind him, checking that everyone who was meant to be following was, checking Tristram was there. He was responsible for Tristram now. He was responsible. He saw something moving ahead, far in the distance, something bobbing above the tall grass. Dark brown hair, white face. A child running swiftly. And he had an urge to run after her. He had been a faster runner than Victoria. He had always been able to catch her. He remembered her laughter that would collapse into screams as he grabbed her. The child swept round and ran for the woods. It took off shortly before the trees. It was a large bird, a shelduck or a Canada goose. It rose ungracefully, disappearing in the blue sky which was turning white with afternoon heat.

Suddenly it was cool and quiet, the swishing grass and sea breeze no longer in Alice's ears. The sun gone. A smell of honeysuckle and pine. Soft, green light. She was glad to be out of the grass, her legs stinging. And out of the sun, which had seemed as strong as it was on the other side of the world. But I'm not there. I'm here, stupid, she said to herself, and took a deep breath of pine air as if to make sure of the fact.

'Shit, I'm glad we're out of that grass,' said Francis, desperate to strike up a conversation with Alice, feeling more confident and secure in the shade of the woods. He had followed her the whole way, and had not been able to say a thing. 'That was a real bastard.' He flapped his T-shirt, making use of the cool air.

'Still, it was worth it. It's marvellously cool in here,' she said.

'Yes, isn't it strange,' he said. Twigs cracked under their feet and the sound seemed to echo deeper into the woods. 'I don't know about the Queen, but you could certainly imagine fairies living here. And a few goblins, that sort of thing.' Francis laughed, wanting to be funny and charming. 'How about that, Tristram?' Tristram smiled shyly and ran ahead to catch up with his father. Francis turned to Alice. 'Has this wood always been here?'

'No, I'm sure not. It's part of the sea defences I should think,' she said.

'I wonder when the trees were planted then?'

'The middle of the last century,' Henderson shouted. Nothing escaped him in the woods. Sound bounced off trees.

'Thanks,' said Francis, having momentarily forgotten Henderson knew everything. Not wanting him to sound too clever in front of Alice.

'You'll find four types of pine here,' Henderson continued, 'Scots, maritime, Corsican. Urrgh, I can't remember the last.'

'Shame,' said Francis quietly, but not so quietly that Alice didn't hear.

'How about Monterey?' Alice offered.

'Yes, that's it. How did you know that?' Henderson was audibly put out.

'I don't know. I must have read it somewhere.' She thought it might have been written on John Baxter's map. She watched Francis pick up a pine cone and fling it as far as he could. There was a small thwack as it hit a tree. 'Francis, see if you can hit Henderson on the head with this,' she whispered, handing him a small cone. She liked Francis. Men who knew too much frightened her.

Carey led Laura along the edge of the dunes, determinedly, as if she knew where they were going, and why. Here the dunes and clumps of grass were small, manageable, and speckled with clearings of sand. And Carey thought how easy it would be to lie in one of these hollows and lose yourself, become invisible, be someone else, do what you wanted. The weight of the wet sand on the beach stretching so far to her left, oppressed her. That was not how she wanted to feel, or how she wanted Laura to feel. 'Try to enjoy yourself,' Carey said. 'We are on holiday.'

'Great,' said Laura, trying hard to remember when she had last enjoyed a holiday. She thought of the time she had gone with her parents to Scotland, and how they had set off each day on hikes that took them to a ruined castle, a deserted inn, or a secret loch. And how much fun it had been discovering these things with her mother and father. How they had been as surprised as she had been when they stumbled upon them: forgotten, hidden. They would become hugely excited and search about, examining everything, and look at each other wide-eyed. Often her father would have to give her a piggyback on the way home because she would be tired out and happy. Laura didn't know her parents had pretended about anything then. She didn't know their marriage would break up later. She still had no idea what really caused the split. Just weariness?

Holidays are precious when you're young, she knew that much. Tristram immediately came to mind. She wished Carey had children, wishing Tristram had someone his age to play with. She knew how important that was, too. For when she thought hard enough she could remember being fought over and misunderstood, and forgotten about at times. Carey had never been there when she had really wanted her. No one had.

'Well let's make the most of it. Come on Laura.' Carey could sense that Laura was still upset, distant. She hated it when Laura was in one of those moods.

Laura suddenly felt unable to hold herself together. She shuddered, feeling her life, her marriage slipping away. At times she felt she was mirroring her mother. Helplessly.

'Forget about the others for a while,' Carey said, thinking just how complicated men made everything. Which was odd, she thought, because most men were really quite simple. 'Tristram will be all right. He wouldn't have gone far. He loves you.'

'Anything could have happened to him.' She remembered the man with the binoculars. 'You see, you don't understand. How could you? You don't have children.' She looked at Carey. 'Sorry, I didn't quite mean that. It's just all so complicated. Henderson's so bloody difficult.'

Carey didn't need reminding. But she didn't feel like talking about him now. Henderson, Francis, Tristram, she wanted to forget about all of them for the moment. And Alice for that matter. 'Laura, darling, let's just forget about them for a while.' She put her arm around Laura, and Laura nestled close, and they walked together like that for a while, slowly, stumbling, unable to balance properly. The sand hot to step on and getting hotter.

Laura broke free at last, feeling much better, thinking she had to think about herself more. Put herself first occasionally. Carey took care of herself, did what she wanted. Didn't she?

The path widened and flattened out between two small ridges of dunes. A faded, striped wind-break was set up in the middle of the path not far in the distance. They headed for it, automatically, both curious about who was on the other side. They heard no noise as they approached and they stepped lightly to the side, edging the dune ridge, both peering over their shoulders to the middle of the path and the wind-break. Then they came into view, four naked bodies, two men and two women, all lying on their backs with their eyes shut and legs astray. They were pudgy bodies, middle-aged, careless, droopy in places. Carey and Laura looked at each other and both started to giggle. They looked at the bodies again. Pink and brown and sweaty. One of the men opened his eyes and smiled. He started to sit up. Carey and Laura turned away, embarrassed, and walked quickly on.

Shortly they saw another naked body, a man standing on a sand-drift staring out to sea, his right hand shading his eyes, his other hand resting casually on his hip. They passed two naked women lying on their stomachs in a sandy hollow, and an old couple sitting on deckchairs drinking from plastic cups, quite bare.

They stopped at last. Laura laughed. 'Well, it is sweltering.' She took off her T-shirt and shorts, and stood on a sandy mound in her swimsuit. She thought about taking her swimsuit off for a moment. But she hadn't done such a thing since she was child. She was far too shy, and modest.

'That's a good idea. I just have to pee.' Carey disappeared behind a dune.

'Daddy, which way now?' Tristram stopped at the point where the path split into two. A tree had fallen across one of the paths. A scarlet mushroom, large and saucer-shaped, sprouted from the foot of a tree just at the beginning of the other path. Tristram was suddenly frightened, not wanting to go down either path. The mushroom reminded him of a nightmare.

'I don't know.' Henderson couldn't remember. He was lost.

Alice and Francis caught up with Tristram and Henderson, and the four of them stood not saying anything for a while, wondering which way to go. The odd crackle reverberated in the near silence. And there was another sound, a sort of clanking, as if the tops of trees were grating against each other.

Alice got out John Baxter's map. She found it hard to see clearly in the green dimness, but she unfolded it and held it close to her face anyway, and she felt as if she were holding something very solid indeed. 'It might be shown on this map,' she said.

'It won't be marked,' said Henderson. 'They're not going to mark the Queen's beach hut on some stupid map.'

'They might,' said Francis. 'Why the hell not?' Fuck you, he said under his breath.

Henderson studied each path. A sense of foreboding rose in him. But he knew he was in charge and he was damned if anyone else was going to show him the way in his woods. My fairy woods, he said to himself. Victoria, he felt like shouting. If you were here Victoria, we'd be able to find it. 'It's this way,' he said loudly. 'Come on, Tristram, let's go.'

'I don't want to,' Tristram said. 'I want to go back.'

'Oh, come on Tristram, it's this way, really. Don't be so silly.' Henderson sensed Tristram might be frightened. 'It's quite safe. The Queen uses this path. She might even be there. Imagine that. Come along.' He held out his hand for his son.

Alice gave up looking and put her map away carefully. 'It doesn't look like we've got any option,' she said, quietly to Francis, raising her eyebrows, then smiling sweetly. But she knew she had the map.

Henderson didn't know whether he was leading them on the right path or not. He trod heavily, trying to crush pine cones into the ground, pulling Tristram behind him. He had to find the beach hut. For Tristram, for Laura, for himself. He shut his eyes and tried to imagine running, branches slapping his arms and legs, Victoria dashing ahead. But nothing was any clearer when he opened his eyes. No Victoria, no idea where he was going. And he felt himself start to panic.

Whether it was the hazy green light that seemed to close in on her, or the way in which the pine forest seemed to thicken and the path lead deeper into nowhere, Alice didn't know, but she felt her mind was turning in on itself, receding, and she thought of Billy. His wild, thick hair, and brown eyes that looked black from a distance. She first spotted him by a camping store in Ceduna and they spoke later that day in a bar. She told him she was on her way to the Head of Bight to watch the whales and paint the limestone cliffs, and then she was going to travel along the rest of the Eyre Highway, all the way to Norseman. And he told her he was heading as far as Yalata, then inland to a place called Maralinga, in search of where his ancestors came from. 'My grandmother was an Aborigine,' he said. 'She was known as Joongura and she used to tell me about the Sun Mother, who rose from a cave below the Nullarbor Plain and when the Sun Mother opened her eyes the darkness disappeared as her rays spread over the land.' He was proud and charming and naïve, and Alice was immediately entranced. They arranged to set out together the next day as they were both initially going in the same direction across the plain. Alice remembered now how Billy had told her that Ceduna came from an Aboriginal word that meant to sit down and rest. But Billy could have told her anything then and she would have believed it. She knew little about the Nullarbor Plain or Aborigines, but neither did Billy. He had lived all his life in Melbourne. He had gone to Ceduna to find something out about himself. She had gone for the same purpose, as naïvely, she supposed now.

They set off in her VW and were soon passing sand dunes that shimmered and grew mountainous. A harsh whiteness. And, 'Hey,' Billy said, 'why don't you come to Maralinga? I could return to the highway and travel on through to Norseman, too. I'm part Aborigine and I haven't been anywhere.'

Carey startled Laura, creeping up behind her. She was carrying her clothes and her swimsuit. 'God, this feels great,' she said, dropping her stuff on the sand and spreading her arms wide.

'Carey,' Laura pulled back. 'What are you doing? You can't stand there with nothing on.'

'I can. It's lovely. I think you're meant to here anyway.' She twirled on the spot: a pale body, short auburn hair. 'Go on, take yours off.' She felt quite at ease. Quite herself.

'No.' But Laura was tempted. 'What if the others see us?'

'They won't. They're nowhere near here. Besides they haven't been gone long enough. Go on.'

Laura hadn't seen Carey behave like this for years, so frivolous, light-minded, not since they were children. Then she would do anything Laura dared her to do, because she was stronger and more capable and outward-going. Sometimes Laura would follow. 'Do you remember the time when you took your clothes off and walked around the wall at the end of your garden?'

'Yes,' laughed Carey.

'And your mother came outside looking for us and we jumped into the lane at the back and ran off. I must have taken my clothes off by then, too.' Laura suddenly felt warm inside, a heat spreading out from her stomach. 'We had to hide behind that shed and it smelt of cigarettes and pee.' She remembered the smell clearly now, and the feeling of doing something she shouldn't have been doing. The feeling of danger and being naked, their bodies touching as they scrambled behind the shed. Laura stepped out of her swimsuit, and felt the happiest she had felt since she had left London. She felt free. And sensual.

Francis was convinced Henderson was leading them in the wrong direction, because he couldn't understand how anybody could know where they were going in the forest. The path was narrow and branches blocked their view ahead and flung back enclosing their tracks. He was trying his hardest not to say anything about it. He clenched his fists and carried on silently. Alice was walking just behind him now, and he kept turning round to look at her. He'd raise his eyebrows, as if to say, where the hell is he taking us? Though it was cool, and the further they went Francis found he was increasingly absorbed by the eeriness of the forest: the strange sounds, the way odd shapes and figures would form out of the trees and shadows. He thought he might even paint a forest scene when they got back to the windmill, if they ever got back. He thought he could become quite serious about painting. A new venture. Something vocational for once. Alice was a painter.

'Daddy, are we lost?'

'No, Tristram. Of course we're not.'

'Well where is it? Where's the Queen's beach hut. You said we'd see the Queen. I want to see the Queen.' Tristram felt let down again. Why was it that everyone was always promising things which never turned up? He was becoming cross, but he knew he wouldn't run away here, not in the woods. It was too dark and he kept thinking he saw horrible things, creatures.

'It's not far now. I'm sure of it. Hey, just beyond that ridge,' Henderson said, hopefully, trying to calm himself. But still he didn't know where he was going as he tried to crush the pine cones below his feet with fresh vigour, stamping on them uselessly. He had remembered the way to Gun Hill. He had an excellent sense of direction. But the woods somehow disorientated him, shutting out the world, the past. It had always been such a mad rush, a blur, in the woods. And he needed to see it all clearly now. He kicked a cone and thought he would go in the direction it landed. But he wondered whether chance was really all he had left.

'There, is that it?' Alice suddenly shouted, pointing. She could see what she thought was a roof, over to her left. She had good eyesight. She was used to spotting things in difficult places.

Carey watched the insect crawl up Laura's arm, onto her shoulder and into the dip by her collar bone. She wasn't sure what it was exactly, but it was dark red, nearly black, and looked like it had pincers that could bite. It was horrible. She leant across Laura, casting a shadow over her breasts and face, and brushed the insect away.

They had sat in a soft hollow, hidden from the beach and dunes, feeling they were hidden from the rest of the world, and talked about what Carey had got up to when they were children. The time she had thrown mud at passing cars in the lane, the time she had pushed Hilary Scot off the coal bunker, the first time they had smoked a cigarette, and the first time they could remember thinking about sex. They had shown each other their bodies, comparing, touching. Both intrigued but shy. Later they used to masturbate together in Carey's bedroom, but they didn't talk exactly about that now, instead Laura said, 'It's funny how you lose interest in your body. How you'd rather just hide it than show it.' Carey responded, 'You've still got a lovely figure, Laura, really. I'm jealous.' She sighed, and continued, 'I don't think it's my body I have the problem with though, but Francis's. I suppose we're just a little bored of each other at the moment.' Carey stood up and looked around for any sign of anybody, before sitting down again. Laura lay down awkwardly and shut her eyes. She felt her body tingle despite the heat, too aware of her nakedness. And she thought of the times in Carey's bedroom. How most girls must have had similar experiences. How unfulfilled she was now.

Laura felt the sun suddenly ease off her, and the light beyond her eyelids darken. She opened her eyes and saw Carey leaning over her: her face, her lips, the faint fur just above her top lip, inches away. She remembered what they had been talking about. 'I like Francis.'

Carey backed away. 'So do I. Shit, we've been together long enough. It's just that he can be so, well, distant. Noncommittal, I suppose you could say. It really annoys me. I can't stand people who don't know what they want. Who can't just get on and do what they feel they should be doing.'

'Maybe he hasn't found out exactly what it is he wants to do.'

'That might be part of it. But I think he can't make up his mind whether he wants to be with me or not. Whether he wants to have children with me. Ha, ha, could you imagine that?'

'But isn't that your problem, too?' Laura asked. 'I thought you couldn't decide whether you wanted to marry Francis, whether you wanted to have children with him.'

'It's not that easy. I know what I want,' Carey said angrily, without thinking, so used to saying it. She hated admitting she was indecisive or weak or wrong about anything. But she could see Laura looked suddenly hurt. 'It's just that the longer you're with someone the harder it becomes.'

'Maybe you're afraid Francis will leave you?' Laura said. She didn't think she was afraid of Henderson leaving her any longer. Often she thought it might be her and Tristram who left first.

'Oh, Christ, I don't worry about that,' Carey said, but she did. She worried about betrayal and commitment more than most things, and she couldn't help expressing this sometimes. 'I suppose whatever happens to you and Henderson, you'll always have Tristram.'

Laura realised that Carey might be jealous of her, something that hadn't occurred to her before. 'Yes, I have. I'm extremely lucky. Children are wonderful. They give you something to hold on to. When there's nothing else,' she laughed. And she couldn't help thinking that Carey had become so serious, so grown up, as she had got older. How wild, how carefree she had been. That she wasn't as strong and determined as she made out. Laura shut her eyes again, wishing they could both forget about the present for a while. Waiting for something to happen.

'The Queen, the Queen,' Tristram shouted, starting to run after his father, who was leaping through what might have been a trail, or just a patch of woodland that wasn't too dense.

Alice and Francis started to run after them, through the

ferns and fungi, both suddenly smiling and excited and uneasy, not because they had found the hut, but because they were acutely aware of each other. Henderson looked over his shoulder and caught sight of Alice's brown hair, recognising Victoria, her brown hair, the way it would trail behind her as she ran. He blinked and said shit under his breath. And he was short of breath and his heart was heaving and he thought he might even collapse.

'Daddy, where's the Queen then?' Nothing stirred around the hut.

'I, I don't know,' Henderson replied, distracted by the sudden, unexpected peace.

The hut was large, more like a house, thought Tristram. It was made of wood and brick and had a veranda. Weathered wooden stairs ran up from the spongy, green ground to the veranda. Tristram stopped at the foot of the stairs, desperate to go up, but too nervous to go alone. He didn't want to ask his father, who was puffing and panting, supporting himself against a nearby tree, to come with him. He waited for Francis and Alice to catch up, hoping they would accompany him.

Francis could see Tristram wanted to have a closer look. 'Let's go up and see if anyone's in, Tristram,' he said, climbing the stairs, hearing Tristram's light steps following. Francis went straight to the tatty French windows, Tristram beside him now. He looked into a large room. There was a table with benches around it to one side, a simple dresser, which was empty, and a door at the back. Francis could see the dust and sand on the floor, and on the table and benches and dresser as well, and he thought nobody could have been in the hut this year, if not for many years. He thought he could smell the emptiness, the staleness, seeping out of the French windows. He backed away, not disappointed, but realising how disappointed Tristram might be.

'It's empty,' said Tristram, his face pressed against the

glass, which was sticky with salt and sap. 'Where's the Queen? The Queen doesn't come here, does she?' Still he stared into the room, hoping for some sign of royal occupation. Something plush or sparkly.

'Round the back?' Francis suggested. 'We might find something there.' And he descended the stairs two at a time, passed Henderson leaning against a tree, and slipped down the left-hand side of the hut where there was a gap, Tristram hurrying after him. The smell of staleness, the sense of stillness, was stronger here, but Francis found it not unpleasant, slightly melancholic if anything. There was a rainwater barrel, full and black, and a back door. Francis tried the door just in case, but it was locked and only rattled. There was a small window on the rear wall, but it was too high for Francis to see in.

Tristram spotted the window also. 'What's in there? I want to see what's in there.'

'I don't know. Here, let me lift you up.' Francis was surprised by how light Tristram was, and thin, holding him by the waist and hoisting him above his head so he had a clear view in. 'What do you see?'

'Nothing much.' Tristram sounded fed up. 'It's boring.'

'There must be something?'

'Well, there's a bed or something. And something's on the bed.' He sounded more excited. 'I don't know what it is. A hat or something. It looks dirty. It can't be the Queen's.'

'Hey.'

Francis jumped backwards, nearly dropping Tristram.

'What are you doing?' Henderson even startled himself. He didn't mean to sound so hostile.

'Tristram's seen something in there.' Francis lowered Tristram. And Tristram, thinking his father was angry, tried to hide behind Francis.

'What? Seen what?'

'Nothing,' Tristram said, still hiding behind Francis. 'Nothing, Daddy.'

Henderson realised he was frightening Tristram. 'I thought I heard some people coming in this direction,' he said, as calmly as he could. 'I don't think we should be seen behind here.' He didn't want Tristram to see into the hut, he didn't want to see in himself. Gun Hill had been easy, everyone pushing him forward. Now in the stillness he had a feeling nothing had really changed here, that time had by-passed the woods, and he couldn't bring himself to look in. Nothing could make him. So he led them back down the side they had come round on, and there was an ache inside him now. A weakness he couldn't yet overcome. He knew if they had gone back along the other side, pushing through the brambles, they would have passed the window he used to break open and climb in, pulling Victoria after him. But he couldn't show them that. And he wished he could be young again. Wishing he could go back to the time before he had first come across the hut. He looked at Tristram knowing Tristram had everything ahead of him, untainted and uncomplicated. And he had a sudden urge to be with Laura, a small sense of hope seeping into his mind. 'I think we should head back to the beach,' he said, looking about him. 'Alice, Alice. Where the hell's Alice gone now?' He wanted there to be a future, as though that would dissolve the past. 'Alice.'

God, how boring I must have become, Carey lay on the sand thinking. How fucking boring. Have I changed that much? She couldn't understand how it had happened, how she could have let it happen. Because I wanted to be successful, to be taken seriously that much? Now all I can do is worry about business and having children and Francis. Francis leaving me. Fuck it. Why should I care? My business is successful, I'm still reasonably attractive, though I could be a little thinner. She squeezed her stomach and then half rising off the ground grabbed her right buttock. I wouldn't want to be as thin as Laura. But then it suits Laura. She's always been elegant, delicately poised. She shifted across the sand on her bottom to be closer to Laura. The sand was so fine she thought it felt like flour, not sand anyway. She picked up handfuls of it and let it trickle slowly onto her thighs, making patterns. Laura was lying on her stomach now, and Carey leant over and drew a line down her back with the sand.

Laura didn't notice for a moment or two, then she felt something soft and wonderful trace the small furrow her spine made. Down and back up, down and back up. She didn't look up. She shut her eyes tighter. She was far away. The feeling then moved to her legs, starting at the soles of her feet, tickling slightly, then her calf muscles, lingering by the backs of her knees where she loved to be touched. She felt the line float slowly up the back of her left thigh stopping just below her bottom, powder falling between her legs. Then the sensation floated up her right leg. More than one line now, three or four. Fingers. She shivered.

Alice suddenly appeared from the other side of the hut, holding her hat, brushing twigs and green stuff off her T-shirt and shorts with her other hand. 'Sorry.'

She was smiling, though in a way that made her look almost guilty, or at least as if she were hiding something, Francis found himself thinking. She often had that look about her, he realised.

'We should get back to the beach,' Henderson said.

'Really,' Alice said, 'so soon?'

'Yes,' Henderson said, loudly, shortly. 'The others will begin to worry. We've already been nearly an hour.' It was hard to keep track of the time in the woods, Henderson remembered. The sun and the sky largely obscured.

Alice could tell Henderson was anxious, and she thought
Tristram looked disappointed. He was staring at the ground,
digging his toes into the moss. She had noticed him doing
this before. 'You know, there's a window on that side,' she
pointed to where she had emerged from by the right-hand
side of the hut, 'which is coming off its hinges. We could
easily open it.' She saw Tristram lift up his head.

'No, no way,' shouted Henderson, starting to walk into
the woods on a faint path. 'Come on, let's go. Tristram.'
Tristram looked at Alice expectantly. 'Tristram,' Henderson
yelled. He walked towards his father, his head dropping.

'Francis,' Alice said quietly, 'how about it?'

Francis looked at Alice. He suddenly felt afraid, but he
wasn't sure why. 'I don't know. I don't think we'd better.
Henderson said he heard some people coming this way.'

'Well it's not going to be the Queen, is it?'

'No,' said Francis. His mind racing, confused. 'You don't
think we should keep an eye on Tristram? We are all
responsible for him, you know.' He raised the pitch of his
voice, trying to sound like Laura.

'Henderson is his father.'

'The others, we shouldn't keep them waiting.' He thought
of Carey, trying to imagine what she would think if
Henderson and Tristram arrived without him and Alice.

'Oh, well, never mind.'

Francis didn't know what to do. He was starting to sweat,
the palms of his hands moistening. 'OK, OK, let's go and
have a quick look. Yes, I'd like to do that.' He moved
towards her. 'We'll catch you up,' he shouted to Henderson
and Tristram. 'We won't be a minute.' And he was suddenly
glad he had made this decision as he followed Alice, as they
pushed through the branches and brambles by the side of
the hut. 'Here, let me go first,' he said, worried about the
brambles scratching her legs.

Henderson took hold of Tristram's hand. 'I'm sorry the

Queen wasn't there,' he said. 'Don't be too disappointed. There'll be many other things to see.' He started to walk quickly, wanting Laura to know that he could take care of Tristram. That they were still together, a family. Tristram stumbled on a root, but he got back up without saying anything, Henderson barely pausing before pulling him along faster. 'Let's go and find Mummy,' Henderson said. 'Do you want me to carry you?'

5

Francis got to the window first. It was just above waist height. The room inside was dark and small. He saw a sink and a sideboard. A cupboard attached to one wall. He could see where the window was coming away.

'I reckon you should be able to open it if you pull here,' Alice said, as she pointed to the bottom left-hand corner. She had learnt to be practical.

Francis could feel her breath in the stillness, his heart beating. He was shaking slightly. He looked at her as if to say, do you think we really should be doing this? He tried to listen for voices, people in the woods. But all he heard was Alice and himself breathing.

'Let me,' she said. She moved forward, forcing Francis to step sideways. She grabbed the bottom of the window and tugged. It creaked and came away from the frame without much effort. She thought it must have come away before. She put the window on the ground. 'Do you want to go first?'

'No, no, you go. I'll help you in.'

Alice pulled herself up, Francis trying to help her, holding her unnecessarily by the waist and pushing. She was light and agile and slipped into the room. Francis followed, awkwardly. Alice walked across the room, confidently, and opened the only door, which led into a thin corridor running across the width of the hut. She could feel the sand on the floor through her shoes. She had been in huts like this before, sand and dust everywhere, dim and still and sheltering. But those huts had smelt of dry heat, roasting wood, sweat perhaps in the afternoon. The smell now was of damp, thick air. She moved forward in the dimness, discerning three more doors, one to her left, which she thought must lead to the main front room, one directly ahead, which she could tell was the back door from the way in which light glowed around the edges and through the lock, and one to her right. She could feel Francis's presence behind her. She opened the door on her right. Light from a window high up the back wall poured in and onto a bench, or a sort of couch. 'What do you think the Queen gets up to in here?' she said.

Francis laughed, feeling the tightness inside him relax. 'You tell me.'

There was a blue cotton sun hat on the bench. Alice picked it up and examined it. It was stained, with patches of greeny brown. It was a small child's hat. She lifted it to her nose and smelt it. It smelt of damp. But there was also a hint of baby oil or something like that, a baby's smell anyway. She threw it to Francis.

'Let's take it back for Tristram,' said Francis, stuffing it into his pocket. 'I think he spotted it through the window earlier.'

'Yes,' she said abstractedly, suddenly not interested in the hat. She sat on the couch thinking of the heat and the smell of sweat. The afternoons she and Billy had spent hiding from the sun. The first night she had spent with him in a motel near Yalata. It had been in a room much like the one she was in now, on a bed not much bigger. She remembered the coolness of the night, but still how their skin had stuck to each other. She had got up some time before dawn wanting fresh air, to be on her own for a

few moments, away from being so close to someone she
hardly knew. And she remembered how he hadn't let her
leave the hut without him accompanying her, saying it was
dangerous. How he had hated to let her out of his sight.

Francis was still standing by the door. She looked at him,
looking for Billy in him, but it was just her brother that
came to mind again. She thought Henderson was more
like Billy, not in the way he looked, but in the way he
was. His awkwardness, his temper, the way he thought
he knew everything. And the way he was probably hiding
something.

Francis looked at Alice sitting on the couch and wondered
what he should do next. He was not sure why she had led
him here, away from the others. He wondered whether
she wanted what he believed he wanted. But it had been
so long since he had been in a similar situation he wasn't
sure whether he could read her clearly. He hovered by the
door for a while longer, moving his weight from one foot to
the other, neither of them saying anything, then he went to
sit beside her. His leg touching hers. He knew they shouldn't
be here. That was all he really knew.

'We should get dressed,' Laura said.

'Not just yet. Let's lie here for a little longer. Please.'
Carey was beginning to feel like her old self at last. She
didn't want to put her clothes on. She stretched her legs,
pointed her toes.

'What if the others find us?' Laura was suddenly very
conscious of where she was, her nakedness, what they had
been doing.

'They won't here, there's no way.' Carey didn't care who
came across them.

But Laura didn't feel comfortable any more. She stood
up. She felt sticky. She wanted a swim.

*   *   *

Henderson and Tristram emerged from the woods into an area of scrub, nearly running. Across a vast plain of rippled sand the sea appeared as a thin blue wedge, absorbing the sun, which was turning it a deeper blue. Henderson could just hear it, sound waves washing over the sand. He was relieved to be out of the dark woods and into the brightness and breeze, and he took deep breaths once they had stopped to get their bearings: clearing his lungs, clearing out his system. He puffed. They stood on a mound of grass-fringed sand for some time, Henderson deciding on where exactly Laura and Carey should be.

'Look, Daddy,' Tristram pointed to his right. He saw horses, three or four, moving across the sand.

Henderson could just make out the riders, the flap of bright clothes, fraying hair. 'Yes, I see them.' They were galloping now and Henderson watched, quickly becoming mesmerised. 'Wonderful,' he murmured. He had never been riding, but he wanted to be on a horse now, galloping across the beach. The feeling of power, surely. Of being able to move so quickly away. He watched as the horses reached the sea, the spray as they thundered through the water. But he knew he had to lumber on. That there was no easy way forward for him.

Tristram quickly lost interest in the horses. 'Come on Daddy, let's go.' He clapped his hands, in the way his father often did when he was in a rush. 'I'm tired.'

'OK.' Henderson saw a path worn through the scrub and marram edging the beach and going in what he thought was roughly the right direction. He set off not able to get the horses out of his mind, imagining the motion, wondering how far they could go in a day. Unable to concentrate on where he was really going. Then he saw a man walking along a ridge of small dunes some way in the distance. After a while he realised the man was naked. He turned to Tristram not sure if Tristram had seen him.

'Tristram.' Tristram wasn't behind him, he was nowhere in sight. 'Tristram,' he shouted, running back along the path, panic growing, over a rise in the ground. 'Tristram.' But Tristram hadn't moved. He was still where they had first stopped. 'Tristram, what are you playing at? What's the matter?'

Tristram was sitting, rubbing his eyes, bewildered. 'I'm tired.'

'Here, climb on.' Henderson knelt and Tristram climbed on his back. He stood up, worried that Tristram was much lighter than he should be. He held onto his legs and Tristram grabbed him round the neck. They set off again, the path widening and flattening out between low dunes. Henderson kept scanning the dunes but he didn't see the naked man again. They crossed the jetsam of an old tide mark: dried seaweed, pieces of wood, bits of plastic, old buoys, soft drinks bottles worn translucent. 'See here, Tristram,' Henderson tried to point and hang onto his son at the same time, 'the sea comes up as far as this.' It had always amazed Henderson quite how far, and fast, the tide moved here. And he wanted to tell Tristram about it now. Explain what made the tide go in and out. Explain to him all sorts of things he had never had the chance to tell anyone. He wanted Tristram to listen to him.

But Tristram was too sleepy to be interested. He didn't want to get down to have a closer look at what had been washed up, even if there might have been something he could have taken home for his box. He shut one eye and the sun made hazy rings in the other. He saw a butterfly, a large tortoiseshell drifting just above him. He reached out, instinctively, but the butterfly was out of his grasp.

Henderson moved to the side of the path well before the faded wind-break, not wanting to intrude on anyone's space. Then he saw the four bodies, old and naked and shocking. He leapt into the dunes, through the grass, jogging Tristram violently.

'Daddy,' Tristram cried, banging his head against his father's neck. He too saw the naked people. 'They've got no clothes on, Daddy. They've got no clothes on.' Tristram couldn't take his eyes off them. The women were so much larger and floppier than his mother. Their breasts falling to their sides or lying low and flat on their stomachs. He had never seen bodies like them. 'Daddy.'

'Shut up, Tristram.' Henderson hurried through the dunes, Tristram bouncing and giggling on his back. Henderson had taken his clothes off in places he shouldn't have, but he couldn't understand how people could just lie on the beach without any clothes on, not with bodies like that, not in the middle of a path. He thought of Laura's body, firm, bony even. But young still. The ancient couple he then spotted, sitting on deckchairs eating with nothing on, made him feel quite sick.

Alice sprung up, suddenly aware Francis might have misunderstood her, the situation. God, she was tired of people misunderstanding her. No one knew how she felt. They always got it wrong. They always played games with her emotions. She thought for an instant she was going to cry. Then the injustice of not being understood made her angry and defiant. And she realised she didn't really care what Francis thought, because he could have no idea what was going on in her mind, which was drifting uncontrollably back to Australia. 'I once stayed in a hut very like this, in Australia. I can just picture it,' she said

Francis cleared his throat. 'Where?'

'Oh, miles from anywhere. In the outback. South Australia.'

Francis tried to imagine transplanting the Queen's hut to the outback. God, how he would hate to be marooned there, even with Alice. He thought of the snakes and all the other poisonous things, more of them than anywhere else in the world.

'It was in the Nullarbor Plain. Nullarbor means no trees in Latin.' She suddenly remembered Billy telling her that.

'Oh, yes, of course,' said Francis, still sitting on the bench, pretending he would have understood the Latin. He then tried to imagine a place with no trees, the Nullarbor Plain, but all that came to mind was the beach earlier. 'It must be like here. Well not exactly here, in these woods, but on the beach.'

'Yes and no.' She went to the door. That's it she thought. That's enough.

Francis understood that she didn't want to continue the conversation. Still he didn't want her to leave the room. He thought something else must happen, be said. He changed the subject. 'You're a painter, aren't you? What do you paint? What sort of pictures?' Unsubtle questions, he knew, but he couldn't think properly, so quickly. 'Big, small?' Stupid.

Alice raised her eyebrows, but not in a perturbed way, expansively really. No one took an interest in her painting. She moved away from the door, back closer to Francis. Pleased he'd asked. Prepared to give him another chance. 'I used to paint, oh, I don't know, I suppose you'd call them abstract pictures. They were big paintings. I thought of them as landscapes. They were based on the landscape, and what made up the landscape. You know, what happens underneath, where you can't see, the rock formations, the strata.' Light from the window poured on her. She rubbed her left eye. 'Well I started painting regular landscapes, literal interpretations. Then as I progressed and thought more about the form, what made up the land, they just became more abstract. Really they were about taking off layers and looking underneath, as well as trying to show what it looked like, or how it came across as a whole, a complete form, all at the same time.'

Francis was confused. 'Do you ever paint people? Did you ever?'

'Oh, I suppose so. I did life drawing for a while, of course. But I was never so attracted to people. I found them much harder to unravel. Pick out the layers, if you like. People are not as defined as places. You don't know where you are with them, what they are formed of. In a way people keep reinventing their past, hiding things, making things up. The land can't do that. I suppose I could have managed bits of people.' She paused, turned away. 'I always made a mess of them. I don't paint anything now anyway.' She left the room.

'Shit,' said Laura. 'Oh, shit. I think I've just seen Henderson.' She crouched, trying to hide behind the marram and sea couch.

'Where?'

'It is him. He's coming this way. He is, really. He's giving Tristram a piggyback. Shit.'

Carey was still lying on the sand. She yawned and stretched again. In a way she wanted Henderson to find them naked together. Shock him. 'I'm not moving.' She thought it was about time he noticed Laura properly, took an interest in her. About time he thought about someone other than himself.

Laura was now sitting on the ground pulling her swimsuit on, putting her legs into the wrong holes. 'Oh, come on Carey. Get dressed. Please.'

Carey sat up. She leant over and patted Laura on the shoulder. 'OK.' She stood and brushed the sand off her thighs and bottom, seeing Henderson with Tristram coming from the direction of the woods. He was not far away and she wondered whether he would be able to recognise her.

She reached down for her swimsuit, shook it and pulled it on. It had not occurred to her that Francis and Alice were not with them.

'Laura,' Henderson shouted. 'Laura, Carey.'

Laura scrambled to her feet. 'Henderson. Tristram.' She could feel her face flush. 'What are you doing here?' She was breathless. 'I mean, how did you find us? You shocked me.'

'What are you doing here?' He could see she was surprised to see him. And Carey, who was untwisting the straps of her swimsuit. They looked guilty, he was sure of it. But he had no idea why. He lifted Tristram off his back, saddened because he had been looking forward to meeting up with Laura, thinking she would be pleased to see him. He had wanted to bring Tristram safely back, bring them all together. And it wasn't at all how he had anticipated.

'We've been sunbathing, chatting, forgetting the time. I thought we were meeting on the beach, further over there?' Laura was getting her breath back. 'Tristram, come here darling.' She wanted to cuddle her son, mask herself from Henderson. But Tristram stayed where he was, tired and not understanding his parents.

'Well where do you think we were going?' Henderson looked at her, her heaving ribcage, her flushed face. 'Why on earth did you stop here?' he asked. 'You're surrounded by nudists.'

It's a public beach, Carey felt like saying. We can go where the hell we like. But she didn't say anything.

'Oh, really,' said Laura. She tried to laugh, but just a nervous giggle came out. 'I thought I saw a naked man. I must have.'

'Well, I'm not lingering about here,' Henderson said. 'No way.' But he didn't walk away either, he kept staring at the ground Laura and Carey had lain on, their clothes and bags in some disarray. He looked up and caught Carey's eye. He didn't like the way she was looking at him. It was as if she were keeping something from him and was enjoying the fact that he didn't know what. He suddenly wanted to hurt her. 'I don't know where Francis and Alice have got to, I imagine they'll meet us where we said we'd all be.'

Laura didn't notice Carey flinch. 'Didn't they go with you to the Queen's beach hut, or whatever it is?' Laura asked Henderson, now annoyed they might have gone elsewhere when they should have been keeping an eye on Tristram.

'We left them there, they wanted to stay behind. Alice wanted to break in or something and Francis said he would help.'

'What?' Laura didn't quite believe Henderson. 'Break in?'

'That would be the day,' Carey scoffed. 'I can really imagine Francis would be a great help.' She suddenly felt better about Francis being with Alice, knowing he would be useless if they actually were trying to break into the Queen's beach hut. And probably terrified. She knew how pathetic he could be. 'Ha, ha,' she laughed. Serves him right, she said to herself. Serves him bloody well right. But she wanted to get going now, get to where they were meant to be meeting, hoping she wouldn't be there first.

Alice wasn't in the beach hut, and Francis suddenly found he was afraid on his own. He tried to calm himself. He stood still listening for voices, before climbing out of the window. He caught his shorts on a screw in his haste and they ripped just below the pocket. The screw grazed his leg also and blood started to ooze and smudge onto the flap of material. But he didn't notice that as he struggled to replace the window. He pushed his way back through the brambles and sharp branches, panicking, sure he heard voices, scratching and cutting his legs further. Knowing he would have no idea how to get back to the beach and the others on his own. Carey. Christ, he said to himself. 'Alice,' he shouted, just before he saw her sitting on the veranda steps.

Alice looked up to see Francis approaching, red-faced, blood on his legs, and she laughed. 'What the hell happened to you?'

'I thought I heard someone,' he said breathlessly. He sat beside her, relieved, forgetting there might be any awkwardness between them. Alice had unfolded John Baxter's map. 'Will it show us how to get out of here?' he asked

'I don't know. That was why I was looking at it.' The map also gave her strength, as all maps did, making some sense of where she was, her way forward.

Francis leant over. 'Christ, it's hand-drawn. Where did you pick that up?'

'In the windmill. But it's a good map. The person who drew it knew what he was doing. I do know a bit about maps.' Alice started to look at maps seriously when she couldn't look at her paintings any more. She thought that maps would help her find the true shape of things again, the formations. The way things should be. She tried drawing her own maps, still tried, but they weren't very clear. She felt she had lost her ability to read the land. Indeed, nothing was very clear. And she thought it should be clear now, in the country of her childhood. Somewhere that had existed in her mind irreproachably. Blast it, she said to herself, then bent closer to the map knowing she couldn't stop yet, wondering whether she would ever be able to. 'Look, see where he's drawn the marshes,' she said excitedly, 'look at the detail. All those channels and gullies he's marked, the paths leading across the marshes and mud-flats. He's even marked which paths to use for high and low tides. Where it's safe to walk.'

'Well what about the woods?'

'Wait a minute.'

Francis noticed the blood on his legs. He tried to wipe it off with his hands, but it just smudged further and he ended up wiping his hands on his torn shorts. He worried about what Carey would think when she saw him. God, he knew how difficult she could be. He didn't want to be here anymore, sitting on the Queen's veranda with Alice. He wanted to be out of the woods and with Carey, with the others, where everything would be normal. 'Have you found the way out of here yet?'

Alice could detect the urgency in his voice. 'Yes, I think I have. I knew it would be marked, despite what Henderson said earlier. I don't know what his problem is. Here.' She pointed to the map. 'We're here. Look, he's even called it the Queen's beach hut. Gun Hill's marked, there, where we had lunch. We could take that path, the way we came, or that one which leads straight out to the beach, and then walk across.'

'That one. Straight out to the beach definitely,' he said, leaping up.

They set off on a barely discernible path, but a path none the less: Francis bloodied, and Alice buoyed by the small success of John Baxter's map and the way that one route at least was clearly marked and seemed to be reliable. They emerged a short while later in a field of waist-high grass, that reminded Alice of elephant grass. The sun was on them and the fluffy heads floating in the breeze. There was the soft sound of the sea, and they both felt warmed and secure.

Tristram screamed, but he didn't turn away. 'Mummy,' he then shouted, rooted to the spot. 'Mummy.'

Laura ran to him, 'Oh, God, come away.'

'What is it?' Tristram asked, not moving, fascinated by

the dead animal, the maggots writhing in the eye sockets and the burst gut.

'It's a seal. Come on darling.' She smelt it then. It made her gag.

Carey and Henderson crowded round, unable not to. It was grey brown and scarlet where the rot had set in. Carey even noticed the seal's whiskers on the bubbling face. But neither Carey nor Henderson could bear to look at it for long, both having grown quietly squeamish over the years. 'Come on,' said Henderson. 'Leave the poor thing alone.' He walked round it and on across the hard drying sand.

Tristram wiped his hands on his shorts, as if he had touched the dead seal. He thought it was the first proper dead animal he had ever seen. He couldn't stop thinking about the maggots. Wondering where they came from, if they were inside everybody, himself even.

Laura felt stickier and stickier walking out to the seashore in the swelling afternoon heat, her swimsuit adhering between her legs. She also wanted to have a pee. She couldn't wait to get into the sea. She tugged at the bottom of her costume while walking, straightening her back.

'I wonder what happened to the seal?' Henderson said to Carey, gravely. The seal had disturbed him, the way it had suddenly appeared on the sand, staining something so vast and unblemished, so pure. He didn't want to hurt Carey now. He didn't want to hurt anybody, momentarily realising how fragile life was. How violent. 'Just stranded by the tide, do you think?'

Carey didn't want to think about the seal. 'Who cares?' she said. She was angry and worried and kept looking about the sand for two figures. Where the fuck are they? she said under her breath. She increased her pace and soon she had separated from the others.

'I'm dying for a swim,' Laura said to Henderson. She suddenly felt sorry for him, his head red and sweaty, his long limbs reddening too. He looked awkward and uncomfortable, hopeless even, marching across the sand. Sometimes she did feel sorry for him, believing in him again. Believing their marriage wasn't hopeless. 'Are you going to come in again?'

'Yes, if, if it's not too shallow.' He was hesitant. He often found himself stumbling for words when Laura asked him something. He had grown unused to conversing with her.

'I want to swim,' said Tristram, excitedly. 'I love swimming.'

'I'll take you in,' said Henderson. 'It's not much further.' He could see small waves breaking, white water, the width of wavy wet sand. Tristram was walking between himself and Laura now. He had an urge to hold his son's hand, for Laura to hold Tristram's other hand. Swing him in the middle, like he knew you were meant to. But they didn't.

Carey looked back. She couldn't see any figures that might have resembled Francis and Alice. She just saw Henderson and Laura, and Tristram in the middle of them. They're not much of a family, she thought. They should be swinging him, one, two, three.

'It's a magnificent beach, isn't it?' Henderson suggested to Laura, realising they had lapsed into silence again. Their feet on the sand making no noise.

'Yes. Is it how you remember?'

'In a way. There are some places I suppose you just don't forget.'

'It depends what happened there, I believe, and who you were with.' An image of a Scottish loch flashed in front of her, startling her. She shook her head. She caught sight of two figures behind her, but the sun was behind them and all she could see were silhouettes. 'You can certainly alter the picture of a place in your mind.'

'That's them,' Alice said. She could feel the hard ripples of sand on her insteps, and the further they walked out onto the beach the more her feeling of security evaporated. She kept thinking she was somewhere else again. Billy shifting in the distance, a shadow. She couldn't bear it. And for a moment she felt an incredible urge to run, to run back into the woods, run away, away from Nullarbor. And the past. But she strode on, knowing, hoping Laura and a different world were ahead.

Francis could only see two people and a child, then he saw a third person beyond the group by the sea. He waved. No one waved back and he started to jog. He wanted to get to them well before Alice.

Henderson heard panting. He turned and saw Francis jogging up to him. 'Francis,' he shouted.

But Francis didn't stop as he neared. He had discerned Carey by the shore. He raised his hand to Henderson as he swerved round him and Laura and Tristram, panting on, finally slowing. He didn't think Carey had yet seen or heard him. 'Hi,' he said, catching his breath suddenly beside her, smiling.

'Where the fuck have you been?'

'What do you mean?'

'You're ridiculous, breaking into the Queen's beach hut. Honestly. Where's Alice? I suppose you got scared and left her there.'

'Oh, don't be so stupid.'

'Don't be so stupid? Git.'

'Calm down. There's no need to get hysterical.' Francis knew Carey hated to be told to calm down. He knew she couldn't bear the thought of not being able to behave rationally, of not being in control. 'Really, what's your problem?'

'You,' Carey said.

'Great,' Francis said. The sand was wet and soft, the consistency of slushy snow. The water was much warmer now, as it flopped in, over Francis's feet. 'Come on, let's go for a last swim.' He started to undress, thinking even swimming would be better than standing here with Carey. 'Carey?' He moved closer to her, struggling with his shorts in the sinking sand, and tried to kiss her cheek.

She pulled away, confused. 'Christ, Francis you're pathetic.' And so am I, she said to herself. Grow up.

'Hi, Laura.' Alice reached Laura's side, bounded up as if it had been twenty-five years ago. 'The Queen's beach hut was not that interesting.' She didn't want Laura to feel she had missed out on anything special, knowing how children hated to miss out on things. And for an instant she saw Laura as a child, thin and gangly and left out. And she wanted to comfort her, while comforting herself.

'Oh, Carey and I had a nice time in the dunes, relaxing, chatting. We talked about what we used to get up to when we were growing up. I think it made us both feel quite young again.' She smiled at Alice.

There was a roar and a splash, and Francis jumped and belly-flopped into the shallow sea, grazing his stomach on the bottom. Laura dropped her things and ran in after him. Henderson struggled with Tristram's armbands. Alice helped him, as she had helped Laura earlier. They both then held Tristram's hands and swung him into the sea, Tristram shrieking joyfully, Alice imagining Tristram to be her son, Henderson imagining what life would have been like had he married Alice, or someone like her. Carey was the last in, but she didn't go far out this time, keeping close to the shore, sitting on the bottom, digging her hands into the sand, trying to remain balanced as the small swell rocked her. Laura swam and swam, finally stopping. The water still no deeper than her waist. She squatted down so it came up to her chin. She then hooked her fingers round the leg holes of her swimsuit and peed, feeling the warm liquid flowing over her thumbs.

Francis reached a sand bank, proud of himself. He didn't know whether it was the one he had bumped into earlier. He stood up and walked through ankle-deep water until there was none. He walked on seaward for a while, leaving deep footprints. He stopped well short of the next shoreline and watched as the water started to creep over the sand towards him, he was sure of it. Brown foam soon curling by his feet. He turned to see the others. They had got out and were towelling themselves and running on the spot. He thought Alice was waving at him for a moment, then he realised she was drying her hair. The water was over his feet now. He started to walk back to them, reaching the deeper water. As he swam and waded, suddenly desperate to be back on dry land, a sense of *déjà vu* flooded through him.

Sticky with salt, they drank the rest of the water and squash and packed up their stuff for the last time. 'The trouble with going to the beach for the day is that you have to carry so much bloody stuff,' Francis complained. They lugged themselves and their sandy damp things back across the enormous empty beach, the heat creating streams of shimmering water that weren't really there. On in the vague direction of the windmill, that was obscured by the dunes and the distance. Laura felt the heaviness of her limbs, quite unused to so much exercise, or the intensity of the day. Tristram marched ahead, but soon found the ripples in the sand hurt the bottoms of his feet. The sun, much lower now, dazed him. His head hurt inside. He had loved being in the water, and he wanted to be able to do what the others could do. But he was beginning to realise he was just too small; he couldn't go any further, and started to whimper. Henderson picked him up, thinking that they had perhaps been a little too ambitious for the first day. He was ambitious, though, never knowing when to stop, always going too far, pushing himself and whoever he happened to be with. Alice was fit and she felt refreshed after her last dip. But she also felt increasingly that she was not a part of the group. She had noticed the looks Carey had been giving her, and Francis's awkwardness, the way Henderson leered at her. The way Laura seemed to not open up to her at all. She felt detached.

'There's no way I'm going back the way we came,' Carey announced. 'No way.' She was carrying the biggest bag, and she felt quite justified in demanding they went a different way. Even if it turned out to be slightly longer. She knew everyone would appreciate it later, they always did.

'Well how do you want to get back?' Laura asked, her voice tired and concerned. She didn't want Carey to be difficult and dogmatic now. The sun split into shafts of late afternoon light and there was a growing haze in the air which made everything seem quite tranquil.

Francis tutted to himself, knowing they would be going back the way Carey wished. He looked over to Alice and thought she looked rather sad, dejected even. But he didn't want to walk beside her because he was unsure of Carey's mood, whether she was still angry with him. She didn't forget things easily.

'Henderson, there must be another way back?' Carey asked. She hated asking Henderson anything, but she had no choice.

'I'm not sure. There might be a way around the end of the dunes, and across the harbour creek and over the marshes that side. Certainly I should think when the tide's out. But I don't know it, I've never done it. I suppose it could be quicker. You would cut out the embankment.' The image of the seal had reappeared, and it was mixing itself up with an image of Victoria, and then he saw the look in Carey's eyes when he had stumbled upon her and Laura amid the nudists, a look that said she knew something he didn't. He didn't feel like helping her, even if he had clearly been able to. In fact he wanted her to make a mistake.

Alice thought about getting out John Baxter's map: she knew that if there were a way back it would be marked, she remembered he had even named the marshes. But she felt hurt and shunned by Carey. If Carey was so determined she could find the way herself. Besides she knew Henderson would only deride the map again.

'Well let's try it,' Carey said. 'The tide's still out. Come on, it would be so much more interesting. I don't think I could bear to walk all the way back along that embankment.' She started to walk towards the end of the dunes and the harbour mouth, cutting across the beach. 'Come on,' she yelled.

'Carey,' Laura shouted, but Carey ignored her, so she turned to Henderson. 'Do we have to go this way?' she asked him. 'Is it really a good idea?'

'I don't know.' He was still struggling with the images. 'You know what she's like. If she thinks she knows the way, she knows the way.' He could tell Laura was anxious. 'Look, the tide's still a long way out. It shouldn't be a problem.' Henderson hoisted Tristram further up his back, and the images disappeared and it occurred to him instantly, shockingly, just how valuable Tristram was, and Laura. 'Don't worry. I'll look after you both.' He felt useful for once.

Francis somehow found himself walking beside Alice. She had put her hat back on, and he could see the dark brown curls that escaped it were still wet, some sticking to her neck, droplets clinging to her pale skin then letting go. 'Carey can be very determined,' he said, almost as if that were an excuse for his behaviour too.

Alice didn't feel like giving any credit to Carey at the moment, but she said, 'Well she does have a point. I hate going back the way I've come.' You have to keep

finding new ground, she added to herself, new terri-
tory.

Francis was conscious of every step he took, the way
his feet stuck a little too far out. He slung the bag he
was carrying onto his other shoulder. 'I enjoyed—' he
started, but Alice interrupted him before he could finish
his sentence.

'Sorry, you go on,' she said.

'No, you,' Francis said, urgently, forgetting what he was
going to say.

'I was just going to say, I'm glad the sun is not so
strong now.'

'Yes,' he said, looking up at the sky. 'I suppose the days
are already drawing in.'

'Of course they are,' said Alice, realising it would soon
be autumn here. Her second autumn in a year. Her mouth
suddenly felt very dry and bitter. She tried to swallow, but
couldn't, couldn't get her tongue out of the way.

The dunes ran out and they reached the harbour mouth,
the sun glistening on the water, and the water appeared like
mercury rising onto the shingle banks. Beyond the channel
was Scolt Head Island. It wasn't much of an island, just low
dunes and marram-tufted bluffs pushed westward by the
wind and the sea, but like all islands Henderson had found
it mystical when he was young. He told everyone that a
warden lived on it in a hut during the summer months.
Like Robinson Crusoe, he said for Tristram's benefit. But
Tristram hadn't heard of Robinson Crusoe, or if he had
been told he had forgotten. 'At least a warden used to,'
Henderson added, because he couldn't see any people on
the island, or anyone now anywhere, which was unusual
for the time of year.

Carey turned inland, keeping to the bank, not sure
exactly where they should be heading. The others followed
her, and it became noticeably quieter as they moved by

the harbour creek. The noise of waves breaking receded into the distance, and they thought they were leaving the sea behind. But they weren't, the sea was following them inland, quicker in fact than they were going. Up the harbour creek, and all the other creeks and gullies that spread out across the marshes in a maze.

Tristram was the first to comment on the ark. 'Look, Mummy,' he said, 'an ark.' He knew what an ark was. He had been told about Noah at school, seen pictures in a book. 'It's not very big.' He had imagined the real ark to be enormous, bigger than his house in London, bigger than the biggest building he had ever seen. The ark was beached well above a shingle bank on fine sand surrounded by clumps of shrubby seablite. 'Down,' Tristram demanded, suddenly reinvigorated. And Henderson swung him over his head and onto the ground. The small boy ran to the ark and tried to climb aboard the rotting wooden structure, half expecting to hear animal noises from inside. But there was nothing except the smell of tar and dry wood, so Tristram soon gave up and walked back to the group. 'It's empty.' Why's everything empty here? he thought. Why does nothing work? He thought of the Queen's beach hut, the windmill. How nothing works properly on holidays.

'It's for birdwatchers,' Henderson said, for the benefit of everyone, not just Tristram. He knew what it was, of course he did. 'See, see the flap. That's where they poke their binoculars out. At least that was where they used to. It looks abandoned to me.' He scanned beyond the ark, seeing no one.

'Sure you don't want to break in and have a closer look?' Carey asked Francis, annoyed that he was talking to Alice. Francis didn't answer, he just looked at her blankly. Carey then told everyone to hurry up and follow her, she was getting impatient, eager to prove she could get them back to the windmill quicker than the way they had come.

'Sure you know where you're going?' Francis asked.

A tributary split off and appeared to curl round the island while the harbour creek, continuing inland, narrowed noticeably. Beyond the harbour creek was a large stretch of sand, edged, Carey could see, by mud and marshes. She walked down to the water, and holding her shoes and bag to her chest, started to cross. 'It's easy,' she shouted, delighted, once across. The water had not come much above her knees.

Henderson wasn't sure about crossing here, he knew the marshes the other side could be dangerous, that you could get cut off. He didn't think he had ever ventured onto them, not that he was allowed, preferring the sand dunes and the woods, which were less open, less exposed, and much better for hiding in. He could see the embankment they had come on was now not that much further ahead. That they could reach it without crossing the harbour creek, or any other major obstacle, and that it wouldn't take too long to reach the staithe. He could see Laura looked uneasy still, and his concern for her and Tristram was growing. 'I think it might be just as quick to join up with the embankment there,' he shouted to Carey, pointing.

'What? I'm here now. It's easy. All we have to do is cut across those marshes and we'll be back.' She thought she could see the edge of the harvested field that lay next to the windmill, rising above the marshes and pasture, golden and lovely in the sinking sun. It was the same field. She was not mistaken. A hundred yards or so on and she knew she would be able to see the windmill, clear of the staithe and the coppice behind the staithe. She never got lost. 'Don't be so boring.'

Alice was next across the channel, and Francis followed her, exactly.

But despite his concern for Laura and Tristram, Henderson found himself edging towards the channel. He wasn't sure what was urging him on: whether it was because he hadn't been onto these marshes before and he felt compelled to go somewhere so familiar yet new, or whether it was because he just wanted Carey to make a mistake so Laura could see she wasn't perfect. He picked Tristram up. 'Here,' and he held out his hand for Laura, holding Tristram onto his back awkwardly with the other. The current was strong as the water poured inland. Pebbles and shells were hard and sharp on the bottom. He tightened his grip on Laura's hand, still holding on once they were across. Though he was unsure about being on this side of the creek, he felt somehow stronger, more useful, Tristram on his back, and he squeezed Laura's hand before letting go.

Carey marched on. The sand was soft and heavy-going and it took her much longer than she thought it would to reach the marshes. She climbed up a bank of mud, slipping, but managing to grab hold of a bed of matted sea lavender going to seed before she lost her balance completely falling onto the top. She picked herself up and wiped her hands on her shorts, surveying the wet land ahead. She had thought she might see a path but there was nothing resembling a path, just an expanse of marsh, laced with muddy channels and gullies. Some were already deep with water. She couldn't see the windmill either, and it occurred to her, just for a moment, that she shouldn't have insisted on coming this way.

The others scrambled onto the marsh and waited for Carey to decide where to go next. 'It's all yours,' Henderson said to her. 'We're just following.'

Francis could see no logical way ahead. He would have started to panic had he not been aware of Alice and the calm she exuded.

Despite Carey's momentary lapse, she was still confident. 'Do you want me to help you with your bag?' she asked Alice, annoyed that Alice seemed so unperturbed, so calm about their predicament, about everything. She still couldn't work her out.

'No, of course not, but thanks,' Alice replied, sharply. God, she thought, this bag's nothing. Neither's this terrain. Come on, let's get going you bitch.

Carey moved ahead, knowing she'd find a way, skipping and jumping across the small gullies and over the shallow pools of salt water mirroring the sky.

The others followed, then stopped because Henderson stopped, spotting a bed of samphire. He lowered Tristram to the ground and began pulling at the samphire, freeing plants, their roots blackened with silt. 'Hey,' he said, 'supper.' He tugged at the stuff manically, soon collecting a large pile. 'Isn't anyone going to help? Alice, this is samphire. Samphire, the stuff I was telling you about last night.'

Alice dropped her bag and began picking, finding the plants almost slipped out of the ground. She was not used to plants that gave up so easily. Or plants that were so green and tight with moisture. She had a sudden craving for samphire. Something so easy and different.

'Keep to the really green stuff,' Henderson directed. 'The reddish ones have had it. We're lucky there's so much left this late in the season. We're bloody lucky.' Henderson soon forgot who he was with, the time, the tide, where they had to get to. He felt he was pulling up his past, with each root came a tingling of recognition in his lower back. Voices, birds, the burble of the marsh mud. He stood up, dizzy, seeing Victoria beside him. 'Look how much I've got,' he said. 'Look at my pile.'

Tristram picked at the samphire too. He thought it felt rubbery. He bit into a stem, spitting it out immediately. 'Yuk,' he shouted, his mouth full of salt and stringy fibre.

He spat and spat, his face becoming covered in green spittle. He started to cry again. His body shaking.

Laura watched a shingle ridge in the distance. Sun catching the stones and sand-polished shells, and it was not still. Then she saw what she was looking for. Black legs, shaggy crest, short tail, yellow tip to black bill, she muttered to herself. Yellow tip to black bill, yes, I'm sure of it. She shielded her eyes from the glare with the flat of her hand, watching the tern, waiting to see it find its mate. But the small bird stepped gingerly, awkwardly about on its own. 'We should move on,' she said loudly, her eyes straining, unable to watch the tern any longer. 'We must get back. Oh, Tristram, what have you done?' She bent down and wiped his face with the corner of a damp towel.

Carey came running back, her knees and hands covered in mud. Mud on her cheeks even. 'I've found the way. Come on. What are you doing with all that muck?' She didn't direct the question to anyone in particular, bemused by the two piles of samphire. 'You're not bringing that back, surely?'

Henderson had unrolled a towel and was placing the samphire in the middle, the way he had carried samphire before. 'Of course.'

'Henderson,' Laura said.

Alice squashed the plants into her bag. She wasn't going to miss out. She wasn't going to be ignored. She'd see to it.

'I do think we should get going,' Francis said. 'Carey?' He set off with her, hoping the others would hurry up.

The sun swept across the marshes burning the pools of water and slick mud with a fiery thickness. Gulls, redshanks and oyster-catchers were busy feeding before the sun set and a pair of mallards flighted overhead. There was movement everywhere, and a smell of salty decay. The dunes, far to their north, were turning red and the tops of the pine woods, just visible, black. The air was much cooler suddenly. They were the only people on Overy Marsh.

They followed a creek for a while, slipping down onto a muddy ridge, their view obscured by the high banks, the creek quite dim in the shade. The creek split in two and they stopped. There was a gurgling, scraping sound. They all stood in silence, and the sound filled the dark creek. A clicking, sucking.

'What's that noise?' Tristram finally asked.

Alice looked at Henderson, just waiting for him to come up with some clever explanation.

Henderson bent down and dug his fingers into the mud. Shortly he stood up holding a cockle. 'It's the shellfish opening and closing.' He started digging in the mud again, soon coming up with handfuls of cockles. 'They do that at this time of day,' he said.

Alice nodded her head, slowly, resignedly.

'For God's sake,' Carey shouted, startling Laura. 'We haven't got time for that now.' She was worried again, the high banks making her feel closed in.

With dismay Francis watched Alice join Henderson digging for cockles. He wanted to get out of the creek, he wanted to get out of the marshes. He had had enough for one day.

But it was Laura who spoke. 'Henderson, Alice, come on,' she said. 'It's getting cold. Tristram's getting cold.' She rubbed her son, his face tear-stained. And Alice and Henderson stopped digging, both slightly ashamed, coming back to their senses.

Alice was first out of the creek, trying to make amends, and up onto the lavender beds. She was the first to spot the windmill again, the black tower on the horizon. 'We're nearly there,' she shouted.

Laura thought it looked miles away, but she was happy she could at least see it now. As was Francis. Henderson had seen it stark on the horizon so many times he wasn't surprised or comforted. It was just natural, how it was always meant to be.

Carey was delighted. 'See,' she said. 'I knew I would get you all back.'

'We're not back yet,' Henderson said.

They headed straight for the windmill, jumping the small channels once again, and wading through others. Francis was carrying Tristram and Carey was thinking about how right she was, how you should never go back the way you came. How you'd miss out on so much. 'Fuck,' she said softly, then she shouted it, 'fuck.' The noise spread out across the marshes, and was echoed by birds and burbling, nothing human. They had come to a creek, much larger than any they had encountered previously. It was filled with fast-moving water, patches of swirling brown scum. Not far beyond the creek was an embankment, and beyond that the tussocky pasture leading up to the windmill. Though Carey, all of them, realised there was no way they could cross here. They headed inland with the current, the channel neither widening nor narrowing, just swirling, none of them speaking. Then the creek joined another creek, as wide and full, cutting off their passage further inland.

'Oh, Christ,' Francis said. 'Where the fuck are we? Where the fuck have you led us Carey?'

'You can see where we are. Look, there's the bloody windmill. We just can't seem to get there. How was I to know that this creek was going to be here?' Carey turned back to sea, there being no other way to go, feeling stupid she hadn't anticipated any such obstacles, having believed they would be able to get back the most direct way. She just didn't understand this wretched place.

'Where are you going now?' Francis screamed. He was sure the ground felt wetter, as if water was seeping up under the tangle of marsh plants, slowly immersing them.

Carey didn't answer. But they all followed her, their feet squelching, as the marshes were indeed getting wetter, soaking up the incoming tide. They walked alongside the creek, against the current, until the creek swept round and into the direction of Harbour Creek, Gun Hill magnificent and pink straight ahead. Laura slipped on the edge of a gully, falling flat onto the wet slimy ground with a splat, dropping her bags and hurting her right arm. She got up without complaining, not wanting to make matters worse, and rubbed her arm. Henderson was now carrying Tristram, and struggling under his weight, the boy having grown so much heavier throughout the afternoon. And soon it became clear they were going to end up back on the sand bank, back by the harbour creek.

'Look,' said Alice, at one point, 'I can get us out of here. I've got a map.'

But Carey was too angry to pay her any attention. And Henderson could only concentrate on the fact that Carey should have listened to him, that they should have gone back the way he had originally suggested, even if that had meant largely going back the way they had come. There was a lesson in that, he thought. Seeing his greater predicament, he believed more strongly than ever that you have to retrace you steps, go back to places at certain times in your life to enable you to move forward. Had he been feeling more himself he knew he would have remained in control, and that they would have followed him and he would not have got them in this mess. Nevertheless, he realised he had learnt something, or at least had had something confirmed. He hoped. Trying to ignore the weight of Tristram he quickened his pace. He was worried the tide might have risen too high and Harbour Creek be uncrossable.

He was right to worry. The sand bank they had trudged across not much earlier had virtually disappeared and the creek was now a lake. Francis and Laura sat down near

the edge, neither bothered by the wet, both on the verge
of despair. The water rose as they watched it. And Tristram
looked at the lake in amazement. He couldn't understand
why it hadn't been there before.

'A boat will pick us up,' Henderson said, trying to reassure
Laura, Tristram still unaware of their predicament. No one
said anything for some time, all listening and watching for
a boat. Masts were visible in the direction of the staithe,
but they were sail-less and there was no boat anywhere
near. The sun was a ball of fuzz behind them, the lagoon
suddenly still and scarlet.

'I'm sorry,' Carey said, angrily. She was too cross to cry.
'I haven't been here before. I don't understand it.' I don't
understand anything, she said to herself.

Alice calmly got out John Baxter's map, squiggly and now
smudged in places, but still reassuring. She reckoned the
lagoon was Cockle Strand. She could see that if they stuck
north, skirting what must be Little Ramsay as far as Plover
Marsh, then on by Plantago Marsh they would reach Norton
Marsh and the grazing land leading up to the windmill. She
could see where they had gone wrong. They had taken too
direct a route and hit Trowland Creek. They hadn't gone far
enough north. 'Look,' she said, 'there is a way back. Carey,
Henderson, stop being so arrogant and bloody-minded and
listen to me.' Alice knew they'd have to listen to her. She
knew she couldn't be left out.

'That scrap of paper won't get us anywhere,' Henderson
said. He didn't like being called bloody-minded.

'Do you have a better idea?' Laura said, raising her
voice.

'Yes, it will,' Francis cried at the same time. 'Why didn't
you suggest it sooner Alice?'

'I did.'

6

The birdwatcher was happy. He had seen a whimbrel, a number of greenshanks, a kingfisher, a meadow pipit, and a rock pipit which was early for the time of year, and a common sandpiper. He had hoped to catch sight of a roseate tern and he had been paged by a friend informing him a caspian tern had actually been sighted down the coast. That was five days ago, but there was always hope. He had seen a curlew sandpiper, however. That was rare. He flicked through his notebook, the names of different birds he had seen over the last week. He would come here again. He had had no idea what fun salt-marshes and mud-flats could be, or quite how close he could get to the inhabitants, thinking the ark-shaped hide almost perfect.

The light was fast dimming and for the first time in the day he felt a cool breeze against his cheeks and neck. The car was still some distance away, the caravan not even in his thoughts. But he wasn't in a rush, knowing it was duck and goose time, time for the mallards and greylags, the shelducks and Canadas. Maybe even an Egyptian. He knew the place was quite capable of throwing up all manner of surprises. He heard voices, human voices in his bird world, for the second time that afternoon. He stopped and looked out across the marshes, which suddenly seemed still and dense, no place now for waders. He spotted them quickly, four, five people and a child. It's no place for people either, he thought. Now, or ever. Wondering whether the woman he had come across earlier had found her child. Half wondering whether they were amid this group. He turned and carried on.

Some scrap of paper, Alice felt like telling Henderson. But she didn't say anything while she folded the map carefully and slipped it into a side pocket of her bag, unable to stop smiling. She wondered whether Henderson would sulk about it, like Billy used to whenever she proved him wrong. God, he was a child sometimes, she thought, remembering his silences, and worse than that his tantrums. His inability to say sorry, you were right. His lack of humility. Oh, no one knew any better than Billy. Billy couldn't do any wrong. Except he did, Alice thought. He did.

'Thank you,' said Laura, once they were over the embankment and on the firm, dry grazing land.

He never thanked me for anything, Alice thought. There was a tightness in her throat.

'Yes, thanks,' said Carey, her voice stiff and unfriendly. 'I should have listened to you earlier.'

But you didn't listen, Alice thought. You never listened to me.

Francis wanted to kiss Alice, hug her to death. 'You saved our lives,' he said, nearly meaning it. He reached out and touched her upper arm instead. Squeezing it gently.

'I didn't,' Alice laughed, realising where she was, thinking how pathetic Francis was, but sweet. 'Nothing of the sort.' She felt suddenly light-headed, happy.

'You must let me have a look at that map some time,' Henderson said. 'Whoever drew it must know this area like the back of his hand. It's remarkable.' Well it wasn't you who found the way back was it, he said to himself looking at Alice, and for a split-second Victoria. 'We all here?' He moved his head from side to side robotically, chin up, eyes down. He was happy. They were nearly home. He had survived, they all had. He felt Tristram's breath on his neck. Things were looking up. 'Last one back cooks supper. Ho, hum.' He sprinted up the pasture, Tristram bobbing on his back, the windmill looming, its useless sails pink with sunset.

Laura remembered her father saying just that, last one back cooks supper, and herself clutching his shoulders and neck as he stumbled and slipped on a damp Scottish mountainside, her mother running behind. She had always thought she was going to fall off, but she never had. Not until much later, she supposed. For a moment she imagined she were Tristram, sliding down Henderson's back, desperately trying to hold on. Scratching his neck and shoulders. Drawing blood. She started to trot after them, clutching her bags tightly. 'Don't fall,' she shouted. 'Henderson, Henderson be careful.'

Carey couldn't be bothered to run and she was fucked if she was going to cook supper. She wasn't enjoying herself. It wasn't exactly what she had been expecting. She lit a cigarette and puffed furiously, leaving smoke signals as she progressed slowly up the incline. She preferred countryside with its lanes and footpaths and marked trails, she now thought, to the seaside, and these blasted marshes where it was impossible to find your way. The only part of the day she had enjoyed, her time alone with Laura, seemed tarnished now. She took a last, deep drag and stopped while she exhaled, flicking the butt to the ground and stamping on it, telling herself to calm down. Then Alice ran past and her hat blew off. Carey smiled but her smile left her as she watched Alice bend to pick it up, her hair falling over her face, glowing auburn in the pink light. She was lovely. Carey wanted to go back to London. Back to what she knew. Francis appeared by her side. He was little consolation.

Henderson gave Tristram the key and helped him put it into the lock and turn it. 'Let me,' Tristram protested. But he was not strong enough. 'Ow.' His hand hurt as his father covered it with his hand and turned, squeezing. Henderson was met by the smell of sweet staleness. A memory he still couldn't place. It was dark and cool and he went for the light switch.

'Gosh, I'm exhausted,' Laura said, following Henderson and Tristram into the windmill. 'And hungry.' She felt a ripple of pain inside her head, but she was immediately comforted by the round room, the familiarity, and tried to ignore it. 'Home,' she laughed, thinking, here we are, just the three of us.

Alice appeared next, dumping her things on the floor and flopping into an armchair. Though she wasn't tired, it would take a lot more than that to tire her. She couldn't sit still and she leant forward and reached inside the side pocket of her bag for Baxter's map. She touched it but didn't take it out, letting her fingers trail the edges. She sat back, amazed. She couldn't understand how his map was so accurate, how he could have charted the marshes, land that was continually changing. She had had a hard enough time trying to understand land that hadn't changed for millions and millions of years. She felt inspired, properly, for the first time in a long while, and wanted to start work on her own map of the area because her paths would be hers and lead to places John Baxter's could never. She leant forward again, but stopped short of reaching for the map. Her feeling of inspiration and confidence waned and she sunk back into self-doubt, wondering whether her paths would lead anywhere of significance, or indeed whether there really was a language for what she had to say. 'Samphire,' she sighed, looking at the green plants falling out of the front of her bag, drying white with salt, 'what a lovely name.'

Francis walked in. He smiled at Alice, at everyone else.

But it was a forced smile, a brave face. Carey followed him.

'Looks like you're cooking supper Carey,' Henderson said, jovially.

Laura looked at Carey, as if to say don't pay any attention to him. Carey smiled at Laura, a tight-lipped, furrowed-brow smile, and headed straight for the stairs and her room.

'Looks like supper might take some time,' Henderson laughed. 'Anyone want a beer? Francis, Alice?' Laura rarely drank and he had long stopped asking her whether she wanted a drink.

Francis couldn't remember when Henderson had last been quite so friendly towards him. 'Yes,' he said, 'why the hell not.' He'd nearly drowned after all. Yes, he said to himself when Alice said she wanted a drink too.

Alice could really drink if she tried. And she felt like it now.

'On second thoughts,' Henderson said, 'why don't we go out for a drink before supper?' There was a place he knew he had to go to at some point over the weekend. A place he couldn't avoid. It would be perfect in the dusk. He felt better with himself than he had for almost as long as he could remember, he felt he could cope with it. In fact he felt he had to go now, go with the momentum, build on his strength. 'Francis, Alice?' He'd at least have those two in support.

It sat just off the coast road, an old smugglers' inn turned pub. It would still be there. It had been there for centuries. Henderson dimly remembered the interior. He and Victoria had been allowed in occasionally. The tiny, smoky rooms. The thick beams. But he could see it from the outside better, crystal clear. The wonky roof and lopsided windows, the oil tank. The caravan park was at the back of the pub and he'd been able to see the pub from his bed, watching out for his parents returning from an evening drink. The caravan. He suddenly felt hot and excited, the heat of the caravan at night. But he couldn't help shivering somehow and he wondered whether Alice or Francis, anyone, had noticed. He scratched his left arm, trying to disguise the shivering albeit belatedly, and he felt, he really felt himself getting tangled in the net curtains choked full of dead insects, the sheets full of insects too. He could feel the caravan shudder, how it used to in the wind, and when anyone moved violently. And he stopped scratching his arm and blocked an ear with one hand, thinking it would be too obvious to block both, expecting to hear rain on the caravan's roof and other sounds, far worse. But they didn't come.

Alice looked at Laura. And Laura, thinking Alice wanted her approval, said, 'You should go. See what you can while you're here.'

'But what about you?' Alice asked. 'And the supper?'

'I can do without a drink. Besides I've got to get Tristram something to eat and then to bed. We can all do supper when you get back.'

'Are you sure you'll be OK?' Henderson asked his wife, dropping his arm to his side, relieved. There was a breathlessness to his voice.

Laura wasn't expecting him to be bothered about her. 'Urrgh, yes, of course.' She was pleased he had asked. 'Go. Go on. I'm happy here.'

'Well let's go then folks,' Henderson said, about to clap his hands and say chop chop, knowing if he didn't move quickly, if he dwelled on what he had to confront for too long, he'd put it off until tomorrow, or much later. But he caught Tristram's eye, and remembered seeing Tristram copying him earlier. He didn't want his son to pick up all his mannerisms, all his problems. So he just thought, *vite, vite*, instead, mouthing it. 'Action,' he then added audibly.

'Wait a minute,' Francis said. He rushed to the stairs and

leapt up two at time, running his hand against the wall to steady himself. Carey was looking out of the window, through the sail and over the dim neatness of the fields and hedges and stately woods. Lights were coming on in farmhouses and cottages, and in the village she and Laura had bought the picnic from that morning. Proper countryside, she was thinking. Calming, peaceful, falling into darkness. She suddenly felt old, not seeing why she had to prove anything anymore.

'Carey,' Francis said quietly. He walked up to her and put his hand on her shoulder. She didn't turn round. 'Henderson wants to take us to the pub before supper. Do you want to come?'

'No,' she said, softly. She turned to him. 'It's all right, you go.'

Francis didn't move, not sure of her tone, what she really meant. He looked at her quizzically, raising his eyebrows, hoping she meant what she had said.

'I'm not angry with you,' she said. 'I just feel like being on my own for a while. Go on. Have a good time, if that's possible with Henderson. Besides I've got to cook supper.' She laughed without opening her mouth. Then she said, 'Look at you. You can't go like that.' She tugged at the loose flap of his shorts. 'What on earth happened? What's that? Did you cut yourself?' The brown stains reminded her of the sock she had found behind the door earlier.

'Oh, I caught my leg on something in the woods.'

Carey turned to the window again, the night noticeably thicker. 'You should look where you're going,' she said, hearing him change. 'You've never been any good at finding your way, have you?'

'What do you mean?' What about you? he felt like saying, too, but he didn't want a confrontation now. She was letting him go, and he just wanted to get going. Henderson, and Alice were waiting.

Tristram was crying when Francis returned to the sitting-room. He had thrown his crayons and the pad he had been drawing on across the floor so the pages had ruffled up. Some were torn.

'Leave him,' said Laura, when she saw Francis approaching. 'He's overtired.'

But Francis walked straight up to Tristram, noticing the picture he had drawn that morning torn on the floor. 'Here, Tristram,' he said, 'look what I've got for you.' He handed Tristram the blue hat that smelt of babies. Tristram sobbed and drew breath and slowly stopped sobbing and took the hat from Francis. 'It's the hat from the Queen's beach hut,' Francis added.

'It's not the Queen's, though is it?' Tristram asked, catching his breath, turning the hat over in his hands. 'I bet it's not.' But now it was in his hands he was beginning to believe it might be.

'It could well be,' Francis said. 'If not it certainly belonged to someone close to her. You have it. Keep it safe.'

'What the fuck,' Henderson started to say, edging closer to his son, his hand outstretched, but he caught Laura's eye, and saw her face begin to collapse, and knew he had to control himself, let it pass, so he turned and said, 'I'll be waiting by the car.' He walked out, breathing deeply.

Alice saw Francis had put on fresh clothes. He looked quite different, more manly, more attractive. She decided she wanted to change, too. Her legs were cold and her back tingled with salt. She ran up the stairs saying she wouldn't be a minute, wishing she could have a long bath.

Henderson thought not of the hat, but how glad he had been when he saw the photograph of the windmill in the brochure. And he looked up at the dark tower, drawn to the bright windows one above the other. It was not dark enough for the lights to illuminate much outside, but the interiors were clear. A naked figure then crossed the highest lit window. Small, firm breasts, childlike, Alice's. Henderson moved further out into the garden, his heart beat quickening, trying to see further in. Then Francis appeared in the garden and he looked out towards the sea instead. The North Star was already visible, hanging low over the drowned marshes. Henderson couldn't help himself. He looked up at the window again, fleetingly, catching sight of nothing, then he brought his left wrist up in front of his face as if that had been what he had intended to do. But he wasn't wearing a watch. 'Women,' he said, when Francis reached his side, 'they always keep you waiting. Alice appears to be quite a natural at it.'

Francis laughed, out of politeness. 'Really?'

The two stood side by side, silently, Henderson trying not to look up at the window, Francis thinking Carey never kept anyone waiting. Henderson shifted his weight from one foot to the other, while Francis looked at the ground. Francis said, 'So where are we going?'

'There's a pub, I suppose it was a smugglers' inn once, a few miles along the coast road. Actually I must check the map in the car.'

'How do you know about it?'

'There's a caravan park behind it. That's where we used to stay.'

'Lovely.'

'Well, it's not exactly a caravan park, it's a small field with a few caravans parked in it. At least that was what it used to be like.'

'Twenty, thirty years ago,' Francis said. 'God knows what it could be like now.'

'It'll be pretty much the same, I'm sure.' Henderson felt his heart beat again and he took a few short, deep breaths. 'Nothing seems to have changed much around here. Where the hell is Alice? Alice.' He shouted her name.

There was no echo as the sound sunk into the night air,

but a breath of wind blew back, reminding Francis of the impending autumn.

From her bedroom window Carey watched Alice step out of the windmill and into the garden. And she watched Henderson and Francis move to meet her, Francis reaching her first. She saw them get into Henderson's car, Alice in the front. The car turned in the driveway, and Francis got out to undo the gate. The car swept out of the driveway, and on along the coast road without Francis. Francis rushed into the middle of the road waving frantically. Carey laughed. The car reversed into sight and Francis got back in. Its headlights came on and Carey watched the car and the faint wedge of light ahead of it move along the darkening coast between the marshes and the fields of proper land, thinking how pleased she was she wasn't in the car. At that moment she was not interested in where Henderson was taking them, or the surrounding countryside anymore; she was slightly afraid of it. She lit a cigarette and exhaled into the clean, thick air, watching the smoke being whipped around the black tower. For an instant she felt she was a child and she shouldn't be smoking and that someone might catch her, that she was trying to conceal a secret. And all she could focus on was the thought that Henderson was taking Francis and Alice to some secret place which would change everything for ever. That Henderson, not Alice, was taking Francis away because he knew where to take him. She wondered what she would have left to believe in. Eventually she gave up on the view and the cigarette and what she was thinking, knowing simply the next time she looked out she'd be looking into complete darkness. She sat on Francis's bed, first throwing his torn, bloody shorts and T-shirt off, aiming for the corner behind the door. She was exhausted.

Henderson told Alice the name of the village and Alice

found the map light and the road map, and shortly the village. 'Yes,' she said, 'you're right. It was left on to the coast road. It looks about five or six miles from the windmill.' And it suddenly occurred to her that she might not have needed to use John Baxter's map to get them off the marshes and that Henderson might have known where to go all along. He knew how to find Gun Hill and the Queen's beach hut after all. 'When were you last here?' she asked. He was reminding her of Billy more and more. It was exactly what he would do. Pretend he didn't know a place or how to get somewhere. It was just another one of the games he played to give himself an advantage, to take advantage of her. And she thought if Henderson was concealing something like that she would reveal it. She bloody well would.

Henderson didn't answer immediately, but he looked at Alice, the map held tightly in her hand, close to her chest. Exactly how she had looked the evening before when they were driving in the opposite direction. Victoria was there all right, shockingly so in the mouth, the nose, the hair, the eyes even. But it was a distant, adult Victoria. Someone whom he didn't know. 'Ages ago,' he said, and looked back at the road, the surface grey and rippled and potholed under the headlights and the harsh, wide-changing weather throughout the year. He pressed his foot on the accelerator, eager to get there quickly, his stomach beginning to ache. He was going back to the caravan. Back to Victoria.

'You've got a bloody good memory,' Alice said, not looking at him. She let go of the map with her left hand and scratched the side of her head, ruffling her hair. She could feel Francis watching her. It always made her uneasy when she thought someone was watching her. She turned round, but Francis was now looking out of the window.

Francis didn't like the way Henderson kept looking at Alice. He was driving too fast and Francis thought about saying something like, watch the road. Alice didn't keep looking at Henderson, he noted. But he tried to forget about the speed and he looked out of the side window instead, marvelling at the way it was dark then suddenly light as they passed gates and broken down bits of hedge. He pressed his face against the window, feeling the window sticky and greasy against his nose and cheek, as if someone had pressed their face or hands against this part of the window while they were eating sweets. He could see more clearly through the dark patches now, discerning the rough road, the potholes and faded markings, the drainage ditches by overgrown verges, and the hedges of brambles and shrubs; the odd bit of farm machinery lying there, too dark to tell whether it was rusty and broken, and a child's bike. Definitely. Surprised, he pulled his head away from the window.

They passed through a village, where high walls made of flint lined the road at first, closing it in. It was hard to see clearly the houses and cottages behind the walls, but Alice caught the glow of interior lights, knowing people were at home. They passed a pub called The Jolly Sailors' where customers were crowding the bright windows, and an unlit petrol station that had boats on its forecourt. And then the houses ended and it was back between the hedges. A flint church suddenly appeared quite on its own, as if it had been built for a different village or the village had forgotten about God or found something better to worship and uprooted and left it behind. Alice checked the map. 'It must be the next village,' she said.

'Yes,' said Henderson, 'I know where I am now.' The church hadn't so much triggered his memory as confirmed he could not only remember the way but also everything of note on it. 'Thank you,' he added. He knew they would have to pass the turning to the nature reserve first, also a telephone box by itself and a pillbox sinking into the ground at an acute angle, as if it were capsizing. Then they would come to the village, again constructed largely of flint. Not far into this village would be an old school built more like a church, which was always dark and deserted, and inexplicably linked with his father in his mind. And in the middle of the village would be a church, much bigger than the one they had just passed all on its own: a church no one could ignore or easily walk away from. Just beyond the church would be the turning, marshward. At the beginning of this road would be the village's only shops, a butcher's and a general store. The road would soon narrow and any markings disappear. It would lead out of the village, alongside a pasture of reclaimed land where cows would be looming in shadows, and a row of poplar trees shading the stars and the moon on clear nights, to the old smugglers' inn. Behind the inn would be the caravan park, hidden by fences and hedges and small trees, as if it were something to be ashamed of.

Laura walked into Carey's room. Her eyes weren't used to the dimness so she stopped just inside the door to listen. A car passed along the coast road, as its engine died away she heard Carey breathing. With her eyes growing accustomed to the light Laura moved over to Carey, who was stretched out on top of the single bed. She put a hand on her shoulder, bent over her and whispered her name.

Carey opened her eyes, blinked, startled. 'What?' She shook her head. 'Laura?' Laura came into focus. Her face was inches away. So close Carey felt she could kiss her lips with little effort. She angled her head on the pillow, so she was closer to Laura. She felt her hair pull on the back of her scalp. 'I was dreaming that we were still on the beach. I must have fallen asleep. What time is it? Have I been here long?'

'It's past nine. No, about twenty minutes. You must be tired.'

'Oh, God,' Carey said, a thought filling her mind. 'I'm sorry about nearly drowning you all this afternoon.'

'Oh, nonsense. We got back. Forget it,' Laura said, adding, 'we weren't in any danger.'

'Alice got us out of it. I don't feel I've been very nice to her. She's beautiful isn't she?' Carey didn't wait for Laura to reply. 'And she's so bloody relaxed about everything. I wish I was like that.'

'She seems removed, if anything, to me. Carey, you're hardly the hysterical type. You're the most together person I know.' Though Laura was beginning to realise that something really was unhinging Carey, and she found it made her feel more together herself. More positive about her own situation. 'I'm certain Henderson would have found the way if Alice hadn't had that map. He's most resourceful. Seems to know everything about this part of the country. Incredible, he hasn't been here for twenty years or something.' And thinking about him she felt surprisingly happy. 'Francis and Henderson seem to be getting on better, don't you think? It's nice to see them talking and going off to the pub together. We should organise more of these holidays.'

'Oh, God,' Carey sighed. 'What's come over you?'

Tristram came into the room clutching the hat to his face, recognising and enjoying its smell. 'I want to go to bed now, Mummy.'

'Darling,' said Laura, laughing, 'you haven't had your supper yet. It's cooking. It won't be long.'

'Carey's in bed and I'm not hungry anyway.'

'She's getting up,' Carey said, sitting up. 'She's going to eat a huge supper before she goes to bed. Come here sweetie.' But Tristram stayed where he was, sucking the rim of the hat. Carey stood up trying to untangle her hair with her hands, giving it more bounce than it would naturally have. She then held out a hand for Tristram. 'Come on, darling,' she said.

Tristram didn't take Carey's hand but he walked beside her, out of the room and down the stairs, keeping to the outside where the stairs were wider and easier. Carey ran her fingers along the wall, above Tristram's head, steadying herself. Laura was a few paces behind. They crossed the well-lit sitting-room, strewn with Tristram's crayons and crumpled pictures and toys, and the beach bags half unpacked with samphire falling onto the floor.

'What the fuck are we going to do with that? Excuse my language, Tristram,' Carey said, noticing the samphire.

Laura knew exactly what she was talking about. 'Wait till the others get back. Henderson can deal with it. It was his idea. Come on, let's go into the kitchen and have a drink. It's cosier in there.' Laura pushed the small wooden door open and the smell and sweat of Tristram's supper hit them: steaming tomato sauce and starchy pasta, left over from the night before.

Carey went to the window. She rubbed the condensation clear, not thinking what she was doing, then opened it. Fresh air rushed in and she stuck her head out into the cool. It was not as dark as she had expected but blue and shadowy. She looked up and caught the moon, one night off being full. Then the clusters of stars faint in the moon's glow. She pulled her head back into the kitchen feeling much clearer-headed and happier, and determined, nevertheless, to get drunk. She looked at Laura, knowing Laura would be able to tell what she was thinking. But she said it anyway. 'What should we drink?'

'Gin?' said Laura, smiling. She drank so rarely just saying gin made her feel deviant.

'Gin,' said Tristram. 'Yuk.' He started to make vomiting noises, getting louder and louder.

Cars were everywhere. 'It must be happy hour,' Francis said, as Henderson eventually found a parking space some distance from the inn. They got out, all noticing the night air, the heady mixture of oxygen and salt and fresh cow dung. Henderson led the way and as he brushed past, Francis smelt sweat. The hum of noise coming from the pub grew louder and the far off wash of the sea diminished. Henderson stopped by the entrance, blocking it, and looked out across the pasture and the marshes for a moment, forcing the others to do likewise. He drew in air fast and sharp so he made a shrill gusty sound.

The sky in the north was still in twilight, and Alice thought she could discern the horizon. 'I keep forgetting how far north we are,' she said.

The pub was even smaller than Henderson remembered, yet he was stunned by the way everything was suddenly so familiar, so toy-like: the beams, the pewter jugs around the bar, the iron junk hanging on the nicotine-stained walls, the black and white photographs of old fishermen, still with their bushy beards and stupid grins and unlit pipes hanging from the corners of their mouths. The bar was crowded, and Henderson felt conspicuous, sure everyone was looking at him. He noticed an extension had been built at the back, where once there used to be a paved garden, but he couldn't see beyond the black windows of that room, no caravan roofs, no aerials. He stood on tip toes, feeling himself tower above everyone else, but he saw no further. He dropped back to his heels, finding himself by the bar and the smell of spilt beer overpowering. 'How about a pint of the local ale?' he shouted to the others, who were standing close by.

'Yes, sure,' said Alice, 'I'm parched.'

'OK,' said Francis. He didn't think he would like it, he was not an ale drinker, but he thought if Alice was having one he would.

Alice said to Francis, 'I suppose there's not much point in looking for seats.'

'I don't know. I'll have a look,' Francis said, disappearing.

'I didn't mean—' she gave up. Smoke and voices enveloped her and she tried to make sense of the conversations nearby, thinking these people are not locals, but tourists like myself. There were teenagers joking, impressing each other, couples quietly discussing their day, parents trying to ignore tired small children.

Henderson appeared shortly with two and a half pints of dark brown beer. 'Here,' he handed Alice the half pint.

'I get the little one, do I?'

'Oh, I'm sorry, I didn't think you'd want a whole pint. Have mine.' His voice was calm, considerate even, but distracted. He didn't sound like himself.

'No, it's all right, I'll wait until the next round.'

Henderson sipped his beer, but it didn't go down well, sitting in his stomach like a heavy ball, feeling it could come back up. He continued to drink nevertheless, nervously, watching the people in the bar. He tried to find a family of two adults and two children: a shy, fair woman and a purple-faced man with a little ginger hair and thick sideburns; a boy, something like himself years ago, and girl, simply a young version of Alice. He bit the glass of his beer mug, tasting something sharp, chemical, dishwasher fluid perhaps. But the room was too crowded and no one seemed to be with whom they belonged. The adults were enjoying themselves too much and the children were just children, behaving in normal, bothersome ways. Besides the clothes were all wrong.

Alice observed Henderson looking about the bar, his thin lips sucking the glass mug, his dishevelled hair thickened with salt and sticking out at the back. She could see his eyes clearly. Narrow and set back, they were a grey green, perhaps with a tinge of blue also. And they were deep and questioning and sad. She presumed he was looking for something, someone he might recognise. Or something he had lost even. He was tall and angular and awkward. His awkwardness counterbalancing his arrogance, she thought, seeing he didn't fit in, believing he wouldn't fit in anywhere. But she saw something else in the pub light, something she hadn't seen before, an innocence.

'There are a couple of seats through the back,' Francis said, eagerly, reaching out for his beer Henderson had placed obviously on a ledge. 'Should we go through? Alice?'

'Oh, I'm OK standing here,' she said.

'No, let's,' said Henderson, swallowing, trying to dislodge the solid thing in his stomach. 'Francis, lead the way. Quick before they go.'

Alice took her first sip of beer. It was warm and sweet and earthy. She took another, longer sip, drinking half the glass, before walking through to the back room and the others. Francis was hovering behind one of the seats and Henderson motioned to the other. She sat down, not really wanting to. And Francis sat next to her. There were more children and noise and ketchup-stained napkins in here. There was a stove against the old inn wall, and Alice followed its iron chimney running up the wall and through a transparent plastic corrugated roof which she couldn't see through. The stove was not working and people had put glasses on the top, and propped themselves against the chimney. Alice could tell the room had recently been added on and wished it hadn't.

All the windows were open but condensation still dripped from the plastic roof, a drop landing on Henderson's shoulder, soaking straight through his T-shirt onto his skin. 'It must be because of the bank holiday,' he said, the crush beginning to get to him.

'But it's not as if we saw hordes of people today. What do they all do during the day?' Alice asked, finishing her beer before anyone answered.

'I don't know,' Henderson said. He couldn't think clearly. He took a large gulp of beer and it made him gag slightly.

Alice found it most untypical of Henderson not to know. She waited to see if he was going to elaborate further, then offered to go to the bar to buy the next round when his silence suddenly became strained.

'No,' said Francis. 'It's my turn, really.' He leapt up, gulping his beer that he had only just started.

'I'd like a pint this time, please,' Alice said. And when Francis was gone she told Henderson, who moved onto Francis's chair, about bars she had come across when travelling along the Eyre Highway. A particular bar just west of Ecula, in a place called Mundrabillia, came to mind. She described the flies and the smell of beer and sweat, the backpackers trying to hitch rides and the size of the truckers who stopped there and drank such vast amounts despite the distances they had to cover. She didn't mention that it was there that Billy got beaten up because he was drunk and out of control. Or the fact that it was there she realised she could drink more than him. That was her advantage, but it wasn't big enough in the end.

'You haven't forgotten much about this place have you?' she said, having become more and more intrigued by him and what he might know throughout the day.

'I don't know. No, I suppose not. Things you thought you had forgotten seem simply to come back when you return to a place,' he replied, slowly and unusually quietly, as though he wasn't sure of what he were saying.

'Sorry?' Alice said, leaning towards him. She thought he might be blushing, although it was hot and clammy in the plastic-roofed room.

He repeated himself, but he needn't have, Alice had heard the first time.

'I don't know whether that's always a good thing,' she said.

'What?'

'Returning to places, retracing your steps.'

'It is,' he said, loudly, firmly. 'It has to be.' Then he jolted sideways, involuntarily, knocking over his beer with his arm. There hadn't been much left in the glass, but what there was pooled on the table, then the tension gave way and it ran off the edge. Francis returned with more beer and packets of crisps, and noticed the spilt beer, and Henderson heard him say something about being just in time. Henderson tried to wipe the liquid away from running onto Alice, with a beer mat. He looked at her, not seeing Victoria, at any age, but someone he didn't know, someone simply as troubled as himself. Her eyes didn't focus on anything for much time, shifting, blinking, as if she didn't want to dwell too long on a particular subject. As if she had to keep moving, he recognised that. 'I'll be back in a minute,' he said, suddenly leaping up, wobbling the table and sending more beer onto the floor.

'Remembered something?' Alice shouted after him. But Henderson didn't answer and she watched him push his way out of the room, thinking perhaps he was going to be sick.

Francis took Henderson's seat. He was getting used to the beer. He was becoming more confident.

Carey topped up her glass with gin, cursing Laura lightly to herself because she always made exceptionally weak drinks. She lit a cigarette and exhaled, watching the smoke rise, attracting the light from the bare kitchen bulb, then drift in a wavy band towards the open window. She got up and put Tristram's dirty plate and cutlery into the sink, and moved back to her chair, not quite restless enough to wash up. She smoked intently for a few moments longer, got up again and walked over to the window. The night sky calmed her, and she finished her cigarette, blowing the long last puff outside. The air was almost still, unusually still. Carey leant further out of the window. She was sure she felt a tension in the air, as if the pressure were about to change and a storm come rolling in. Or something bigger, like autumn.

'He went out like a light. Nothing will wake him tonight,' Laura said, as she returned to the kitchen.

Carey moved away from the window on hearing Laura and sat down once again, taking a sip from her glass. 'I think the weather's going to break,' she said, swallowing.

'Well, I certainly wouldn't mind if it wasn't as hot as today. I feel really quite burnt.' Laura hadn't sat down and she went over to the sink and ran the tap. 'Tristram was exhausted. I just hope he's not too tired and grumpy tomorrow. Do you know what he asked me before he went to sleep?' She turned from the sink to face Carey, holding a dripping plate. 'He asked me what a birdwatcher looked like.'

'A birdwatcher?' Carey laughed. She picked up the gin bottle. 'Let me make you another drink.' She poured herself a large measure then started to fill Laura's glass.

'Not too strong,' Laura said. 'I already feel a bit woozy. I wasn't sure what to say.'

The air hit Henderson. It was cool and peculiarly solid. He stopped and took a few deep breaths, trying to calm himself. He moved away from the back of the inn and the muffled chatter, finding the path that led to the caravan park. The path was unlit but Henderson had no difficulty seeing where he was going. Ahead the field opened out and the caravans glowed in the moonlight against a pale sky. Stainless steel sparkled instead of stars and inside lights shone from a few of the caravans through paper-thin curtains and cracks in doors and other cracks, making the grass look brown. But the only noise now was far away,

a faint rustle of the sea perhaps and a car traversing the
coast road. There was no one else about. Henderson was
aware only of his breathing as he moved from one caravan
to the next, keeping in shadow and to the grass. There were
twenty, twenty-five caravans. A hedge cut the field in two,
affording some sense of privacy. Henderson remembered
the hedge, but he thought it seemed shorter than before.
With a jump he would have been able to look over it.
He remembered the layout of the field, exactly. It hadn't
changed. And the caravans seemed not to have changed
either, still facing south with their backs to the sea. Not
one out of place. They were old fashioned, with wood and
metal trimmings. They had flat roofs and were coated with
a dull grime. And couldn't be towed. None of them had
gone anywhere in the last twenty years.

Henderson stepped off the grass and onto the gravel,
which was underneath and immediately surrounding a
caravan in the far corner of the field. There were no lights
on in this caravan and the curtains hadn't been drawn, but
net curtains hung over the main windows, ghostly white,
as they always had. He ran a finger along the side of the
caravan, feeling the salt and the dirt build up. A child
suddenly started to cry. It was not loud, coming from a
caravan in the other section of the field, but Henderson
shuddered. He left the gravel and walked round to the back
of the caravan, by the dustbin and the power-supply box.
He stood on the box, as he used to, and pressed his face up
against the window. The moon was behind him, the net
curtains didn't meet in the middle, and he could see in. The
two beds were bare, without even their mattresses. There
was nothing else in the small room. No hint of himself or
Victoria, no hint of what he had done to her. The child
was still crying, more desperately, and Henderson jumped
off the box. He slumped to his knees, then sat so his back
was propped against the power supply box. He looked up

and saw the wonky roof of the inn, the lopsided windows, homely with light. The oil tank wasn't there though. And he felt as though he'd been removed somehow, too. Removed from his life, his family. The child's wailing continued, and Henderson found he was crying also. Silently. Steadily.

He didn't know how long he sat there for, he was not wearing a watch. At last he wiped his eyes and cheeks on the bottom of his T-shirt. He felt goose-pimples on his arms, and realised how cold it had become. He pushed himself up and started to make his way back to the pub. Rounding the hedge something hard smashed into the side of his head with a terrible crack. He stumbled but didn't fall.

'Are you all right?'

Henderson heard a man's voice. He didn't recognise it.

'Are you hurt? Christ, I'm so sorry.'

'I don't know.' Henderson rubbed his head. 'What happened?'

'Let me have a look,' the man said.

Henderson began to focus on him now, as he came closer. He was large and laden with cameras or binoculars, Henderson wasn't sure. The man put a number of bags and objects onto the ground, and Henderson felt him put a hand on his shoulder.

'The light's not very good,' he said.

Henderson felt the man's other hand on his forehead. and he smelt his breath. There was a greasy, fatty smell. He had been eating chips. 'What happened?' Henderson asked again.

'My tripod must have hit you. I just can't see.' The man ran his hand over Henderson's head again. 'A bump's coming up, but I don't think you're bleeding. Do you want to sit down?'

'No.' Henderson felt faint, but he said, 'I'm all right.'

'Can you walk? Where's your caravan?'

'I don't have a caravan, not any more.'

'Look, that's my caravan, there.' The birdwatcher pointed to Henderson's father's old caravan. 'Why don't you come back and I'll make you a cup of tea. It won't take a minute.'

'No,' Henderson cried. 'I don't want to go in there.' He stumbled on.

'When did you last see Victoria?' Carey asked Laura.

'Oh, years ago. She doesn't come over much, not that we'd see her anyway. Henderson's mother occasionally tells me what she's up to. But they don't get on either.'

'Really? I didn't know that. What a shame, don't you think?'

'Yes, of course. Maybe they haven't tried hard enough. But, Christ, families are complicated.'

'Is she really that difficult?'

'I don't know. Perhaps not. Henderson won't talk about her. They had a tough upbringing, that's for sure. Henderson's father was a complete tyrant by all accounts. I think Victoria blames her mother in a way for sticking with him.'

'What does she look like? It's hard to imagine a female version of Henderson.' Carey laughed, and cleared her throat, which was becoming hoarse with cigarettes and gin.

'Now? I wonder. She used to be lovely, quite unlike Henderson. Ha, ha. She had lots of brown, wavy hair. And deep brown eyes.' She paused. 'Rather like Alice actually.'

Carey went to the fridge and found the ice tray and popped some fresh cubes into their glasses. She then added more gin and tonic to both.

'Just a little,' said Laura. 'I'm getting drunk.' Her head throbbed, slowly and steadily, from the alcohol and lack of eating anything for a long while. 'Maybe we should start thinking about supper? It's getting late. God, I don't know whether I can get up.'

'She's in Australia, isn't she?'

'Victoria? Yes.'

'She wouldn't know Alice, would she?'

'No, no. Wrong side of the family, of course.'

'Are you all right?' Alice asked Henderson. She thought he looked pale, green even, and she could see his eyes were bloodshot. 'You've been ages. Has anything happened? Were you sick or something?'

'Surely you didn't get lost?' Francis said. 'No, that would be impossible.' He then noticed that Henderson really didn't look very well. And he was sure Alice frowned at him. He regretted his words. 'Another drink anyone?' he stood up, grabbing hold of the edge of the table, now full with empty beer glasses and crisp packets and damp, sticky patches.

'Yes,' said Henderson. 'I want a drink.'

'Shouldn't we be going?' Alice said, but she was feeling talkative. She felt good. She really wanted another drink.

'I want a drink,' Henderson said, again. 'We'll be all right. What's the time anyway?'

'Quarter to ten,' Francis said, heading for the bar.

'It's OK.' Henderson rubbed the side of his head gingerly, shutting his eyes, feeling the bump. Then he rubbed his eyes, and pulled his hands down his cheeks, so for a moment his eyes were completely red. 'I suppose you just forget the things you don't want to remember.'

'What?' said Alice, trying to sound jolly, not wanting to talk about such things now.

Henderson squinted, looking into the middle distance. He was quite unsure of where he was. Not wanting to be removed. He didn't repeat himself.

Francis returned with the drinks and Henderson sipped his beer in silence. But Alice and Francis chatted. Alice was glad Francis was next to her. He told her he was thinking of getting out of business altogether. That he wanted to do something creative. She said she wondered whether she would actually go back to Australia. She couldn't stop looking at Henderson, however, thinking perhaps he hadn't been sick, though unable to imagine what was troubling him, what he'd remembered. She felt Francis's leg against hers and it wasn't unpleasant.

Henderson finally got up to leave and he led them out of the back door and into the caravan park. He was sort of crouching along the path, as if he didn't want to be seen. 'Oh, Christ,' he said when he realised his mistake at the edge of the field, 'I forgot where I was.' Alice and Francis had followed him, having had too much to drink to know where they should be going.

'Are you sure you're fit to drive?' Francis asked once they were in the car.

'Yes, of course,' said Henderson. 'Of course.'

Alice got in the back because she didn't want to have to look at the map or have anything to do with getting them home. She didn't want that responsibility. She wanted to just lose herself in the evening.

'It'll be a full moon tomorrow,' Henderson said, leaning forward and looking up, the car gathering speed on a straight section of the coast road.

'Henderson, keep your eyes on the road,' Francis said, aloud this time. He wasn't drunk enough to not care about the driving.

'That's why the tide was so high this afternoon. It'll get higher, and faster still over the next two days,' Henderson said, looking out over the marshes, dark and draining. Urging the tide on. Damn it.

'Henderson,' Francis said.

What if I don't go back to Australia? Alice reasoned with herself, knowing, hoping she was moving further and further away from that continent and everyone she knew there. She slid down in the seat, tilting her head back, so she could catch the moon and the stars in the rear-window. Who'll care?

'Henderson,' Francis shouted. The car swerved violently, flinging Alice against the back of Francis's seat. Francis banged his elbow on the door's hard arm rest.

'Sorry,' said Henderson, braking.

Francis rubbed his elbow and reached over and tried to help Alice back onto the seat, touching her hair and shoulder. She didn't pull away from him.

'I'm fine,' she said. 'I'm pretty tough.'

Francis pushed open the kitchen door with more exuberance than he intended, and it banged against the wall, adding to the dents in the plaster already there. They entered the kitchen, all feeling pretty numbed. Carey and Laura were flushed and numb also, a mess of bottles and melting ice and lemon on the table in front of them. They looked up simultaneously and Carey slurred, 'What happened to you lot?'

A huge saucepan was bubbling away on the cooker. Amid the steam a tangle of green could be seen. Henderson noticed this. 'Samphire,' he said. 'You're cooking the samphire.' He moved over to the pot and pulled out a sprig with a fork. He waved it in the air, saying, 'You mustn't overcook it, whatever you do, or it'll be ruined. It mustn't be ruined.' He bit into the end. The plant was hot, but fell to pieces in his mouth. 'Christ, it's done. Oh, Christ.' He turned off the ring, and with some difficulty managed to drain the samphire. 'Come on, let's get organised. Someone lay the table.' He suddenly felt very lucid, pushing the bottles to the side of the table and placing the pot on a mat in the middle. He went to the fridge and came back with butter. He watched the butter slowly melt and froth over the samphire, adding a gloss to the dull green. For a moment he felt he was presiding over a religious ceremony. 'Quick,' he said, '*vite*. It's getting cold.'

They all managed to sit around the table. Francis found and opened some wine, while Henderson heaped the plates with the mushy marsh plant. Laura got the stalks stuck in her mouth at first, then worked out how to eat it despite being drunk. No one talked. And butter spread across everyone's faces. Henderson watched the piles disappear, the pain on the side of his head subsiding. Francis watched Alice, admiring the way she pulled out the clean stalks, slowly and determinedly. He felt someone kick him on the shin, hard. He looked across to Carey, who was staring at him. Her lips were smudged with butter and comical. He laughed and she kicked him again.

They drank more wine with bread and cheese, and after a while Laura said, 'Look, I don't think I can stay up any longer.'

'What?' said Alice, 'it's early.' She wanted to dance or play games at least.

'You're not a mother,' Laura said, getting up.

'I'll come,' said Henderson. He wanted to lie down. His head was fuzzy again and throbbing, and he didn't want to go upstairs on his own.

'Francis,' Carey said, thinking she couldn't drink as much as she used to be able to. Wondering whether it might just be because of the sea air. Something to do with this bloody place anyway.

'But there's all this opened wine left,' he said.

Carey followed Laura and Henderson out of the kitchen, looking back at Francis with hatred just before she disappeared.

Alice filled her glass and motioned to Francis with the bottle.

Francis shook his head. 'No,' he said. 'No. I'd better go to bed.' He looked towards the kitchen door, which had been left open for him.

'Oh, well,' she said, her large, brown eyes blurring Francis. She really didn't want to go to bed. Not alone tonight. She stood up and walked over to him. She put her right hand on his shoulder, stood on tiptoes and kissed him on the lips, quickly and gently. She then winked at him and returned to her seat, expecting him to rush out of the room.

7

The windmill was not completely dark. The air was bluish, leaden. And Alice thought it seemed to groan. She bumped heavily into a chair crossing the bottom sitting-room, sending it skidding into the table. But it didn't topple. She felt her way to the stairs, and climbed slowly, catching her breath. She paused by the window on the first floor landing, but not for long enough to see any detail outside. There was no noise from the two bedrooms on that floor. She proceeded up the next flight of stairs, pausing again by the landing window. As shapes were becoming discernible a sudden, creaking sound emanated from the bedroom, as though someone was turning unhappily in their bed. She hurried on, sure nevertheless she hadn't woken anybody. She passed her bedroom and reached the top sitting-room. She found the light switch. The sudden brightness made her blink and the room seem like it didn't belong in the windmill, but in an ordinary house. She stood quite still in the middle wondering whether she was elsewhere, her mother's home in Melbourne. But not for long, and she was relieved. She saw a lamp on an old desk against the wall across from her. She was surprised the lamp worked. But it did and she left it on, turning off the main light. The room was now unmistakably part of the windmill, waning and eerie.

She sank into an armchair, which seemed to collapse around her. The cover was worn through on one arm and a tangled mass of black horse hair was spilling out. She stuck her fingers into the stuff and scrunched it. A spring just beneath the horse hair scratched her index finger, but she didn't pull her hand away immediately, wondering whether her finger was bleeding. She now wished she had something to drink, and had brought up a bottle of wine. But she couldn't face going back to the kitchen. She took a book from the top of a bookcase nearby. It was old and dusty, the hard covers coming away from the spine. The lamp made the faded front cover look warm. She could depict an engraving of a sailing ship, a magnificent three-masted warship, and the words *HMS Victory*. Above the ship was the title, *Lord Nelson's Norfolk*. She flicked through the book carefully. There were numerous engravings: portraits of Nelson, the rectory where he was born, his father's church, the windmill owned by a nephew. And there were extracts from letters and certificates of baptisms and weddings. She began reading the middle of a letter . . . *Probably I shall never see Dear dear Burnham again but I have a satisfaction in thinking that my bones will probably be laid with my fathers in the Village that gave me birth* . . .

Alice put the book back, not noticing the print of Nelson on the wall above the bookcase, and stood up, too quickly. She felt faint for a few moments, in need of air. She started to climb the ladder before she had fully realised what she was doing. She reached the trap-door and pushed. It creaked loudly, but opened easily enough. She pulled herself through the gap and into the bare room with the stone star in the centre of the floor. The four windows were black but there was a fresh blueness to the air in the room. She looked up, her head not swirling any more. The cogwheel was just a dark shape, more prominent than the other, awkward shapes around it. She saw the light switch, but ignored it. She heard the wind sigh and drift through the top of the windmill; the cap was riddled with holes and cracks and bits missing. She climbed the last ladder and remembered to duck on the platform before she had a chance to hit her head. The door was rattling slightly in the wind. She kicked the bottom of the door and it flung open. Wind rushed in and swirled about her. It was cool and sobering. She suddenly felt very awake. She crouched as she walked out onto the fanstage. She then stood erect, holding onto the fantail. The sky was moving and shadowy, thick clouds scudding across. There were no stars, but the moon was visible from time to time as clouds thinned out or parted. But it was never completely clear, at the most veiled and soft. The marshes were almost indistinguishable from the sky.

Then she heard a scream. The noise seemed to be sucked out of the tower and pulled apart in the autumnal air. She froze. There was a second scream, which didn't die away, but developed into a loud wailing. It made her shiver, because she felt for a moment that the screaming was catching up with her. As if it had finally found the person to whom it belonged.

Laura didn't switch the light on, she didn't want to startle Tristram. She walked quickly over to his bunk bed, stood on tip toes and laid a hand across his forehead. He was wide awake. But he didn't sit up immediately. He whimpered, catching his breath. His forehead was hot. 'It's all right, darling. It was just a bad dream.' Her throat was dry. She was terribly thirsty.

He wriggled in his bed, before pulling himself up. 'I saw the seal,' he said, in between short breaths, 'with things crawling all over it. And then they were crawling all over me.'

'It was only a dream,' Laura said. 'It's nothing to worry

about. Everyone has horrible dreams.' She climbed onto the edge of the bottom bed so she could get closer to him. She stroked his forehead and his cheeks. His pyjama top was damp with sweat. She thought she should change it. She walked over to the light switch.

'But it wasn't a dream. I did see it,' he shouted, terrified.

She rushed back to him. His eyes swollen and red in the bright light. 'I'll read you a story if you like. Let me just change your top.' She found a clean top. It always made her realise how fragile he was when she saw him naked. His tiny chest, the ribs perhaps too prominent.

She read him most of a story, while he slowly settled himself and eventually closed his eyes. She listened to his breathing, and decided after a short while he was asleep. She kissed him gently on the forehead, and walked out of the room leaving the door open and the light on.

Henderson stirred purposefully when she entered the bedroom. 'Is he all right?'

'Yes, he's gone back to sleep.'

'A nightmare?'

'Yes.' Laura hovered in the middle of the two beds, then walked over to Henderson's bed. She sat on the edge and put her right arm across him. Henderson rolled onto his back so he faced her. She leant down and kissed him on the cheek and then the lips. He reached up and pulled her to him. 'Get in,' he said.

Tristram climbed out of bed and down the little ladder. He couldn't sleep. Every time he shut his eyes for long he saw writhing maggots. He lifted up the corner of the mattress on the bottom bunk and pulled out the sock and the Queen's hat. He sat on the floor and played with them for a while, stretching the sock, checking it over for holes and smelling it. He rubbed the brown stains, but they wouldn't come off. He tried sucking. The sock quickly became wet in patches and the stains seemed to smudge. He kept sucking, not minding the salty taste. He heard something knocking next door, in his parents' room. And he heard a creaking sound. He stopped sucking for a while, listened, then carried on when he realised no one was going to come in. He tried to ignore the sound, but it was growing louder and he thought he now heard someone moaning or crying. He stopped sucking the sock again, but didn't let go of it. He put the hat on, pulling it hard down on his head so the rim felt like it was cutting into his scalp. He walked over to the door and peered out. It was dark everywhere except where the light, coming from behind him, flowed. The noise was getting quicker. It was a sort of panting, he thought, as if someone was out of breath. The longer he looked into the darkness the further he seemed to see. He stepped out onto the landing. He thought he could see light coming from the top of the stairs also.

Henderson closed his eyes. He saw Victoria again. Felt her beneath him, moving with him, not struggling now. And he was tired and kept his eyes shut and Victoria stayed in his mind. And he felt himself recoiling. He stopped moving and opened his eyes, catching the whites of Laura's. He was sure she had been staring at him, studying his face, his expressions, in the dimness. Sweat was trickling down his forehead and his neck was burning and veins standing out. He shut his eyes again, not wishing Laura to see all of him, his unbearable shame. And Victoria's face reappeared immediately. Now he pushed on, feeling angrier and angrier, gripping Laura tighter by the upper arms, expecting them to be thinner. The bed seemed to be moving, the caravan rocking, shuddering. It was all too vivid. He braced himself for the terrible noise, the noise of a child giggling, gurgling, screaming. He pushed into Laura for the last time, hearing her expel air. He collapsed onto her. Still she pulled him closer. And he felt her kissing him, searching out his ears, his mouth. He rolled off her and onto his side, feeling the pillow press against the bump on his head, and her body spoon into his. And he knew he couldn't give up.

He lay there for a long while, with Laura snuggled next to him breathing heavily, loving him. They didn't say anything. He was hot and felt his skin sticking to hers. The bed was far too narrow for both of them to sleep comfortably. He felt he couldn't sleep now anyway. He kissed her gently on her hot cheek. He climbed out of bed and she immediately spread out unconsciously into the space his absence made. He found his shorts and a T-shirt in the darkness and walked out of the bedroom, opening and closing the door as quietly as he could. The light from Tristram's room poured onto the landing. He didn't look into the room, however, but headed downstairs. The sitting-room floor was cold on his bare feet. The lino in the kitchen was sticky and wet. He stood in a puddle of something warm and thick. He cursed to himself and felt the wall by the door for the light switch.

Carey heard something brush and scrape by the door. She thought it sounded just like a dog. Or a large rat. She heard it breathing and sniffing. Then it was silent for a long while and she shut her eyes trying to forget about it. She heard the wind outside, realising it must have picked up. And then she heard the thing moving about on the landing again, brushing against the wall and door. There was a tapping sound for a while. Then she heard someone humming. Humming. 'Francis,' she whispered. 'Francis.' But Francis didn't answer. She sat up. There was no moonlight now and the room was very dark. 'Francis,' she said, louder. She couldn't even see his bed. She lay back down and listened to the wind. And it suddenly occurred to her she couldn't hear Francis breathing. That he wasn't there. She sprang up again. 'Francis.' She got out of bed and rushed across the room. She prodded his bed wildly.

He grunted. 'What, what's going on?'

'Francis,' she sighed, suddenly relieved and feeling foolish at the same time. 'There's something outside the room, an animal or something.' She wasn't going to say a ghost.

'What? Don't be so stupid.' He hadn't moved. He was lying on his stomach and he mumbled into his pillow. 'Go back to bed, for Christ's sake.'

Carey couldn't hear him clearly. 'What? There's something on the landing, I'm telling you. Listen. Sshhhh.'

Francis couldn't hear anything. Not even the weather outside. He felt too tired to hear anything. He fidgeted angrily, trying to block Carey out.

'There,' said Carey. She heard the thing moving again.

'Please leave me alone. It's the middle of the night.'

'But there's something out there.'

'Well go and see what it is if it's concerning you so much.'

She moved away from his bed, able to see better now. She still felt foolish, but also annoyed Francis hadn't woken up properly. He was always so bloody difficult to wake up. She walked to the door on tip toes, subconsciously believing that she would make less noise walking that way. She stopped by the door, put an ear against it and listened. She heard nothing. She opened the door. She squinted, then she saw Tristram sitting on the stairs with a hat on his head sucking his thumb. Faint light was falling from the floor above, or the floor above that. After a few moments Carey realised Tristram wasn't sucking his thumb but a piece of cloth or a rag. He carried on sucking it, looking at his feet or the step below. He didn't acknowledge her at all. 'Tristram, darling,' she said, softly. 'What are you doing here?' She walked over to him and crouched down. She placed a hand on his shoulder. 'Have you had a bad dream?'

He nodded a yes.

'Come on, I'll take you back to bed.' She stood up and held out her hand for him to take. But he didn't move. 'Tristram, come on darling, you must go to bed.' She returned to him, and tried to make him look into her eyes. She crouched so low she had to look up at him. 'Please,' she smiled, her eyes pleading.

'There's something knocking down there, and other noises,' he said.

'What do you mean, darling? Where?'

He shook his head. Neither a yes nor a no.

'Come on, I'll be with you.'

'It got faster,' he said. 'And louder. Someone was crying or something.'

'Where? In the sitting-room?'

He nodded another yes.

She took hold of his hand and the thing he was holding in it, and stood up, pulling him. She didn't think she had the energy to carry him. Then she heard something bang above her, a window perhaps. She felt Tristram shiver, but she didn't say anything, hoping he'd ignore it. They walked slowly and carefully down the stairs to his room. Tristram refused to go in until Carey had checked there was no one hiding anywhere. 'See, there's no one here,' she held her arms outstretched. 'I can't hear any strange noises either. I'm sure it was nothing.' She helped him onto his bunk and took the wet rag out of his hand, and his hat off. Almost immediately she realised what the rag was and she thought she was going to retch. But she handed them straight back, because Tristram suddenly looked desperately in need of them. She tucked him in and kissed him on the forehead. 'You're quite safe,' she said. 'Your mummy and daddy are next door and I'm just upstairs. I'll leave the light on.' She blew him a kiss as she retreated out of the room backwards. She closed the door, and feeling something shiver behind her, leapt round to face a shifting figure. Alice. 'Alice,' she said, shocked. The light seemed to disappear and darkness fell like a blanket, and all Carey could see of Alice was the shape of her head and hair, moving away from her. Carey felt herself recoil backwards, quite involuntarily.

'Carey,' Alice said, nervously, breathlessly. She found she was suddenly short of breath.

Then the stairs creaked behind them. Carey heard Alice draw a breath. It made a peculiar, warbling sound. Neither could move any more and they stood, frozen, while Henderson loomed into view. He seemed to bring the light of the kitchen with him, because he was clearly visible.

'Henderson,' Carey said, now baffled, her muscles relaxing. 'What are you doing?'

'What am I doing? What are you doing?' he said.

'I, I found Tristram sitting on the stairs outside our room. I've just put him back to bed. Something had disturbed him.' She could feel her heart beating, and wondered whether her neck would be reddening. It did when she felt accusatory. 'Some noise, he said, a knocking and moaning, coming from the sitting-room downstairs. It woke him up.'

'Sshhhh,' Henderson whispered. 'We'll wake him again.'

'You'll, you'll wake him again, you mean,' Carey said.

Henderson didn't answer. He couldn't understand what Alice was doing with Carey. Alice's presence made him feel quite unsure of himself, and he didn't like the way Carey was looking at him either. 'Come on let's all go back to bed.' He moved to the door of his bedroom.

Alice had forgotten that she had been heading for the kitchen, to fetch a glass of water. 'Yes,' she said. She started to climb the stairs, tiredness and drink swamping her all of a sudden. She heard Henderson open the door to his room and Carey's footsteps hurrying behind her on the stairs.

'Alice,' Carey whispered, loudly, urgently, just before

they reached the next landing. 'What the hell were you doing?'

'What?'

'What were you doing with Henderson?'

'With him? I wasn't with him. Look I'm really tired. See you in the morning.' She left Carey on the landing and carried on up the stairs to the next floor and her bed.

Henderson felt he was sinking, deeper and deeper into a bog. He was lying on his back and he was going down bottom first, as though he would eventually be bent double, his joints ripped out of their sockets. The mud made a sucking, squelching noise as it pulled at his back. It was pitted with sharp shells and stringy plant remains. The plant remains became more solid and as he sank further he grabbed hold of these chunks, which began to feel like pieces of rotten wood, trying to find something solid enough to support him. 'Arrgh,' he shouted, waking himself up. He was amazed how light and dry he suddenly felt. He raised his pelvis from the bed, arched his back, tucking his hands under it, realising it was the bed that had been trying to bend him double. The bed creaked and shifted as he thrashed about, stretching. He sighed loudly.

'For goodness sake,' Laura said, 'what on earth's the matter?' Daylight fell on her and she had been awake for a long while, enjoying the scatty rhythm of the soft wind. She hadn't heard a noise from Tristram, which was unusual for the time of morning, but, God, she was thankful.

'This bed, it's agony,' he said, then realised he was in Laura's bed.

'Now you know what I had to put up with.' She smiled to herself. She was content. 'So where are we going today?' She tilted her head back so she could see under the useless curtains. But the sky still wasn't clear to her. There was a whiteness, but nothing more discernible than that.

'I think the summer's over,' Carey said. She was standing in her nightdress peering out of the window. 'That's it, gone.' And she was surprisingly glad.

'It was too hot yesterday, anyway,' Francis said, not fully understanding what she had just said. He could feel sunburn on his back and the backs of his legs. He rolled onto his stomach, which felt gaseous and delicate.

'Perhaps we should leave today, get back to London. We'd miss the traffic and all the fuss tomorrow. There's nothing worse than bank holiday traffic.'

'Go, today? Don't be so ridiculous. We haven't come all this way for just one day at the beach, surely. Besides I'm enjoying it. I like it here. It's unspoilt and beautiful.'

'Christ, you've changed your tune,' she said.

'Well I thought it was you who needed to get out of London so badly. I thought it was you who needed to escape to the country for the air and the space. What more could you want than here?'

'Look, I'm not really sure what's going on, but I don't feel very comfortable staying here. And you're not helping matters.'

'I don't know what you mean,' he said, sleepily, yawning loudly.

'I'm sure Laura wouldn't mind if we left this afternoon. Just look at this weather.'

Francis rolled back onto his back. He then sat up. He was becoming aware that Carey might actually mean what she was saying. 'Carey please. It's quite comfortable here, the windmill's fine. Even Henderson's not being too bad. Nothing's going on, not that I know what you're referring to.'

'You don't understand, do you?' she said.

He got out of bed and joined her at the window. He put his arm around her. 'It's not too bad. It could be raining.' The sky was a vast cloud, the marshes a band of dull greens and browns and purples below. He kissed her on the cheek. 'Try to enjoy yourself, please. We've only really got one more day. Of course Laura would mind if you left.'

Francis's last sentence stuck in Carey's mind. She wondered for a moment whether he entertained the idea that she might go back alone and leave him here. Because that's what she thought it sounded like. Of course Laura would mind if *you* left, she repeated to herself, emphasising the you. Turning the word bitterly in her mouth.

The gloom and thickness of the cloud had drifted into the sitting-room, which smelt fusty. Everyone was quietly eating or drawing, or staring into space. The long walk and the sea air the day before had taken its toll. Yet they all knew they had to get up and go somewhere today, visit something else. It might have been the middle of the long weekend, but Carey thought, surely we've seen everything there is to see, and that it was all the same here anyway. Laura wasn't gloomy at all, and wished everyone would just be thankful and enjoy the fact that they were on holiday. However, holidays always take a while to settle into, she thought. Francis thought he would be quite happy to go anywhere as long as they didn't have to have another picnic; the weather didn't bother him that much, he knew it wouldn't bother Alice. While Tristram knew it didn't make any difference what he thought or where he wanted to go, Henderson couldn't actually decide where they should go next, where he had to go next. He was thinking of the whale skeleton and the wreck, but thinking they would be better if it was warm and sunny, better another day.

No one noticed Alice come in. However, everyone suddenly became aware of her as she stood motionless by the table. She didn't make a noise. She didn't have to. She had a strong, uncanny presence. Henderson looked up. He saw she had tied her hair back, but a few strands, wayward, or perhaps purposefully, fell about her ears and face. She was wearing a blue-and-white striped French top and a pair of jeans.

Carey studied Alice carefully. But she didn't think Alice looked tired, or indeed sheepish. There was nothing to suggest she'd been up half the night with Henderson. Indeed Carey thought Alice looked pretty and confident, exactly how she wanted to look herself. Perhaps nothing had happened between them, Carey thought, or else Alice is remarkably good at concealing the truth. But she couldn't help noticing that Henderson kept glancing at her. As did Francis.

'I couldn't get up,' Alice said. 'It's most unusual. It must be the sea air. That and the walk yesterday. I thought I was fitter.'

Carey nodded to herself.

'Well, you certainly don't look tired,' Laura said, smiling. 'Wait until you have children.'

Alice ignored Laura. 'So where are we going today?' she asked, flicking a curl off her forehead, looking at Henderson. She had intended to get up early, return to the fanstage, and make a start on her map of the marshes, she knew she had to at least give it a try. But she had woken late with a dull pain in the back of her head. The weather hadn't inspired her and she had lain fitfully in bed for a long while. She hadn't fallen back to sleep because of the headache and a feeling that something hadn't been resolved. It nagged at her, but she couldn't place it. She had pinned her hair back because it made her feel more sure of herself and purposeful, stronger really. And now she was up she wanted to get going. She wasn't in the mood for sitting around, just waiting for something to happen while everything caught up with you. She still had to keep moving. 'Henderson, you must have thought about it?'

Everyone looked at Henderson, Carey resignedly, waiting their fate.

'Well,' he said excitedly, 'I think we have to see the tank.' The tank had come to mind a few moments earlier, out of the blue. And he had a strange feeling about it, quite different to his earlier feelings about Gun Hill or the Queen's beach hut, the caravan even. He felt instantly compelled to go, not at all afraid of what he might find there.

'A tank,' said Tristram, looking up from his drawing, 'a real tank? Can I go in it?'

'No,' said Henderson, 'of course you can't. It doesn't work. It was used for target practice during the last war.'

Tristram went back to his drawing, huffing, not surprised to hear that the tank didn't work, not even disappointed. He preferred drawing to anything this morning anyway. He was drawing the marshes and the lagoon which had suddenly appeared from nowhere. He made it muddy coloured and put patches of red where the sun had shone.

'God, there must be something better to see than a bloody tank,' said Carey. She looked at Francis, with a look that she thought said, I want to leave for London immediately.

'I agree,' said Laura, yawning.

'There's not just a tank, of course,' said Henderson, still excited. 'There's a nature reserve, and a marvellous stretch of beach. They found a tusk there earlier this century, and a few remains of a prehistoric forest.' He suddenly remembered his dream of sinking into a bog, reaching out for rotting wood, saving himself, and it all clicked and he was even more sure about going, and eager. 'Come on, you don't know what we might find.'

Tristram was interested again, the tusk was better than a tank that didn't work. He pushed himself off the chair and walked over to Henderson. He stopped just before him, looked down at the floor, and shifted his weight from one foot to the other. 'Where did the tusk come from?' he asked, shyly. 'What animal?'

'An elephant or maybe a woolly mammoth. I don't think they know exactly,' Henderson said, not remembering very much about the prehistoric remains, or ever having seen any. It was the tank he and Victoria had been taken to see on one of their first holidays here. His father had been fascinated by the tank. And Henderson remembered now how angry he had become when he and Victoria had spent the whole time collecting shells. What was left of the tank had been full of shells, razor shells. They collected buckets of them because they had thought they were pretty and hadn't seen shells quite like them before. Victoria couldn't have been much older than Tristram was now, he thought. And he must have been under ten, eight perhaps. 'It's not far, four or five miles along the coast. There won't be any problem parking.'

'Well, let's go then,' Alice said, 'now.'

'Aren't you going to have any breakfast?' Laura asked her, surprised by her abruptness.

'Oh, no. I'd rather get going. Besides I'm not hungry.'

'Shouldn't we sort out a picnic?' Laura turned to Carey.

You can, but Francis and I won't be here, Carey wanted to say, but she just said despondently, 'No, I don't think it's the weather for a picnic. I'm sure we can find a pub or something.'

'Try not to sound too enthusiastic,' Laura said.

Francis caught Carey's eye.

Alice was outside, waiting by the car, long before anyone else. She thought the weather made the marshes look dull and wet and inhospitable. They were no longer new and enticing, but old and somehow full of memories better forgotten. She was surprised how quickly they had lost their novelty, their charm. The tide was in and the wind rippled across the channels of water in thick bands, white horses appearing with the bigger gusts. Squalling gulls and flocks of tiny birds were swept in and out of the sky, which was getting darker despite noon approaching. The noise of the wind and the birds and the distant surf buzzed in Alice's ears. She turned to the windmill, the empty sails remarkably, stoically still. She admired the way it stood up against the weather, how it must have withstood anything that was thrown at it for so long. She didn't care now that it no longer worked. It was enough that it had survived. And then the gusting suddenly stopped. She felt a drop of rain on her cheek. Another, a moment later, on her eyebrow.

Henderson appeared. 'They're not going to like the rain.'

'No,' said Alice, 'but it doesn't bother me.'

'It's not going to hurry them up either. I always seem to be waiting for Laura.'

But that second Laura came running outside. She was followed by Tristram and Carey. Francis appeared a few moments later carrying a bundle of clothes, but not in time to hear Carey say that they were heading back to London in the afternoon if the rain didn't stop. Laura thought she was joking.

They crammed into Henderson's car. Francis sat up front with Henderson, Carey and Alice on the seat behind, while Laura and Tristram were on the collapsible seat in the boot of the estate. Only Laura and Tristram talked, about what prehistoric meant, and the sort of animals that would have lived in a prehistoric forest. She mentioned rhinoceros, bison, hippopotamus, anything big and grey and prehistoric-looking that came to mind. Tristram giggled when she said hippopotamus. And she tried to describe to him such a forest, imagining vast trees, the trunks comparable in thickness to the windmill's tower, which would be draped with vines and ooze dark sap. She told him it would always be in the shade, and damp and peaty smelling. The ground would be soggy and writhing with reptiles. It wouldn't be a place, she concluded, you'd want to go today.

'Why are we going then?' he asked. 'We always go to horrible places.'

She said, 'It's not like that now, darling. That was thousands of years ago. Everything has changed since then. I expect there'll be a tea shop there now. You can have an ice-cream if you like.'

The windscreen wipers swept across the windscreen every four seconds or so with a quiet, hypnotic hum and a squeak of rubber on glass. It was barely raining now. Not enough for the slowest wiper speed. The noise was annoying Carey. She couldn't understand why Henderson didn't switch the wipers off. She looked out of the window, trying to ignore the noise. But the view of wet marshes made her even more annoyed. She was glad when the hedges got in the way, and concentrated on trying to identify the wild plants. She had named four to herself when she saw a child's bike in the overgrown verge, seemingly abandoned. It puzzled her. The bike looked new.

Alice recognised the way from the previous evening when they passed through the village with high flint walls, The Jolly Sailors' pub and the petrol station. The village ended and Alice knew the church would appear shortly. When she and Billy returned to the Eyre Highway a couple of years after they had met there, she remembered all the settlements and even numerous buildings. She would anticipate them in just the same way she found herself anticipating the church now. Over the miles, hundreds of miles in many instances from one settlement to the next, she would become more alert. A pain would develop in her stomach, not unlike a period pain. And as they came to these landmarks the second time she would try to recall if she were seeing them exactly how she saw them before, or whether time and how she felt about Billy had distorted them. For most of the journey she found very little had changed. The windmills of Penong with their sails like helicopter blades were still turning silently, the Yalata Roadhouse with its corrugated roof was as empty as before, no one had yet painted out the graffiti scrawled on the huge fibreglass kangaroo at Eucla. And she was thrilled.

Billy drove mostly, hot wind ruffling his hair and dusting his forearms and sweat-stained T-shirt. The whites of his eyes became yellowed and bloodshot, as they had before moving from South Australia to Western Australia. Billy was the same. The pain in her stomach eased after each place, each time she caught sight of the Billy she loved. They didn't stop at the bar in Mundrabilla where Billy had got into a fight. Then at Madura she suddenly became very confused. She didn't recognise the Hospitality Inn. Nothing was how she remembered. She asked Billy if they had come this far before, even though she knew they must have. Billy slowed as he drove past the motel, the few ramshackle houses and stores, thinking about Alice's question. He turned to her. Alice didn't recognise him at first, then she saw a blankness in his eyes, and she wondered for the first time whether he really loved her. Months of worry seemed to pour into her mind in that moment and she felt her heart buckle. They continued in silence for an eternity, then he suggested that they turn off the highway and have a last look at the sea at Twilight Cove, where he knew there was a place to stay, before they had to head inland. 'Cocklebiddy, Caiguna, Balladonia, that's all that's left,' she now remembered him saying, and how cheerful he had sounded. But she couldn't remember leaving the Eyre Highway, or the track to Twilight Cove. She couldn't remember anything distinctive after Madura. Just a sandy blur.

The church was harsh and grey, the flint cold and not glinting. Its short but perfect Norman spire was topped by a weather vane. In place of the cock was an old fashioned square-rigged sailing ship. A brig? A warship? Whatever, it reminded Alice of the print on the cover of the Nelson book, and the tightness in her empty stomach left. The ship was sailing out to sea. Poplar trees surrounded the graveyard. They were bent inland. They had never had a chance to grow in any other direction.

Henderson saw the sign for the nature reserve carpark and pulled off the coast road. 'Shit,' he said. 'Look at all these bloody cars. This is new. There never used to be a carpark here, not a proper one. Christ, you even have to pay and display.' He drove round the carpark once, not finding a place, then followed a track leading to an overflow carpark. There were fewer cars here; the ground was dirt and orange builders' sand. He stopped at the far side. 'I'm not paying to park here,' he said, getting out. 'No way.'

The air was damp, but it was no longer spitting. Henderson strode defiantly across the carpark, forcing a couple of people to step out of his way. The others followed. A neat path took them through some young trees, past a toilet block, to a shop and information centre built from brick and wood and fashioned to look old and natural, like it had always been there. But it didn't. Henderson stood by the entrance shaking his head. 'This was never here before,' he said. And his confidence and certainty that this was where they should be evaporated momentarily. 'Maybe we should go somewhere else,' he said, wishing he had taken them to the whale skeleton, or the wreck, despite the weather.

'We're here now,' Laura said. 'You're always wishing you were somewhere else. There's no need to keep moving from one thing to the next all the bloody time.'

'OK,' said Henderson, remembering he wasn't afraid anymore.

'I'm going to the toilet,' Carey announced. Her stomach had been feeling strange all morning. She wondered whether it had anything to do with the samphire.

Tristram saw an ice-cream sticker on a window by the entrance to the shop. He set off in search of one. Laura followed him inside. Alice, too, saw the sticker. She felt faint and in need of sugar. Francis didn't want to be left with Henderson so he headed inside also. The shop smelt new. It was crowded and the shelves were loaded with ornithological books, maps, charts, camera film, plastic birds and animals, and all sorts of other toys and knick-knacks for bored children and adults who hadn't yet grown up. Francis bumped into Tristram and Laura by the plastic animals.

'Which one's a hippopotamus, darling?' Laura said.

Tristram fiddled with the grey coloured shapes for a while, then held out a rhinoceros. 'This one,' he said.

'That's a rhinoceros. That's a hippo.' Laura pointed to another shape.

Francis left them to it without commenting and moved an aisle down where he found Alice. She had picked up an inflatable whale. Her hands were shaking slightly.

'I can't work out what this is doing here,' she said.

'Oh, you do get whales around here madam,' a woman said, stepping up. She was sixty or so, with short, thick grey hair, a red face and glasses. 'They're not very common of course. And sadly those you do find are mostly stranded. Are you both members?'

'Of what?' Francis asked.

'The RSPB, of course.'

'No,' Francis said.

'Well we're offering a special discounted rate at the moment for families. Do ask at the desk.'

Alice smiled at Francis. A customer had backed into her, forcing her to within inches of him. 'How odd she should think we're married,' she said. He blushed immediately and she added, 'I need an ice-cream.' She pushed gently past him, touching his upper arm. She reached the small freezer, with Francis just behind her, at the same time as Laura and Tristram.

'Where are they?' Carey asked.

Henderson could see Carey looked pale, almost green. 'Are you feeling all right?' he asked.

'Perfectly,' she said curtly, looking over his shoulder into the shop. But she couldn't see anyone inside, just the reflection of Henderson and herself, the dull grey of the day and a bird shimmying across the glass.

'I think they're buying ice-creams. Are you sure you're feeling OK?'

'Ice-creams?' she said. 'It's hardly the day for ice-creams.' She immediately felt queasy again. But she couldn't help thinking of the ice-creams they had all had the day before by the staithe, and how promising and fun everything had seemed. Then the taste of stale ice-cream came to her. And she thought today was one of those days that are never filmed by cine cameras, or video cameras for that matter. But nevertheless how it was a day you would always remember. 'Look, I don't think that samphire agreed with me,' she said.

'I don't think it's possible to get food poisoning from samphire. It must be from something else.'

'I would know. Thank you.' She looked at Henderson. He instantly looked away. He's guilty, she said to herself. He's guilty. But her moment of certainty didn't last either. He turned back to her, rubbing his eye, and she saw something she didn't think she had seen in him before, an innocence, a vulnerability. But she couldn't feel any concern for him. Too much had passed between them for that.

'Well, is there anything I can do, or get you? Do you

want me to drive you back to the windmill?' he asked, now pinching his left cheek.

The others emerged from the shop with ice-creams and leaflets, Alice and Francis walking out side by side.

'No,' Carey said, shaking her head determinedly. 'I'm coming.'

'Well, from what I can remember it's not too far to the beach,' Henderson said, adding, 'but then I was much smaller then.'

They followed a sign pointing to the reserve and the beach, and joined a public footpath which ran along a raised bank, separating the reserve on the right from grazing land on the left, saltings stretching beyond that. The path was full of people in earth-coloured and all-out camouflaged jackets and trousers. Many had stopped in specially widened sections to peer through stubby telescopes supported on tripods or one-legged telescopic stands. They were all pointed in the same direction and angle over the reserve, the first few hundred yards of which was an expanse of reedbeds. The wind picked up as they walked along the path, Henderson striding ahead, and the reeds, as tall as they ever got, lurched in groups and whispered loudly, as loudly as the birdwatchers. The reedbeds ended neatly and marsh and lagoons took over. A smaller path deviated off and led across the mud to a hide. This path was congested and Henderson paid it no attention. He was looking the other way, at the pasture and saltings seeping slowly into what there was of a horizon. He was looking to see what he recognised because there was nothing in the other direction, the people and the man-made reedbeds and marshes had not been there before. There had simply been a public footpath that ran across protected, natural land. Even the path had been smoothed and trimmed with concrete edges. Sweeping inland he saw a line of poplar trees, thin and rakish, and he wondered whether they were the trees which lined the road to the smugglers' inn and the caravan park. They definitely lined a road or a field, or someone's garden. But he couldn't tell what exactly.

'Excuse me,' a woman shouted.

Henderson didn't apologise for bumping into her, for knocking her telescope out of line, but continued quickly ahead. He only slowed when he thought he heard Tristram whining above the ever-present cacophony of birds, the names of which were being hurriedly scribbled in hundreds of damp notepads. He looked over his shoulder but couldn't see Tristram or the others for the birdwatchers, so he continued until the final section of the reserve came to an end by a collapsing pillbox and some wooden steps that led over a small sandbank to the beach. He pushed his way through a number of birdwatchers clustered on the top of the steps and at the bottom of the sandbank, and once he was through he exhaled a large lungful of air, only to gasp for another. The tide was out and where the beach had been in his memory was an expanse of greeny brown boggy stuff, rising one or two feet above the surrounding sand. It was so strange and spectacular he knew it could only be the prehistoric forest remains. And he was not disappointed or disorientated because the foreshore was not how it should have been. In fact he felt elated. As if, suddenly, he was seeing everything for the first time, as if everything were beginning again, the remains actually growing not rotting, because that is what it all looked liked. A spit of rain hit his cheek, followed by another and another. He didn't mind. It made everything seem fresher and more invigorating. He was about to make a charge for the forest when he heard Laura calling his name.

'Sshhhh,' a birdwatcher near him exclaimed.

'Henderson,' Laura shouted again, 'wait.' She dragged Tristram down the sandbank and onto the beach. Tristram was crying and she told him to shut up and grow up. 'It's my fault. I've spoilt you,' she said, aloud but to herself. She presented Tristram to Henderson. 'Do something with him, I can't cope.'

'God, we're lucky,' Francis told Carey. They were a few paces behind Laura and Tristram.

'Do you think so?' She left Francis and pushed her way through the remaining birdwatchers to join Laura.

'He's tired,' Laura said. 'I can't do anything with him when he's like this.'

But Tristram had stopped crying. Henderson was crouching, talking to him. 'Look Tristram,' he was saying, 'there's the prehistoric forest. Think, bison and rhino and all sorts of animals you don't see anymore once roamed on that very land. It looks like it's growing again, doesn't it?'

Tristram pulled a plastic rhinoceros from his pocket. And he held it shyly out for his father to see. Henderson hugged him. After a long while Henderson looked up. Laura and Carey were staring at him.

'Thank you, Henderson,' Laura said. 'I just wish you wouldn't rush ahead. It's not fair. I need your help. More often.'

'I knew it would rain,' Francis was saying, 'because I bothered to bring my waterproof just in case, and I left the bloody thing in the car. Typical.'

Alice wasn't listening. She'd read in the information centre that the tree remains were around ten thousand years old, and that they had belonged to a swampy, deciduous and pine-forested area which grew after the last Ice Age and stretched to what was now Denmark and the Netherlands. The forest had then been slowly submerged by rising sea levels when the North Sea – or German Ocean she supposed, wondering indeed what it was known as before then, took shape. What struck her now as she looked across to the remains was the greenness of it all and the way the forest seemed to be sprouting out of the ground. And like Henderson she too couldn't help thinking that the forest was growing once again, relieved of the sea and sand, and the weight of the glacial past.

'A marsh harrier,' someone whispered loudly. 'There, two o'clock.'

'The light's not very good,' someone else said. 'Yes, got it,' he added excitedly.

Henderson thought he recognised the second voice. But he couldn't think why on earth he should. 'Come on Tristram, let's go and explore.' Henderson stood up and took Tristram's hand. They started to walk across the rain-pitted sand towards the ancient forest. 'Tristram, try to imagine what it was like all those thousands of years ago. Imagine we're entering the forest.'

'Like the forest we went to yesterday?' Tristram asked.

'No. You've never been anywhere like this one before. It's tall and dark. The ground's wet and slippery. Careful where you step. Hear that? What do you think that was? An elephant, a woolly mammoth, a rhino, or something completely different, something no one's ever seen before?' Henderson had excited himself. 'Listen, listen Tristram. You don't want the animals to see you though, or have any idea where you are.'

Tristram hesitated, he put the rhino back in his pocket, then told his father to be quiet. 'Daddy, Daddy, they'll hear you.' Panic was in his voice. With his other hand he held his father's hand tighter. He felt his father walking quicker, and he tried to slow him down, but he couldn't. And he didn't want to be left behind, so he started to trot.

It stopped raining and Francis ventured after Alice onto the beach, joining Carey and Laura. The four of them then set off after Henderson and Tristram, automatically, without saying anything, and blocking much of the birdwatchers' view. But they were looking ahead and they weren't aware of the birdwatchers, or the fact that the birdwatchers were only interested in catching another glimpse of the marsh harrier.

'Get out of the sodding way,' one of them shouted. He knew he shouldn't have shouted, but he was fed-up with bloody townies who didn't understand about birds or nature. Who just got in the fucking way all the time. He was too angry now to steady his telescope. He contemplated going back to the caravan, but it was only lunchtime and he only had Monday left.

8

Henderson let go of Tristram's hand and they moved ahead, soon separating, Henderson imagining he was Tristram's age for a moment, and that he was walking further and further away from his father. He even looked over his shoulder to see if he was following. But he wasn't, the thin ginger hair and bushy sideburns nowhere in sight, and Henderson smiled to himself and knew that his father had no hold over him now.

Tristram scrambled after his father, often using his hands and knees. The ground was patchy, mostly mud and thick moss, more like a lush green, stringy seaweed. But hard clumps of rotten wood stuck up here and there. Tree trunks also lay scattered in various states of disintegration, some trunks hollowed out. The ground was slippery and squelched as they progressed. They found pools of sea water, some two or three feet deep. In other places the forest was cut away, revealing a strange honeycomb structure, and fjords of clear sand leading out to the sea. Tristram stopped by a pool and knelt. He saw nearly-invisible shrimps darting below the surface, and insects hovering and diving across the top. The water was oily, the bottom of the pool dark and murky. Tristram put his hand into the pool, forgetting to pull his sleeve up, wondering whether something vast would latch onto his hand and drag him in. The water was warm and dense. He felt the shrimps. Nothing more violent or sinister. He looked up and couldn't see his father. Then he snatched his hand out, clambered to his feet and hurried away from the pool with the sleeve of his top dripping. 'Daddy,' he called.

Alice was not far from Tristram, but she didn't yell or beckon to him. She returned to what she was doing: trying to pull a piece of wood from a trunk. She kicked at the trunk, her foot indenting the fibrous stuff, but nothing came away. She kicked again and water spurted out. Still she had increased the size of the indentation and she bent down and grabbed at a chunk. She pulled and there was not a splintering sound, but a ripping, tearing sound. A piece about a foot long and six inches wide came away. She immediately smelt it for some reason. It smelt earthy. No, she thought, it was more pungent than that, truffle-like. She sniffed it again, and found it more putrid this time. She then split the piece in two, as though more clues would be revealed. Nothing was, so she split it again. And she found that in itself was satisfying, because it seemed so easy to just tear up something so old, a fragment of the past. She dropped the pieces, and headed to where the tree remains appeared cut away altogether and a strip of sand stood out clear and fresh.

'This stuff's disgusting,' Carey said. She was having difficulty keeping her balance. 'Here, Laura, I think I need your support.' Laura moved closer and they held onto each others' arms. 'Yuk,' Carey said. Her shoes were becoming heavy with clods of ooze. 'All we need now is a downpour.' The sky was darkening but it hadn't resumed raining.

'Come and look at this,' Francis shouted. He was not far away, and had heard Carey's disgruntled voice. 'It's extraordinary, almost a complete tree.' He was walking along its trunk, balancing with his arms outstretched. He could see Alice by the shoreline.

'I've seen enough, thank you,' Carey said. 'I'm going back up to the dunes.'

'Wait a minute,' said Laura, 'I'll come.' They turned to go, then Laura hesitated. 'Henderson,' she shouted. She couldn't see him, or Tristram. 'Henderson.' Tristram emerged from nowhere, muddy and wet. 'Tristram,' she said, 'darling, look at you.' She bent down and felt his top. It was sodden. 'I thought your father was looking after you.'

Henderson then appeared as muddy and wet as his son. Muddier. His hands were covered in it and specks and smudges were on his face. He was grinning, as though he had just discovered something and was too excited to let on immediately what it was.

'It seems he can't look after himself,' Carey said.

The sea was a shifting grey against which gulls swooped and dived. Small waves rolled in and seemed to pause before finally breaking. Others broke over sandbars and shingle ridges and the reefs of ancient forest a long way out into the Wash. Alice was on the wet sand by the water's edge, her feet sinking into it. She felt a grain of sand or an insect in her eye. She blinked and the eye watered badly. She stuck her little finger into the corner trying to dig the thing out. Her eye watered more. She blinked and blinked and when she tried to focus she found everything was incredibly bright. A flock of late terns swirled close by her, and because she couldn't see properly the waves seemed much bigger, the wind kicking up back spray and rainbows. She had a feeling that she was witnessing incredible power and movement, that she was overlooking an ocean. A figure, Billy, was by her side. They had got out of the VW, stretched and shaken the dust off. The view was overwhelming. They were on the edge of the plateau, watching the Great Australian Bight stretch perfectly to the horizon. Sets of waves rhythmically, exactly, gathered in height and pounded the shore without any hesitation. 'You wouldn't last long in there,' Billy said. He laughed and got back into the vehicle. 'Come on,' he said. 'If we don't hurry we won't make it before nightfall.' He started the engine before Alice had even moved from her spot. She was watching a shadow, or something dark a few hundreds yards out, wondering whether it was a whale. She didn't have time to find out for certain. Billy pulled the vehicle up beside her and made her get in, joking that if she didn't get in she'd have to walk. He drove quickly, dangerously along the track, which narrowed and twisted as it descended the escarpment. Soon the massive dunes of the cove loomed, and the Eyre Telegraph Station grew from a dot. Out-buildings and a couple of caravans became visible as they traversed the mallee scrubland, between the limestone cliffs and the sand dunes, towards them.

As Alice turned inland she saw the birdwatchers still massed by the foot of the sand dunes and something else came to her. A pink cockatoo perched on a post, its grotesque crest erect. The station was now used as a bird observatory. It had been full of birdwatchers. She skirted the ancient forest keeping to the sand and the shells.

Carey had cut across the shortest stretch of forest wanting to get onto the sand as quickly as possible. In fact they were all pleased to get off the stuff, their shoes having become great weights of mud and ooze. They were walking back up by the sand dunes towards the footpath when they were suddenly amid rusted and twisted hulks of steel, which could have been almost anything, except there was a vague shape which suggested a caterpillar track.

Henderson stalled. 'The tank?' he said quietly. 'The tank, of course.' Except it was unrecognisable, and he wondered for a moment whether it really had been a tank. Whether his father had deluded them all those years ago. He looked over his shoulder again half expecting his father to be standing there, watching him, watching Victoria.

Tristram said it didn't look like a tank to him. He said, 'Where's the gun?'

'I don't know,' Henderson said. 'Maybe it wasn't a tank.' The largest section of the tank, or whatever it was, was still full of razor shells, thousands and thousands of them, and that was familiar to Henderson, and he felt his face might be glowing. Razor shells also covered the sand around the structure and the other bits of wasting metal. Henderson remembered just how his father had shouted at him because he had been more interested in collecting these shells with Victoria than the tank. The shells gleamed now in the dull light and Henderson reached down and grabbed a handful. The shells were sharp, but splintered and crumbled without cutting him. The mud had dried on his hands and some of it was scraped off as he let go of the broken shells. He urged Tristram to collect some because, he said, he wouldn't find them in London.

'Of course not, silly,' Tristram said. 'There's no beach there.' Tristram wasn't intrigued by the shells. He'd seen plenty of shells before. And because his father wanted him to collect some, he was even less interested in them. He wanted to know more about the tank, if that's really what it was, because no one seemed interested in it. He thought the bits of metal must have belonged to something pretty big. He wondered whether they had anything to do with the prehistoric forest. But he knew he was not going to get a straight answer from his father or any of the others, so he tried to imagine what exactly it could have looked like. He'd work it out for himself.

Carey felt the rain first, because she had been waiting for it, hoping for it. The first few drops were light and could have been windblown shell fragments or grains of sand. But soon there was no mistaking it. 'Time to leave,' she said.

'Hadn't we better wait for Alice,' Francis said.

'It's pouring with rain,' Carey said. 'We can't wait here. I'm not waiting.'

'Oh, Alice,' Laura said. 'Where is she?'

'I'll wait for her,' Henderson said. The others set off quickly, Laura having to drag Tristram away. Henderson looked across the beach and the new slime of the old forest to the water's edge. A number of people were dotted about, but he couldn't tell if one was Alice. Then she was right in front of him. Raindrops clung to her hair and she mumbled something about birdwatchers, but Henderson didn't catch everything because of the noise of the weather, the sea and the birds, and the fact that he didn't see any hint of Victoria in her now, and he couldn't work out why. Alice seemed distracted and he didn't ask her to repeat herself. Instead he just said, 'Hurry, you're getting soaked.' The others had already left the beach and they set off after them, not talking. Henderson suddenly feeling very exposed and shy. Alice thinking about the Eyre Bird Observatory, trying to remember what exactly had happened there, a shortness of breath and twinging stomach overcoming her.

The hides were packed and the path was bustling with people and their equipment as they rushed to the comfort of the information centre and the carpark. The particularly well-equipped birdwatchers remained where they were, however, causing areas of great congestion. They weren't going to be put off by the weather, and they tried to ignore the people passing. But a few had been disturbed, seemingly all morning, and were running out of patience. One didn't get out of the way on purpose, in fact he moved forward slightly when a group of townies passed, and the small boy toppled over the edge.

Tristram felt someone push him. He slipped, lost his balance completely and started to roll down the embankment towards the mud. He put out his hands but the grass was too wet and slippery. Besides he was going too fast.

'Tristram,' Laura screamed. She found she couldn't move.

Francis slid and tumbled after him, but he couldn't catch him. Tristram came to a halt in a clump of reeds just before the mud. All he could see were reeds. He tried to move but his limbs were tangled in the plants and stuck in the soft ground. He felt his knees sinking. Instantly he imagined he was deep within the ancient forest and that he had to get out. Then he felt something grab his arm. He opened his mouth, but no sound came out and he found his mouth was full of bits of plants. Francis pulled him clear, stood him on the edge of the bank and wiped the reeds and wet plants from his face. Tristram was shocked, but not hurt. He didn't cry. He spat and dribbled the stuff from his mouth.

Carey turned to the large man adjusting the height of his telescope beside her. 'You fucking wanker,' she said. 'That's a child. You could have seriously hurt him. Don't you know any better?'

'Christ, I'm so sorry,' the man said. 'You don't think I pushed him do you? Surely?' The man laid his tripod and telescope on the floor by his bags and started to descend the bank, stopping half-way down. 'Here,' he said, reaching out his hand for Tristram, or Francis.

'For God's sake leave him alone,' Carey said, trying to push him out of the way. 'Just clear off.'

The man didn't move and continued to hold out his hand. 'Here,' he said. 'I'm so sorry. I didn't mean to do anything.'

Henderson saw Laura, then Carey in the crowd ahead. Pushing his way through, he managed to reach Laura. 'What's going on?' he asked her.

'Tristram fell down the bank. He's all right. But Carey thinks that man pushed him.'

'Did he?'

'I don't know.' She looked at the man and thought there was something familiar about him, wondering whether there was just something familiar about all birdwatchers.

The man was still defiantly holding out his hand for Tristram or Francis, neither of whom had taken any notice of him. Henderson climbed down the bank so he was level with the man. But he ignored him too and reached towards Tristram. 'Here Tristram, Francis,' he said. Francis helped Tristram to his father, and they all struggled to the top.

'I didn't do anything. I just wanted to help,' the man said, returning to the top also, his red face wet with rain and sweat. 'Let me have a look at the little boy.' He moved towards Tristram.

'Clear off,' said Henderson.

'I've some tea in a thermos. And some biscuits.' He wiped his brow with the sleeve of his anorak. 'Can't I be of any help?'

The crowd had dispersed and Henderson turned away taking Tristram's hand, and they started to walk on, Laura hurrying to take his other hand, the others following. After a short distance Carey looked over her shoulder and scowled at the man. He was still standing in the path, getting in everyone's way. He had a fat, oval-shaped face. She thought he looked retarded.

Finally the birdwatcher picked up his bags and telescope, and headed for the beach. He was angry with himself for pushing the child off the path. He was angry with himself because it was happening more often, these sudden, uncontrollable rages. He wanted to be helpful, but they wouldn't let him.

The carpark had turned to orange mud and puddles. They got into the car in the same configuration as on the way and Henderson started the engine and windscreen wipers, before he said, 'Where to now?' Rain tapped on the roof and the wipers hummed and clicked. The car smelt of wet. Henderson could see other cars tremble to life, exhaust cloud the damp air. A few pulled out, most remained where they were, drying their inhabitants, windows clouding. He wanted to see something he hadn't seen before. Go somewhere new.

'Burnham,' said Alice.

'Where?' said Henderson, puzzled.

'Burnham, you know, where Nelson came from.'

'Oh. Burnham, Burnham, yes.' He had never been to Nelson's birthplace. He had never been allowed. His father had refused to take him. 'He won't enjoy it,' Henderson could remember his father telling his mother, loud enough so he could hear as well. 'He'll get bored. He's not interested in those sorts of things.' The voice came back so clearly Henderson shuddered, disguising it as a shiver. He had watched his father drive off on numerous occasions with Victoria. She had been allowed to go, she had gone everywhere with him. Henderson remembered being left behind with his mother in the caravan, rain tapping on the thin metal roof. It had always been raining. 'Never mind, dear,' she'd say, 'we can play Cluedo.' Christ, Cluedo, thought Henderson. He pulled the road map from the side pocket and quickly found where they were. 'Which one exactly? There are a number of Burnhams, four, five.'

'Oh, I don't know. Just Burnham I read. You don't know? Really?' said Alice.

'No,' said Henderson, sharply.

'Well let's go to the nearest Burnham and ask,' said Alice.

'What about lunch?' Francis said. 'Look we're near that pub we went to last night, aren't we? That did food. Why don't we go there?'

'No,' said Henderson. 'No. Let's wait until we get there.'

'Nelson didn't exactly treat his wife very well, did he?'

Carey said, not expecting an answer. 'I really don't think I want to see where he grew up. It must be a particularly unpleasant place.'

'Carey,' said Laura, finally running out of patience with her, 'do you have a better idea?'

'Yes, London.'

Francis twisted on his seat and looked at Carey, a look which he hoped said, if you want to go back to London, go, but I'm not coming. I've made up my mind about a lot of things. 'I think Burnham's a great idea,' he said, 'as long as we can get something to eat.'

'Carey, I can drop you at the windmill,' Henderson said, 'if you'd prefer to spend the afternoon there.' Carey didn't answer. So Henderson pulled out of the carpark. The traffic was slow along the coast road, and thick with caravans. Many people had packed up and were heading home a day early, others were heading for the stately homes and Nelson landmarks.

'Who's Nelson?' said Tristram, yawning.

'We should really take you home and change you,' Laura said, rubbing her hand over his shoulders and across his back and lower back, all damp. 'Henderson, do we pass the windmill?'

'He was a very famous sailor, an admiral, or at least a vice-admiral. Most people think he was a hero,' Henderson said.

'I don't think he was then,' Tristram said. 'I'm hungry, Mummy,' he added.

Henderson laughed. 'You can think what you like. Yes we do pass it, Laura.'

Laura smiled to herself and shut her eyes. They hadn't gone far but she felt remarkably sleepy all of a sudden.

'Is the heating on?' Carey asked. 'It's bloody hot in here.' She wound down her window and rain spat in. She looked out of the window, rain wetting her face.

They stopped at the windmill. Laura changed Tristram's

clothes, and on the desk in the sitting-room Alice found a booklet amongst a pile. It was called *Nelson Country*. She flicked through the booklet and saw it listed all the local sites associated with Nelson: *England's greatest hero*, it called him. She found it so easily she knew she was right to have suggested Burnham, that they were meant to see where he was born. Then she noticed it was written by John Baxter. Carey said she wasn't going to sit in the windmill all afternoon, when Francis asked her if she was coming. She said she'd have to come, wouldn't she, because she couldn't drive herself to London. Besides, there were still some things she wasn't sure about. She couldn't go until she knew, until she had made up her mind about Alice and Henderson, and Francis. Fuck it, she said to herself. Henderson left the car only to go to the toilet. He found the windmill strange, different somehow, as if they weren't meant to be there in the middle of the day. Then he waited by the car getting wet, mentally urging the others to hurry up. But they were quick, Laura and Tristram emerging from the windmill first. He felt like hugging them, and wished for the first time the others weren't about, and that they could drive off, just them, just the family. And then the others came straggling out. Carey not talking to Alice or Francis, but looking at the ground, then the sky in disgust, conscious of everything in earshot.

'Burnham Thorpe,' Alice said, triumphantly, once they were all seated. 'I can direct.' She was holding *Nelson Country* open on another map John Baxter had drawn meticulously. Indeed, this map was smarter than his one of the marshes, the words were typed and it was dotted with tiny illustrations of sailing ships, churches, pubs, windmills, and Nelson at various ages.

'Oh, look, here Francis,' Henderson said, ignoring Alice behind him and passing Francis the road map, 'will you find it?'

'He's not very good with maps. I'd check it yourself if I were you,' Carey said. Adding after a pause, 'He has an appalling sense of direction.'

'I can direct,' Alice said again, leaning forward.

'It's easier if Francis directs,' Henderson said, acknowledging Alice, ignoring Carey. 'He is in the front.'

Alice slunk back in her seat, closing Baxter's booklet, but she didn't let go of it.

Francis tried to sound straighforward and confident while giving Henderson directions. But the route was simple enough. They took a lane inland and skirted the village where Laura and Carey had bought the picnic yesterday, which Francis noticed was another Burnham. The harvested fields were a deeper yellow and the verges and hedgerows greener, despite or because of the clouds and the rain. Everything appeared soft and soggy. Clayey. Francis anticipated and spotted the final turning in time and they found themselves on an even narrower lane. The hedges were taller and denser and Carey felt increasingly claustrophobic, as if she were travelling down a tube. That she couldn't turn off or turn round, the only way she could go was forward, and she didn't want to carry on anymore. She pulled her head inside and wound up the window, not wanting to see or be reminded of anything here.

Small streams ran down the middle of the lane, tributaries branching off every so often. The car smashed through these streams, sending up waves of muddy spray and confusing the course of the channels. By the time they got to Burnham Thorpe the windows were so covered in rain and spray and steamed up on the insides that only Henderson and Francis had a clear view through the windscreen as they entered the village. Henderson had been expecting a huge statue or at least something monumental commemorating Nelson, but there was nothing except a football pitch where the village green should have been. The goals had no netting and the pitch no marking. And there were no players. Someone was walking a dog, however; both the person and the dog were slow and old and trying hopelessly not to get wet. A row of modern bungalows lined one side of the pitch, fields and a coppice hiding all but the spire of a church spread out from the two far sides. Old barns, a few cottages, a larger house and a pub followed the course of the road, overlooking the near side of the pitch. Henderson slowed and then pulled off the road by the pub. The pub was called The Victory, but the name was painted simply and modestly on a board above the door. It could almost have been missed. There were no flags or signs of anything nautical or garish. It wasn't much like a pub at all.

Henderson wondered whether they were in the right place. 'Are you sure this is Burnham Thorpe?' he asked Francis.

'Yes,' said Francis, putting away the map. 'Thank you.'

'I told you,' Carey said.

'No one ever listens to me,' Alice said, tiredly.

Laura said, 'Alice, they're men, what do you expect?'

'A hell of a lot better,' Carey said.

'I know you wouldn't have made a mistake, Alice,' Laura said. 'You did brilliantly yesterday. But sometimes you just have to let them have their way. It only proves how stupid they are in the end. They're not worth arguing with.' However, Laura wasn't angry with Henderson, or Francis. She said it because she felt she should for Alice's sake. She knew it couldn't be easy for Alice, being in a strange place with people she hardly knew. She suddenly realised she could have been much more friendly and supportive. That perhaps she had been inconsiderate.

I don't need you to tell me about men, Alice thought. She felt to see if the clip holding her hair up on the back of her head was in place. It was, firmly. It gave her a small shot of confidence.

'This is Burnham Thorpe,' Francis said. He got out of the car, and walked towards the pub. He was furious with Carey. Every time she opened her mouth today it made him increasingly angry. Not just angry, but repulsed. Of course he could read a bloody map. He pushed open the front door, it was stiff and creaked. The hallway was dim, but he could clearly make out the prints and paintings of Nelson and various ships and sea battles, a number specifically of Nelson lying on the deck of the *Victory*. He could hear voices, hushed. He walked to the end of the hallway and poked his head through a doorway on the left. He saw no one at first, his view obscured by the backs of high settles. He moved into the room and found a few small groups of people seated around beer-stained tables, the settles forming cubicles and making the room seem much smaller than it was. He stood on the stone floor watching the customers for a moment or two, feeling quite removed. The people weren't so old, but Francis couldn't place them, by their accents or what they wore. They paid him no attention and carried on with their conversations or silence.

'Yes?' A tall, stooped middle-aged man had appeared from nowhere, and stood looking down at Francis.

'Is this Burnham Thorpe?' Francis asked.

'It depends what you mean,' the man said. He had a strangely distant voice.

Francis looked at him. 'Are we in Burnham Thorpe?'

'You're in a pub.'

'Where's the pub then?'

'Burnham Thorpe,' the man answered, without smiling.

'Thank you,' Francis said. He turned and walked out of the room, bumping into Henderson in the hallway. 'We are in the right place.'

'But are you in the right time?' the man said. He had followed Francis and was standing in the doorway, blocking it. He had slipped one of his hands inside the middle of his jacket, so you couldn't see any of his wrist.

Henderson had misheard him. 'It's not two yet. Of course we are.'

'You weren't born yet?' the man said, questioning but not expecting an answer. 'Of course you weren't.' He disappeared.

Laura, standing behind Henderson, laughed. Then she stopped laughing and reached for Tristram's hand.

Carey said, 'Whose idea was it to come here?'

'Mine and Alice's,' said Henderson, walking into the room proudly pushing past Francis. He found an empty table, and stood pointing at it. 'Here?' he said.

They eventually seated themselves, and Alice asked, 'Where's the bar?' They looked around the room, realising there was no bar. There was a narrow doorway at the far end of the room, that was all.

'This is too much,' Carey said, drumming the table.

Francis got up, and walked into the middle of the room. He looked about him as if a bar would suddenly materialise, the other customers still ignoring him, indeed all of them. He moved over to the narrow doorway and peered in, slowly edging through. But he saw no one or nothing resembling a bar, just barrels of beer lined on a bench. The air was beer-soaked. There was a partition hiding half the room from him, and he was nearing the end of it when he heard footsteps on the other side. But he didn't have time to back away before the barman appeared. Right in front of him, as before.

'Arrgh. An impostor. Out, out of here, out of my galley,' he said, shooing Francis back with his long, skinny arms. He followed Francis to the table. 'I've half a mind to report you to the admiral, yes his Lordship himself and get the lot of you thrown overboard. What's this?' He leant so closely over Laura she could smell his breath, a damp, salty breath. 'What's this you're hiding here?' He pointed to Tristram.

Tristram couldn't avert his eyes. He was fascinated by the man, his thinness, like a shadow. He giggled nervously, sliding closer to his mother.

'A child. Well, you're lucky the landlord's not here. I make exceptions for children, particularly boys. Is he brave? Will he make a sailor? Will you lad?'

Tristram hid his mouth with his hand, and nodded a shy yes.

'Seeing as that is so he'd better have a drop of Nelson's blood. It'll knock some spirit into him.' He then looked each of the others in the eye, his eyes grey and the whites extraordinarily bright. 'And the rest of you, what will I be getting you?' His tone was now urgent, excited.

'I'll have one of those, please,' Alice said, sounding strongly Australian and mildly bored.

'Think you can handle it, the navy's best? You're just a woman. A pretty one, if I may say, but a woman.' He laughed, a high wheezing staccato laugh.

Alice didn't answer, but glared at him, her look saying of course I can. Francis tried to catch Alice's eye, to show he was in sympathy or defiance with her, he wasn't sure which he should be.

Laura noticed how thin the man's lips were as he smacked them. 'I'll have an orange juice.' She deliberately didn't say please, rather wishing that the landlord was there. 'And a Coca Cola,' she added, thinking of Tristram.

Carey said she didn't want a drink, not here, and Henderson asked what beer he had.

'Admiral Ale,' the man said briskly. 'The only beer fit for a hero.'

Henderson ordered himself one, and Francis did likewise, adding, 'Think I can handle it?' The man didn't answer before Francis asked for the bar menu as well.

'Food, what do you think this is? A restaurant? If I recollect rightly the last banquet served here was in the year 1793.' He moved off, swaying slightly like a poplar tree, steadying himself on the back of a settle.

Laura smiled at a couple nearby, but they didn't acknowledge her, and she felt even more uncomfortable. 'Phew, I don't know about this place,' she said.

Henderson was sitting on the settle beside Alice. He could feel her thigh against his, and the rub of her shoulder as she moved. Francis was on the other side of her and Henderson couldn't work out whether Alice was squashed or whether she was trying to move away from Francis and closer to him. Tristram sat in between Laura and Carey, across the table. He was tired and fidgeted ceaselessly. They were all wearing too many clothes and were hot and cramped, too cramped to start taking any clothes off. There was a musty smell, mingling with the smell of beer and damp clothes. The table was sticky, and their sleeves stuck to parts of it.

Laura pulled her arm away, leant back and reached across Tristram to touch Carey on the shoulder. Carey turned to Laura and Laura smiled at her oldest friend. It was a smile to show she was still by her side, almost. 'This *is* a strange place,' Laura said. She laughed, but Carey didn't, managing only a flicker of a smile. Laura continued, nevertheless, 'Do you remember those times when my mother used to take us to the Cotswolds, after Daddy left, and all those frightful bloody tea shops we'd be dragged into. This place reminds me of them somehow. There's something not quite right about it.' She looked at Alice, squashed against her husband. 'That barman's taking an awfully long time.' There was a distant look in Alice's eyes, an unengaged look, and Laura wondered whether she really could be more friendly towards her. They might have been cousins, and good friends once, but Laura thought that that was not enough. They had obviously both experienced such different lives she didn't think they would ever become close again. They hadn't shared enough, not like her and Carey.

Laura sighed, wondering how she could make everyone get on, whether they would get through the rest of the weekend without any major upset. And it suddenly occurred to her, in the way it sometimes did when she would be walking down a pavement and have to pass a certain lamp-post before a car came or something awful would happen, that the weekend was some sort of test for the rest of her life together with Henderson and Tristram. That there was still a chance it would work out, and that they had to survive the weekend together, not just her and Henderson and Tristram, but Carey and Alice and Francis as well, or her life with Henderson and Tristram as a family would be over. She knew she had to hold it all together for the sake of everything. And she felt strong enough, strong even for the first time in as long as she could remember.

She looked at Henderson, not so much for support, but because she wanted to look at something solid, a mirror onto the way she felt. And then she talked on, fast and rather stupidly about nothing in particular, because she couldn't bear it when everyone lapsed into silence. That was failure. She had to engage everybody, she had to talk for them. Carey was driving her mad, scowling, looking elsewhere, worse than uninterested, a liability. And it was so unlike her, Laura thought, more like herself really. Had their lives reversed, she wondered, had Carey become her and she Carey, or had she never seen all there was to Carey? But she didn't have time to worry about these things now, she just had to act. God, she could tell she was going to be busy for the rest of the weekend.

The barman finally appeared. He came bobbing out of the narrow doorway carrying a tray of drinks, slopping them onto the metal tray. By the time he had walked the short distance from the doorway to the table the tray was swimming with liquid, a light brown colour but still see-through, and the picture on the tray, of a rusty *Victory*, floated below the swell. 'Everything in life that takes time is worth while,' he said. He handed the drinks out, remembering who had ordered what, then he handed everyone, including Carey and Tristram, a small glass of dark red liquid. It was thick, moving like syrup in the glass. The barman's eyes opened wide, sparkling even brighter. 'Nelson's blood,' he said. 'It'll preserve you for the rest of your journey, that I swear. Drink up and may God go with you.' He moved back to where he had come from, slowly this time and unsteadily, as if he weren't sure of where he was really going.

'Gross,' said Carey, tasting hers. But she didn't find it too bad, sweet like cough mixture, though with a stronger, rummy kick at the back of the throat. After a moment she felt it in her belly, and it dissipated the samphire ache.

Laura moved Tristram's out of his reach. 'You wouldn't like it, darling.' She took a sip from her own glass and found it much more pleasant than she had been expecting. She took another sip, and didn't think the pub was so bad, or the barman. Indeed she thought it prophetic, the way he had said it would preserve you for the rest of your journey.

'Mine,' Tristram whined. 'I want my drink.' He pushed his Coca Cola to the side, spilling some, and lunged for his glass of Nelson's blood. Alice saw what was coming and moved the glass away, and Tristram went bright red in the face and tears burst out of his eyes before he had even whimpered. 'My drink, give me my drink.' His arms were flailing about now. And he started to scream.

'Tristram,' Laura shouted, shouting it again and again. 'Will you behave.'

'Tristram, just control yourself,' Henderson said, calmly, unrealistically.

'Tristram,' Francis said, trying to help. He could barely

watch as Tristram thrashed and fought his mother, and
for air. Carey was sitting impassively next to Tristram, as
impassively as the other customers, and Francis knew she
was right, that there was nothing she or he could do.

'My drink,' Tristram tried to breathe, 'Nelson's, uuhhh,
Nelson's blood.'

Carey lit a cigarette, and blew smoke over the table and
Tristram, trying to drown him with it. The smoke wafted
in the damp, beery air towards the narrow doorway in a
wavering band.

The barman shot out, he wasn't unsteady or unsure of
himself now. 'Put that out, at once,' he shouted. His face
was still colourless, but his eyes were narrowing and his
ears reddening.

Carey felt spit hit her face, and she was repulsed by it.
'It's a pub isn't it? Since when have you not been able to
smoke in a pub?'

'It's not allowed. That's the landlord's order,' he said,
desperately. 'You have to obey him.'

Tristram was quiet now, sniffing, and he stared at the
man, watching his mouth twitch and the way locks of
his shocking grey hair flew about his head as he shook.
He was fascinating, like no man he had ever seen before.
He wondered whether he had come out of the prehistoric
forest, certainly from some time in the past.

Carey carried on smoking, not looking at the man. She
finished her drink and exhaled a gust of sickly sweet
smoke.

'Out,' the man said. 'Off with you.' He started to collect
the glasses, whether they were empty or not, stacking them
on the tray, his gangly arms fighting the air.

Laura finished her drink in one. She gagged, but she felt
she had to get it all down. 'I think we should get out of
here as quickly as possible,' she said, standing up. 'It was
certainly an experience,' she added, cheerfully.

'There's no bloody food anyway,' Francis said, pushing his nearly empty beer mug across the table. 'Disgusting beer.' He caught Alice's eye, hoping she'd heard him. The beer was excellent but he had wanted to sound disapproving.

Carey barged into him. 'Pleased?' she said.

He wasn't sure what she meant, and looked at her quizzically, frowning.

'Pleased that I've upset that barman who was rude to your precious Alice?'

'He wasn't rude to anyone,' Francis said, turning to lead them out of the room.

It had stopped raining, and the sky was much brighter. Clouds had formed out of the mass of dark grey and were beginning to puff and billow. The air was fresher too, and there was a crackle to it, as though you could hear the water evaporating, everywhere drying.

Tristram pulled on Laura's arm. She tried to ignore him, but he seemed so strong and heavy, and his nails dug into her arm. 'What?' she said, looking down at him, far from pleased.

'I want a kiss, Mummy.' His eyes were no longer red, but huge and innocent and full of love and remorse. He rubbed one eye making it red again, and blurring his vision. Laura bent down, and he moved forward, misjudging where she was because he could only see out of one eye clearly, and smacked into her face.

'Pleased?' said Francis, grabbing hold of Carey's arm.

'About what?' She trod on the stub of her cigarette.

'That it's brightening up. I wouldn't be surprised if the sun comes out later. Think we might be in for a glorious day tomorrow, heh?'

Alice headed out across the football pitch, leaving the others behind. She didn't want to get straight back into the car.

She breathed in deeply, shaking her head, shaking away the fug of the pub and the greater fug of her recent life. But nothing much cleared and she ambled across the damp grass slowly, meditatively, her canvas shoes, already soaked and muddied once that day, growing heavy again. But she found the freshness a blessing. The church tower above the coppice seemed to beckon, and she headed for it. Nearing the far side of the football pitch she turned and saw the others standing by the car watching her. She could have waved goodbye and gathered up speed and marched past the church, on across fields and through villages and towns, and sunk herself into some other existence where no one knew her, nor her past, and start again. But there was still something pulling her back strongly enough for her not to do it. It wasn't family or friends, she thought, but something greater, herself, a sense that she owed it to herself not to. That she couldn't deny what had happened. That she had to live with it, grow with it. Make sense of it. Instead she pointed to the church and mouthed, see you there. She could see Henderson flinging his arms in the air, madly, distractedly, and she wondered for a moment what his childhood memories of this place were, whether anything terrible had ever happened to him. The land rose to meet the church, and although the fug was still with her, the slight elevation gave her a better perspective of where she was.

The churchyard was like all village churchyards should be, thought Alice, quiet and reverential and empty of living people. The grass had recently been mown, and cuttings got onto Alice's shoes because they were wet and she chose to walk across the grass in between the yew trees and the lichened gravestones, and not on the neat path. The names of the dead had faded, and the bumps their bodies must have once made had subsided so the ground was pretty level. A dragonfly shot past her face as she entered the chequered flint church, realising she couldn't have been in such an old church for over twenty years. She had never thought of herself as religious, but the sudden echoey space seemed about as religious a place as she had ever entered, more so. She half expected a priest to appear, and summon her to prayer, and she would have obeyed. There was no one else there, however, the only movement coming from the shadows and the light flickering through the stained-glass windows. Two flags draped either side of the aisle were completely still, and looked, Alice thought, from their tattiness and the dust built up around the creases that they had been that way for decades, if not centuries. She blew at one of the flags, but it was too high and heavy and nothing happened. Dust didn't even puff. She walked up the aisle until she came to a bronze bust in the chancel. It was of Nelson, and she noticed he was looking over his parents, Catherine and the Reverend Edmund, who were buried beneath the ledger slabs at the foot of the pedestal. Alice heard a car horn, it beeped twice, three times, and she moved over to the lectern. On top of the huge Bible someone had placed a booklet. It was opened and her eyes fell upon the text:

'I wonder child that hunger and fear did not drive you home?'
'Fear – I never saw fear, what is it?'

She read on only far enough to ascertain it was Nelson who was replying to the first question. She closed the booklet and saw it was John Baxter's *Nelson Country*, from a section she hadn't come across before. She heard footsteps on the shingle path, the latch and creak of the church door, hard footsteps on cold stone.

'Alice,' Henderson said, his voice deep and reverberating and angry, 'we're all waiting in the car.'

Alice looked up from the lectern. The light from the east

window behind her had intensified and was flooding the nave. Henderson appeared as if bathed by multi-coloured spot-lights. 'Can you see fear?' she asked.

'Alice, we're hungry and waiting.'

'I know, but Henderson please answer.'

'I don't know what you mean.'

'OK, what are you afraid of?'

'I don't know, the usual things.'

'Elaborate.'

'Oh, I don't know. Everyone's waiting.'

'Please, it's important.'

'I suppose violence, losing the people you love, not being loved.' He shrugged his shoulders, disrupting the beams of light, 'The past.'

'So am I.' She left the lectern and joined him and they walked out of the church together. 'But at least you've come back,' she said as they emerged into the full daylight, blinking. 'I can't seem to stop running.'

Henderson focused on his car ahead, catching Laura and Tristram, their funny dark shapes in the very back. 'I realised I had too much to lose,' he whispered.

Henderson pressed on the accelerator hard and suddenly and the big car lurched forward, tearing out of Burnham Thorpe on a wet- and dry-speckled lane. And he couldn't believe how easy it was, the car full and his family still together. He didn't feel left out any longer, or jealous, he had his own family now and he was bursting with that. He doubted he would return to Burnham Thorpe. He had seen it now, seen everything he hadn't been allowed to see, and there was no secret. He realised what he had done to Victoria, realised nothing could change that. And he thought for a moment or two that perhaps it wasn't just his fault, that if his father hadn't behaved in the way he had towards them, if he hadn't, if he hadn't, but he didn't dwell on that. The hedges were beginning to glisten in light that was filling out and warming, and Henderson roared on, pumping the accelerator and the brake. 'Chips,' he said, adding for no logical reason in a sing-song voice, 'cheap as chips.'

'I bet they'll be closed,' Carey said, 'it's Sunday for God's sake. What about—'

But Francis interrupted her. 'I'm not asking you whether you have a better idea,' he said. 'We can only try. Something will be open. It looks huge on the map. Well, bigger than anywhere else nearby.'

'Come on everybody, cheer up, we'll get something to eat there,' Laura said. She rubbed Tristram's head, messing up his hair. Her own head ached badly now, but she tried to ignore it, instead imagining Tristram had her headache and she was rubbing it away.

'Mum,' he pleaded, 'stop it. It hurts.' But she couldn't stop it, and continued rubbing away. 'Mum.' He ducked, holding his hands over his head. In one hand he was clasping a beer mat. He had picked it up from the pub, and the mat showed a painting of Nelson's dying moments, lying in his cabin on the *Victory* with Hardy leaning over him. Laura could just make it out, thinking it odd Tristram should have wanted it.

'I bet we don't,' Carey said, 'it's hardly London.'

'Carey, come on,' Laura said. 'We're not in London now, thank God.'

'You think you know everything, what do you think Henderson?' Carey asked.

'I've no idea what to expect, actually. I've never been there before.'

Francis was map-reading again and Alice leant forward trying to look over his shoulder to see for herself exactly how big and where the seaside town was, because it wasn't marked on either of Baxter's maps, being slightly too far away she presumed. The road was uneven and twisty and she found it hard to focus, then the car hit a pothole. Henderson braked at the same time, and she flew into Francis's seat, knocking her mouth on the head-rest. She bit her bottom lip and felt it swell immediately, pushing at the inside of the lip with her tongue. She sat back and wondered why she had bothered to try to look in the first place. It's only a fucking map, she said to herself. It can't really show you what a place is like. Or what might have happened to you there, where you've come from or how far you've got to go. It's only you who can possibly know that.

And she decided then she wasn't going to paint a map of the marshes, or anywhere else. Maps had been misleading her, she thought, lying to her, showing her ways to places which were in reality far more complicated and hidden. She'd been looking at things the wrong way round, unable to know where she really was and where she was going because she wasn't prepared, or able, to look at where she'd come from. And she knew she wouldn't be able to paint again, properly, until she'd at least sorted that out.

The car arrived at the coast road on a stretch they hadn't travelled before and they sped past a brick wall that went on for miles, pasture then pine trees panning out on the other side of the road. Caravans, confused and slow because they'd been tricked by the weather, were no object as Henderson overtook with a calmness and verve that stunned Francis, who normally hated being a passenger. A gate house interrupted the wall. And they passed a tea shop and crafts centre before anyone had a chance to yell stop. And on they rushed, the coast road wiggling now to avoid drainage dykes and patches of pasture which were still too much marsh. The car hugging the corners, but only just. The coast road swung inland and a smaller road took up its course following the soft coastline. Henderson took that road on Francis's orders. And, 'Bingo,' Henderson shouted as they slowed, entering the town: small fishermen's cottages first, then larger merchants' houses and pubs and restaurants and neon. 'Christ,' said Henderson, 'there's even a bingo hall and an amusement arcade.' The high street was full of people and children in unruly groups, eating chips and shoving one another about. Henderson drove on until one side of the street fell away to a dockside incorporating a narrow carpark edging the waterfront. He parked overlooking the harbour, which though wide was bounded on the far side by a seemingly endless stretch of marsh; the channel to sea lay to the west, slipping directly out between the marsh and an embankment, which protected a caravan park and farmed land behind that. Clinker-built whelk boats without cabins and larger fishing trawlers were moored up two-, three-abreast, with their pink plastic buoys rubbing and squeezing loudly between them. There were splotches of tar on some of the buoys ruining their pinkness.

Carey noticed the boats all had two names: *Allison Christine*, *Valerie Marilyn*, *Charles William*. And she wondered why two. Tristram had noticed the lights and the people with a sudden rush of excitement, negating his hunger. He scrambled from the back of the car desperate to see what was going on in the amusement arcade with the mechanical bucking horse outside. It was about his size, he reckoned. But the others hadn't forgotten how hungry they were clambering after him; Laura hanging onto Tristram's collar, telling him he'd just have to wait, she'd take him in later, fearful he would have another tantrum. It was getting warmer by the minute as the sun was pushing harder behind the clouds, smoky rays bounding through and skipping on the low water of the harbour and the now dry asphalt of the road and the suddenly gleaming greyness of the pavement slabs. Francis wished he'd left his waterproof in the car. He saw Alice had left hers behind.

It was mid-afternoon and Henderson spotted a fish and chip shop that was open. He pointed it out, and Francis said to Carey, 'I told you so.' Carey said she wasn't hungry and would wait for them by the waterfront. She said she wanted to have a closer look at the fishing boats, besides the smell of greasy chips would make her feel sick again. Francis said nothing and Laura watched her walk away, tempted to go after her for a minute, but then thought she would be better off left alone. That she'd snap out of it, when the sun shone through and the gulls shone too, circling and swooping by the fishy-smelling boats. Henderson ordered the fish and chips while the rest of the others waited outside dodging the people pushing past. Many of whom were bad tempered because the weather was getting out nice again when they had already decided that their holidays were over, because they had been fooled.

And then, magically, Henderson came out of the fish and chip shop clutching a stack of newspaper bundles, and the air was balmy and everything in slow motion because that's the way he wanted to see it: sunlight, children and laughter. People had shifted over to the waterfront and were no longer pushing but playing, some children having lowered crab lines into the murk. Henderson carried the bundles across the road and they melted into the happy crowd. He handed out the food and they sat on capstans eating. Henderson saw nothing but what was in front of him: Alice and Francis sharing a capstan, Laura sharing hers with Tristram. He thought, this is where the holiday begins, there's plenty of time left, there's no need to rush anymore. I'll buy Tristram a crab line after we've eaten and help him crab, if I can figure out how to do it myself. He'll like that. I want to do whatever he likes. Love him.

The chips were soggy and too vinegary, but they didn't taste as bad as Laura thought they looked, even though she felt they should have actually been eating ice-creams. Tristram couldn't sit still beside her, not being able to eat his chips fast enough because he now wanted to have a look at what the other children were doing by the water's edge. He'd forgotten about the amusement arcade. And Laura's tiredness suddenly seemed to lift. She was glad that they had come here, and that they had a day left. She remembered how she had felt at the staithe yesterday when everything seemed to have escaped her and she was full of regret. She didn't need any more children. If they came along, well that would be great, but Tristram was enough.

'Here, Tristram,' Henderson stood up, crumpling the

newspaper and the remains into as small a ball as he could make, 'how would you like to go crabbing?' Tristram nodded a yes, leaping up, dropping his opened newspaper and chips on the ground and some on Laura's lap, taking his father's hand. 'Let's look at what these other children are doing first.'

I hope Tristram remembers this, Laura thought. I will.

Carey was on the other side of the main group of crabbers and she saw Henderson's head above them coming her way. She moved backwards and stood behind a car, not wanting him to see her, to see she'd been crying. She watched as he bent down on the edge, peering over, Tristram a few steps behind. She had a sudden urge to rush forward and push Henderson in.

Francis finished his chips and wiped his mouth on the sleeve of his waterproof. But the material didn't take any of the grease off, just spread it wider across his face in fact. Alice's mouth was covered with grease, too, so he didn't mind about his own so much. He liked the way she did her hair up. There was a loud splash and shouting which distracted him momentarily, then he caught Alice's eye, the brown deep and dreamy. He imagined what their children would look like. They'd have to have thick brown curly hair, and brown eyes, he thought. They'd be pretty and perfect. And bound to be artistic.

Alice was thinking how much more of a proper place this was than the staithe. Somewhere that still worked as it should. And she felt she knew where she was. She heard splashing, shouting, and she looked up. Carey appeared out of the crowd, running towards them.

The caravan wasn't just damp, leaks had pooled on the floor of the bedroom and the birdwatcher had stepped into the water taking his boots off and soaked his socks. Now he was walking about, feeling the caravan shudder with his heavy steps leaving their marks. The rain had stopped and sun was coming in and he'd packed up for the day too damn early. 'Blast,' he said, slamming his hand down on the stupid, collapsible table, sun in his eyes so he couldn't see outside, and it hurt. He'd had an awful day, people getting in the way. So many people. I can't bear all those people, he said to himself. He smiled at the thought of pushing the boy off the path. Down he went, down he went, tumbling down the grassy bank, splat into the mud. well nearly. Not so lucky next time, he found himself thinking, pursing his lips, pinching his blubbery cheeks. He could feel himself fall on him, squash him.

They were driving into the falling sun and the sun was catching the dead insects and film of dirt on the windscreen, so Henderson couldn't see much more than that, and the car crept along. Besides he didn't want to rush now, wanting everything to slow down so he could experience things fully, for the first time. Keep it slow, keep it slow, he said to himself. The sun hot on his chest, he stuck his arm out of the window, casually resting his elbow on the ridges where the window had slipped between, his hand lightly gripping the top of the door and the roof. Despite the soft pace cool air was disturbed by his arm and eddied into the car out of control blowing anything loose about and everyone's hair. Alice fought with her free curls, trying to tuck them behind her ears and under the hair that was still pulled back tight by the grip. Tristram giggled because the small crab was tickling his cupped hand. He watched it scrabbling about, bemused, senseless, not knowing where the sea and the sand were to bury itself in. He pressed its soft shell, pinning it to the palm of his hand, the crab's legs flattening out and going still. The reddening light swamped the car and as wisps of hair blew across Carey's face she thought she could see the texture of each strand, as if under a microscope, the light searing through the auburn. She didn't want to see anymore than that. Henderson was blinded as the car crawled out of a dip and met the sun face on. Then the road curved towards the sea for a while, a hedge shielding the sun, and he could see better than before. A view of the marshes and the pine woods beyond them thick with filmy light and damp evening air. Ghostly smoke from the Queen's barbecue lost amid the greater atmosphere. Francis felt a rock, or a weight rocking in his stomach. It was anticipation. He wished Henderson would put his foot down as he had done on the way. He felt he was running out of time, and it was not fair. Tristram tipped the crab into the wet at the bottom of the bucket. It left a leg behind, stuck to his hand. He shook the leg into the bucket on top of the motionless, upside-down crab. Francis twisted round fleetingly, glimpsing Alice, the flutter of her hair, which he suddenly realised was not a dissimilar colour to Carey's in this light.

'I hope that child's all right,' Laura said. She couldn't stop hearing the splash, couldn't get the image of the child being hauled out of the harbour off her mind. The crowd of people round him as he struggled for breath, shivering, bewildered. How easily it could have been Tristram, she thought.

'He should have had someone looking after him properly,' Carey said.

'He was just shocked,' Henderson said. 'He wasn't in the water long. I should think people fall in there all the time. It's not far to fall.' He struggled to see again, saying nothing for a while, then as an afterthought, 'At least the current wasn't strong. The tide must have been on the turn.'

The sharp flint of the staithe cottages glinted pink and shafts of sun bounced off the narrow pavements, making it hard for the few pedestrians to see where they were putting their feet. Out of the staithe and the sun was deep red now, hovering over the grazing land, tangling with the tops of the grasses and weeds, wind rippling across shaking it free every so often. The marshes were waterlogged and on fire. The windmill appeared in silhouette first, majestic, and as they drew near the pinkness of the cap and the sails became clear, the view tumbling away from them, tumbling.

Tristram buried the crab in the garden and felt sorry for having taken it away from its home. Maybe you should leave things where they are, he thought. 'Did I kill it?' he asked his mother.

'Well, it was very delicate. You have to be careful with small things.' She looked at him, sad-eyed, standing by the door to the kitchen. She could tell he was not sure whether he had done something really terrible or whether he should come into the room even. 'It doesn't matter, darling. Come and have your supper.' He climbed onto the chair quickly and relieved, and she watched him yawn at the sight of the food she had prepared for him. Still she would never know whether he was going to eat it, ignore it or just play with it. There was no rationale.

Francis left Carey in the bedroom saying he needed some air and space to think in, borrowing her phrase. He shut the door behind him, shutting her in, and stood on the landing deciding where he would be most likely to find Alice. He went up. The sun had fallen below the marshes and inside the windmill the light was thick and dusky, no one having yet turned on any stairway lights. Francis reached her bedroom door. The door was ajar, a crack of light on the landing wall, and he stood to the side of the gap listening, trying not to breathe. The windmill was not quiet, sighing, creaking, noises he couldn't place, but after a while he was sure Alice was not in her room. He pushed the door gently, shshing it, easing his way into her room with it. Her bed was a mess of crumpled sheets and blankets, clothes and underclothes heaped on it, casually, appealingly. His eyes lingered on the underclothes, then moved over to the other single bed. This bed was covered with thin pamphlets or something, Francis wasn't sure. He edged further into the room, but he didn't want to let go of the door, and he didn't have to, suddenly realising what they were, maps. Maps. On the cupboard in between the beds he could see some paint brushes and pencils, a flat, rectangular tin of something, and a photograph propped against a glass. He leant across, as far as he could without letting go of the door, but he couldn't make out the picture, the light was not good enough or the photograph at the right angle. Then he heard floorboards creak above, a person quite definitely walking around. A light person he was sure, too.

He moved quickly, pulling the door fast after him, reaching the next floor in no time. The door to the upper sitting-room was open and Francis rushed in, immediately feeling relieved and happy, that he was where he belonged. Alice was crouching by the bookcase across the room from him and Francis got as far as the middle of the room before he stopped. She had turned to see who had come in and he said, 'Hi,' breathlessly. 'Hi,' he said again. She looked at him blankly without saying anything. He could see her blink, the slight trembling of her crouching body. She swept some hair off her forehead, still not saying anything or smiling, still looking at him blankly, coldly, as if she didn't know him, and then he knew that he was in the wrong place and the feeling of awkwardness that he had felt with her in the Queen's beach hut came back, but much worse. Then he had felt excited by it, now more deadened than embarrassed. Something seemed to heave up from his stomach so he thought he was going to retch. 'Urrgh, I'm urrgh, sorry to disturb you. I was looking for Carey.' He found he was backing away, wanting to run. And he was freezing.

'Really,' she said, standing up. She leant against the bookcase, folding her arms, obviously not believing him.

'Yes,' he said, looking at her, her eyes, trying to discern whether there was any hope at all, but there wasn't. And he felt totally stupid. 'You haven't seen her then?'

'I should think you'd have a better idea where she is, at least you should,' she said, sort of sighing, her voice in tune with the windmill. She was suddenly fed up of getting herself into situations she couldn't control. She'd had enough of men wanting her, abusing her.

Francis left the room without saying anything further.

'I'll put him to bed,' Henderson said, clumsily grabbing hold of Laura's hand, squeezing it, then leaning into her and kissing her gently on the forehead. He let go of her hand and ran his hand up her back, the back of her neck, his fingers through her fine hair, catching onto a knot. He pulled back. 'Tristram, darling,' he said, holding out his hand for him, 'bedtime.'

'Thank you,' said Laura. 'I'll see what there is for supper.'

'The others can do that,' Henderson said. 'You've done quite enough already.'

'No,' said Tristram, 'I'm not tired.' He turned away from his parents so he was facing the wall.

'Come on, Tristram,' Henderson said, 'you're not a baby anymore. It's late.'

'Tristram, be a good boy, go with Daddy,' Laura said. 'He'll read you a story.' She winked at Henderson. She had a way of doing this, tilting her head down and to the side, raising her left eyebrow, smiling, wrinkles rippling out from the corners of her mouth, that she knew Henderson found charming.

Alice waited until she couldn't hear his footsteps anymore,

and for a few moments longer, and she left the sitting-room, quietly, and returned to her bedroom. The door was closed and she was sure she had left the door ajar; it was a habit she had picked up when living with Billy so she knew if he had sneaked out or where he'd been snooping around the house because he always shut doors, thinking he could do it silently, and never noticed that they had been left open on purpose. But she found nothing had been disturbed and wondered whether she might have closed the door anyway or it had been shut by the draught. She turned the light on, then off, preferring the vague light of the encroaching full moon. She peeled off her top, finding it sticking to her armpits, and struggled out of her jeans. Freer now, cool air tingling her skin, goose-pimpling it, she went over to the window, paused there for a few seconds looking out over the marshes, then in her bra and knickers crossed to the bed covered in maps, careful not to glance at the photograph propped on the cupboard next to it. She spread the maps about on the bed carelessly, some falling onto the floor including John Baxter's map of the marshes, knowing she wouldn't be looking at these maps again, or that the one she was really looking for wasn't there. Still not looking at the photograph she went back to the window, looked out again, saw the marshes in yet a different light, then over to her bed and the unpacked bag half under it. There was a hard flap, made of cardboard or something cheap like it at the bottom of the bag giving it shape. She slid her hand under this, feeling the edges of the folded paper. She felt her bra strap cut into her, restrict her, and she took her hand out of the bag and unclipped her bra, shaking her body, letting it fall to the ground. She pulled the map from under the flap and wiped it on the side of her bed, wiping the grit off it, before unfolding it on top of the bed.

Henderson read to Tristram the story about a Mr Business

who left his office one morning and took a plane to New York for a conference. Except the plane didn't stop there but carried on until the middle of America where it landed at an Indian reservation instead, the pilot saying they had a more important journey to make. Here Mr Business got off and met with the Indians, who were the fattest people he had ever seen, even fatter than he was, but also the kindest. However, they were dying out because their children wanted to go to work in the cities or Hollywood and were fed up with being fat. Mr Business then got back on the plane and the plane took him to a Pacific island, where he met a tribe of people who had to leave their island because the island was only a few inches above sea level and the sea level was rising because of global warming and the island was drowning. Next the plane stopped in Australia in the middle of a city and Mr Business met an Aborigine whose path had been blocked by a new office complex. And the man asked Mr Business if he could help because he had gone that way for thousands of years and he couldn't go any other way. Mr Business flew back to his office in London and asked his secretary to cancel all his meetings. He sat down at his desk and thought about all the people he had met and how to solve their problems. Tristram didn't make it to the end of the story, and Henderson thought he knew what was going to happen, so he skipped the last few pages too. He tucked Tristram in, kissing him lightly on the forehead and placing his bunny on the pillow next to him.

Alice could not see very well and she was distracted by the shouting below, but she found the Eyre Highway and starting at Ceduna she ran her finger slowly along it east to west. She got as far as Yalata before she took her finger off and looked across to Melbourne. She was kneeling by the bed and she stood up folding Melbourne and the rest of

New South Wales away so the map was more manageable. She took off her knickers, having an urge to get rid of everything, before kneeling naked by the bed again, the floor hard on her knees.

Alice hadn't noticed the shouting had stopped, or the stillness of the room, her gaze and concentration only on the map now. Just the light was moving, dimming, the tract of yellow desert faintly luminous. She started at Ceduna again, shortly passing the shifting dunes like snow drifts, and then the windmills of Penong. This time she took the detour off to Maralinga and the crackling dry hut, through the Yalata Aboriginal Land before rejoining the highway just short of Nullarbor, seeing the sapling and scrub lining the asphalt here; such pathetic shade. The pounding at the Head of Bight was close by, like her heart. Her hand began to tremble. The kangaroo at Ecula reared up, shocking and plastic and scarred by graffiti. But on she went, shifting her weight from knee to knee, her pubic bone rubbing against the edge of the bed, scratching. Mundrabilla, Madura, dust. And she sort of fell on the map where the VW pulled off the highway and tore along the track towards the Eyre Bird Observatory, shaking her and rattling. The strange muffling of the massive dunes pierced by the lone, shrieking squawk of a cartoon-like cockatoo. The old telegraph station was packed solid with birdwatchers and a few backpackers looking out of place, but they were told that they could use one of the caravans out the back for forty dollars total, including dinner and breakfast. She remembered it like it was happening.

Billy started drinking as soon as they had brought their things and beer in from the vehicle, and Alice joined him, her stomach feeling quite empty. The caravan seemed to shudder as the waves crashed the other side of the dunes, the bigger sets building up momentum and fixtures fell off the walls. Their feet stuck to the patched up linoleum floor, the parts that weren't covered with sand and dust anyway, as they paced about too hot and angry with each other to sit still. The caravan's curtains were shredded by the sun and wind and hung uselessly smelling of old. They finished the beer and Billy started grabbing Alice as she shifted about the caravan, and a game of catch developed with Alice charging and shrieking about like the cockatoo, becoming increasingly terrified because Billy had locked the door at some point and she couldn't get out. She barricaded herself in the bedroom, shoving what furniture there was against the door and falling on it, adding her weight to it, more sober than he was. But that defence didn't last long, Billy pushing his way into the room, on to her. His hands on her waist, inside her dress, which was little more than a short nightdress, pulling her knickers off. His eyes yellow and red, and his speech slurred, spitting out words and kisses.

She started to fold the map, becoming increasingly impatient with it, the folds not matching up, pushing it together nevertheless, scrunching it, tearing it. Still on her knees she reached across, nearly losing her balance, and grabbed the photograph of Billy, tearing it too, and pressing the bits into the bundle of the torn map.

'Should we tell her now, or in the morning?'

'Oh, God Francis, for once just think for yourself.'

'She's your friend. I really think you should tell her. After all, it is you who wants to go back so badly.'

'I thought you'd suddenly changed your mind about that. If you haven't I'm very happy to go on my own, only take me to the train and don't bother to come back at all.'

'Look, I'm sorry. I do think it's a good idea we leave. I think this place has got to me as well.'

'I'll tell her. You're right, she is my friend. I'm sure she'll understand.' She paused and added, 'She seems to be getting on so well with Henderson all of a sudden I doubt she'd notice anyway.'

'Henderson, just give the others a shout would you?'

'Laura, you shouldn't have. Look you've done everything, you've even laid the table. Darling, you really shouldn't have.'

'Well I thought it would be nice for everybody. You know, it is our last supper here, and we had all this food that had to be eaten. Just give them a shout would you?'

'Oh yes, of course.' Henderson left the kitchen, walked across the sitting-room and yelled up the stairs, 'Carey, Francis, Alice, supper's ready.' The echoes were lost somewhere in the tower, perhaps to appear at a later date. Ho hum, he said to himself on the way back to the kitchen, which smelt of chicken and roast vegetables and warm people, which smelt as if they had been there for a lifetime, because it was their smell only now. Henderson took a sip of his wine and felt that and the heat and the effects of the fresh air earlier colour his neck almost immediately and start to work on his cheeks. He poured Laura a glass and handed it to her, clinked his glass with hers, slopping the wine in both glasses so it spilled down them like tears. 'Cheers,' he said.

Carey and Francis appeared together, quietly, and Laura thought they both looked rather sheepish, as if they had done something they shouldn't have or were in on some secret. Though she could tell Carey was much happier than she had been earlier in the day. She had done her hair in the way Laura liked, so there was a small pony tail at the top of the back of her head. Laura thought it was sort of fun and charming and made Carey look less serious.

'You shouldn't have, Laura,' Carey said.

'It was nothing,' Laura said.

'And you and Henderson found the windmill and organised the whole weekend and everything. I feel I haven't done anything to help. Thank you both.' She sat down, pulling Francis with her. She rubbed his leg under the table, hard, grabbing hold of the flesh hanging from the bottom of his thigh and giving it a big pinch.

'Soon be back to work then Francis,' Henderson said.

'Thanks for reminding me.'

'Anything exciting coming up?'

'I was thinking of jacking the whole lot in and doing something completely different, but I don't know. I think I'll see how the autumn works out.' He didn't fancy himself as a painter anymore. He thought he'd stick with what he knew for the time being.

Carey looked at Francis, not knowing whether he had really thought of doing something completely different, or whether he was just saying it because Henderson was asking him about business. Anyway, not believing for one minute that he would really jack his job in. It wasn't the fact that he didn't have the guts, but that she just couldn't imagine him doing anything else. She was still looking at him when Alice walked in and she saw him flush. There was no mistaking it, his face suddenly transformed, as if it had been a piece of blotting paper dabbed in a pool of red ink, or blood, the red spreading out from a point just behind his nose. She watched him cover his mouth with his hand, rubbing it roughly as if he were trying to rub the red away. The hand moved all over his face, rubbing and scratching. She glanced at Alice and saw she had changed into a ludicrously smart dress and was wearing make-up, and really looked quite different. Not attractive or charming, or mysterious, or vulnerable as she had variously over the weekend. Just distant. And Carey didn't feel threatened by her now. She gestured to Alice to sit next to her.

'Oh, Alice what a lovely dress, you look gorgeous,' Laura

said. 'I didn't know everyone was going to change. I feel a complete frump.'

'You look lovely as you are, Laura,' Henderson said. He made sure everyone had wine and said, 'Well cheers everyone. To bank holidays.'

Francis coughed, some of the wine going down the wrong way, reinvigorating his puce complexion.

'Bank holidays,' Alice muttered, looking round the table. She caught Henderson's eye. He smiled, looking quickly away, but not before she saw an awkwardness, and behind that an unbearable sadness. It was there, still there. And she wondered whether going back was quite enough. She knew you couldn't keep everything to yourself, make it all go away, even if you stared it straight in the face. She knew that the suffering would go on. Branch out and go on. And she thought of the rushing tide, the creeks and channels weaving their way through the shifting marshes.

And we haven't even got to Monday yet, Laura smiled to herself. A whole day by the sea left for Tristram.

Henderson found himself floating in a creek. The water was fast-moving and he was unable to swim against it or swim to either bank. He was just drifting. There was a gurgling, swishing sound. Then the sound of laughter, giggling, small children chirping away. And the creek was suddenly filled with cherubs, tens, perhaps hundreds of them, with round pink faces and taut, rubbery skin like dolphins have. They were drifting on their sides, faster than Henderson, each with an arm crooked like a fin. Henderson reached out and grabbed hold of a cherub by the arm, like a swimmer might hook onto a dolphin's fin. He was swept along.

Brightness fell on Tristram, hitting him in the face. He found everything was orange and hot, even though he hadn't opened his eyes yet. He lay still for a few more seconds, not sure whether he was awake or asleep. Or where he was. Just orange and hot. He felt bunny next to him, the worn fur. Hot. And he opened his eyes and couldn't see a thing, sun right in them. He wriggled onto his stomach and saw bunny, distorted because he was so close, the sun glinting in one of his glass eyes. He knelt up backwards using his arms, pushing the covers up with him so they started to slide off the bunk, gathering speed, and they all went over the edge. Tristram climbed down after them, dazed by sleep and the sun. He slid about on the covers for a while, getting his feet tangled in the sheets, crawling back to the bottom bunk and stretching underneath it. He had an idea that today was his last day here, so he thought he'd pack up his things. He pulled the hat and the sock out first because they were easier to get hold of. Then he searched around for the rhino and the beer mat. He got the rhino, then after much more stretching and feeling around, the mat. It was coming to pieces, the card splitting and layers of paper peeling back. He wished he had some Sellotape or glue with him to repair it, but he thought if he was careful with it, he knew he had to be careful with delicate things, he would be able to mend it when he got home. He lined all his things on the bottom bunk in order of importance. He put the sock at the end because that was the least important thing, then the rhino because that hadn't been found but bought. He then couldn't decide what was more important, the hat or the mat. After studying each, thinking hard about them, he decided that the hat had to go next in line, the mat at the beginning because the picture said something more than the stains on the hat could ever say. He heard a shuffling outside his door, and he looked for his bag to put his things in, carefully, in order, thinking perhaps we're going already.

Henderson crept past Tristram's room, a pool of sunlight warming the floor just by his son's door. And the sun appeared at intervals as he descended the tight stairs, flashing on his T-shirt and jeans. He found his sandals in the sitting-room and a thin v-neck sweater and turned the heavy key in the lock. It took Henderson some time to realise the door wasn't locked, as he kept turning it, jigging it against some iron barrier. Henderson let himself out, thinking nothing more of the door being unlocked. There was a chill to the air which the sun hadn't yet lifted, and moisture on the cars and the short drive; soon on his toes and wetting the worn leather of his sandals. He crossed the coast road, blinking for a moment on the other side, his eyes trying to take in the early morning view, a veil or something like that still drawn across it. There was a busy sound, of birds and insects, and the heavier, more persistent tones of the sea and the thinnest wind imaginable. Henderson felt comfortably dishevelled and, for a moment, that he was sleepwalking. But as he progressed down the thick damp pasture he felt very much alive. Insects buzzing him and his feet soaked and his lungs filling with thick creamy air. He looked back at the windmill every so often, its laughable sails waving to him. The windows like buttons up its front from this distance. He even waved back once, cheerily, thinking of his family sleeping happily inside. Waking perhaps to their last day here. And he hoped this day would be memorable for them and give them something to treasure at least until their next holiday. Tristram growing so fast now. Henderson realised every moment would be significant.

He reached the embankment and climbed up and the marshes rolled out and wavered, the veil lifting and enhancing the colours, adding pinks and blues and near-neon greens. Water curdling in the creek like some river in India, and steaming slightly. He could just see the edge of the staithe, sun on the flints, and the roofs now too. The empty masts of the sailing boats twinkling but noiseless from where he was. There were no people about yet, and there was a calm and timelessness. He turned away from the staithe and set off the other way, following the embankment, climbing onto it as it curled gently round the pasture before straightening out and running on as far as he could see, so he was going parallel to the marshes and beyond them somewhere the sea.

At points reeds grew taller than the embankment and him and obscured his view, and he began to feel the warmth that the day would bring, and it urged him on, wanting to feel everything. The path became dryer and rutted, a double track for a Land Rover or the like. His sandals picked up the dust and grit got under his toes and he considered taking them off, all his clothes even. He imagined himself naked, a thin pink figure skipping along the embankment, not quite believing his luck. He saw something in the distance, something moving directly ahead of him in the middle of the track. A tiny person, just a colourless figure so far, shades emerging with every step Henderson took. He soon realised they were walking towards each other and he had a sudden urge to start running to meet this figure, a similar urge to the one that had forced him out of the windmill earlier. It was a girl, a woman, her longish hair was clear now, and his heart skipped a beat as he increased his pace, the figure overwhelmingly familiar. He looked back at the windmill fleetingly, a dot on the horizon, then towards this woman, smiling, puffing. He stumbled on a rut, snapping his ankle, but he recovered instantly pulling his hands from his pockets, and his arms started to rise and open in greeting before he realised what he was doing and was able to take control of them.

Alice waved at Henderson, wondering whether he was looking for her.

'Alice,' Henderson said.

And by the tone of his voice she knew right away that Henderson hadn't been looking for her. 'Hello Henderson. You're a long way from the windmill.' And she wondered whether her own voice betrayed her disappointment.

'Yes, yes. I had an urge to see a bit more before we go back. I don't think I walked along this embankment before. The others are all still asleep. At least they were. Have you,' he swallowed, 'have you been up long?'

'Oh, I couldn't sleep. Yes. I've been miles. If you carry on here,' she pointed behind her, 'you eventually come to another staithe.'

'I suppose I've gone far enough. I'll walk back with you. The others are probably wondering where we are.'

'Do you think so?'

They set off together, the sun lifting in front of them and a heavy silence growing between them that they both found uncomfortable. Still neither spoke for many minutes, both pretending to be distracted by the marshes, birds feeding, or the distant movement of sun on dunes or pasture. Henderson wondering whether he could discern the movement of time on a timeless place.

'Perhaps we can get off this path and cut across that field?' Alice suddenly said.

'No,' said Henderson, stiffly. 'I think we're better continuing along here. Those fields can get awfully boggy. Better to go back the way we came.'

And the silence fell on them again, heavier and more awkwardly. Then Alice said, 'Why did you come back? Did something terrible happen to you here?'

Henderson coughed. He didn't answer for some time, indeed Alice didn't think he was going to answer at all. 'Yes, yes it did. You see it was my fault. Well my doing if you like, and for ages I didn't think I could live with myself because of it. But I feel better about it now. I think I've come to terms with it. At least I feel I can carry on. Anyway I feel that's the least I can do for Laura and Tristram.'

'Does Laura know what happened?'

'No, I don't think so. I'm sure not. I don't think she needs to know either.' He was becoming more uncomfortable and felt himself blush. 'I dreamt about cherubs last night. I used to have nightmares.' He laughed, remembering the dream more vividly and being swept along hanging onto a cherub's arm, like a fin. 'You said as we were leaving the church yesterday you can't stop running. From what?'

'Oh, I don't know. Something stupid really.' She paused. 'Well it wasn't actually. A game I was playing with my boyfriend went wrong. I couldn't think about it for a long while. He hurt me, terribly.'

'Maybe you should go back and confront him?'

'No, I don't think so. I don't think that would be necessary.'

'So are you going to keep running?'

'Well I came back this morning. That's something I can tell you.'

Silence resumed, but it wasn't awkward this time, or heavy. They both felt they didn't need to say anything further, both understanding each other in the way they wanted to. The windmill grew taller and its useless sails larger and more friendly, and soon they were traversing the tussocky pasture, clumps of plants entangling their feet, both eager to get back, more eager than either could have imagined a day ago, pulling their feet through the clumps with an uncanny strength. Carey spotted them from her bedroom window, and told Francis, but by the time he came to the window they'd slipped into the windmill, which was stirring, Alice to her room and Henderson to the kitchen where he had a pretty good idea he'd find Laura and Tristram breakfasting.

*　　*　　*

'Carey, you can't, you can't.' Laura was suddenly filled with panic, felt her breakfast move up in her stomach and her temples ache. She couldn't have the group splitting up now, they'd nearly made it, they had to stay together. She had to see to it. 'Look, it's the most beautiful day. Henderson says there's a lovely beach nearby. You can drive practically all the way there.'

'I want to go back to the sea,' Tristram said.

'You're mad, Carey. You can't go. What does Francis think?'

'I want to go back to the sea,' Tristram repeated, bumping into his mother's leg.

'He hates bank holiday traffic. It's already late.' She looked at her watch. 'God it's getting on for lunchtime. You go to the beach and we'll do some tidying before we leave.'

'Why don't you come for a bit? You don't have to stay all day.'

'Mummy, I want—'

'Oh, shut up Tristram.'

'No, really Laura, sweetheart, we are going to go.'

'I think you're being ridiculous. I really do.'

'Well, Francis and I have a few things to sort out. It would be better for everyone if we left.' She couldn't look Laura in the eye, or let her look into hers. She felt she couldn't explain to her about her and Francis, or Alice and Henderson, or the fact she felt she was losing Laura, none of it made sense, and it wasn't like her to be so irrational.

'I'm sorry.'

'Are you off?' Henderson said, suddenly beside Carey. 'I do hope not.'

'Yes, we have to get back.' Tristram was still hovering nearby and Carey reached out and started to ruffle his hair, wanting to hold on to him tight.

'Oh, that is a shame. We thought we'd go to this

beach nearby. There's a wonderful wreck on a sand-bank which you can walk to across a channel when the tide's out. Tristram will love it. And I bet there'll be no birdwatchers there.'

'You didn't tell me anything about having to cross a channel,' Laura said.

'Well you certainly don't want me around to drown you all,' Carey said. 'Besides they'll be quite enough of you as it is.' She looked at Henderson with pure hatred. 'You've still got Alice, don't forget.' She didn't know what she had left.

'I'm sure you could change your mind,' Henderson said. But he knew Carey wouldn't, and he was pleased. He didn't want her and Francis about anymore, he didn't want Alice about for that matter. He didn't need them. He just wanted to be with Laura and Tristram. He felt he had so much catching up to do. He didn't want anyone else getting in the way. He bent down to Tristram. 'I'm going to take you to see the wreck. How about that?' He looked at his watch. 'The tide will be out and we should have plenty of time there.' He began to imagine the mystery and intrigue a child would see surrounding something like the wreck. Ho hum, he said to himself.

'But I want to go swimming. I want to go to the sea,' Tristram said.

'That's where we're going, silly,' Henderson said, laughing. 'Say goodbye to Carey. She's not coming.'

'Just don't forget his armbands,' Carey said.

The birdwatcher unfolded the map. He didn't think it was much of a map, hand drawn, handwritten. He could barely make sense of it. But someone had told him it was the best map around and full of secret footpaths and ways across the marshes and sandbanks that not many people knew about. I just don't want to see any people today, he thought. Please don't let there be any about. He found a route that he could take, passing through grazing land, freshwater marsh, saltmarsh, dunes, tidal flats, and onto a shingle ridge out near an old wreck you could only reach at low tide. He thought he'd have as good a chance of seeing anything going that way, than if he went back to the reserve. They'd be late terns on the shingle ridge, he could at least be sure of that. Besides, he thought, it would be better to go somewhere he hadn't been before. It was his last day. He checked his tide table and hurried into his gear, sorting out his binoculars and stands and notepads filling up nicely. He'd have time. He'd just have time.

Francis passed Alice on the stairs, climbing rapidly, her perfume, he hadn't noticed her wearing it before, lingering with him. 'Bye,' he said, not waiting for a reply. He carried on up, past her bedroom, trying to see through the crack in the door but not being able to. He came to the sitting-room. Books were strewn all over the place, a torn piece of paper or something on the table. But he didn't pay much attention to the mess, finding the ladder and rushing up it. He pushed the trap-door open and pulled himself into the bare room. He shut the trap-door and thought, I could hide from Carey here. He stood still for a few moments wondering what the silence would be like, the peace, life without her. He looked up and saw the wasting bits of machinery and the last ladder leading to the small platform. He climbed carefully here, feeling something pulling him back. He reached the platform, crawled onto it and saw sunlight framing the small door. He shook the handle, but the door wouldn't open. He then moved himself around so he would be able to give it a good kick. The platform creaked under him, worse than that, a sharp splitting, tearing sound. He grabbed hold of the beam just above, wondering whether the platform would give way. He kicked the door and it swung open, he thumped into the side of the cap and the platform tipped down to the right a few degrees with a comically slow groaning sound. He edged himself out backwards onto the fanstage, still feeling something pulling him back, as if he were attached to a piece of elastic that was nearing the end of its elasticity. He felt the sun on his back and the terrible warmth and stillness of the day. Gulls swooping into that stillness, cracking it. He heard people on the gravel below, car doors opening. He looked above him, the fantail electric white against the blue sky. He held onto the side rail and pulled himself up, clasping. He moved out and had a view of them getting into the car: Henderson and Laura and Tristram and Alice. Carey standing close by. He didn't wave or shout but watched the car move away from Carey, Carey waving, Laura waving back from the car, making Tristram wave too. His small hand just visible as the car pulled onto the coast road then swept away. The car appearing now and then, further and further along the road, the sun reflecting on it as if on a mirror. A flickering of hope beside the filling marshes.

Gorleston

HENRY SUTTON

Dilapidated beach huts, a crumbling pier, neat bunga-lows: Gorleston on the Norfolk coast looks like many a quiet seaside town that has seen better days. As a retired widower, Percy leads an uneventful existence there – until he meets Queenie, a flame-haired, flirtatious widow, who has no intention of behaving her age. She becomes his obsesssion, lacing his days with excitement and passion, and gleeful flouting of convention. But as Percy grows suspicious of Queenie's elusive behaviour and enigmatic past, he is also forced to look into the shadows of his own life.

'In this odd, touching, beautifully written first novel he lays out for us with rare sympathy the frightening and exhilarating fact that age does not necessarily bring serenity. Or even respectability'
The Times

'A wildly original, funny and affectionate first novel'
Elspeth Barker

'A small gem of a book'
Marie Claire

'A finely judged first novel . . . [a] wonderfully inventive and moving finale'
The Sunday Times

'Wry and touching . . . Sutton brings the affectionate tone of Alan Bennett to his depiction of the world of the retired and to the dowdy, humble Percy'
The Times Literary Supplement

∫

SCEPTRE

Trick of the Light
JILL DAWSON

Mick, Rita and their small daughter abandon London's East End for a broken-down cabin in a remote corner of Washington State. Rita soon adjusts and revels in the mountainous landscape, despite her fear of its wildlife – but what she cannot admit is her fear of Mick's violent temper. In this riveting novel, Jill Dawson portrays a father destroyed by his own childhood and a young mother struggling to protect her child.

'A moving, beautifully written tale, taut with narrative tension and memorable for its superb descriptions of landscape and a multitude of deft touches that always seem just right. Above all, this is a genuinely romantic novel, a double love story of love that is raw and raunchy as well as romantic'
The Times

'A taut, compelling story that quells any easy theories about abusive relationships'
The Times Literary Supplement

'Dawson has demonstrated that she can write with genuine passion and power'
Daily Telegraph

SCEPTRE

Sam Golod
SOPHIA CRESWELL

In post-Communist St Petersburg, Natalie, a young English teacher, joins the food queues and tries to adjust to a strange new place. Introduced to a group of illegally resident artists and seduced by the charms of one of its leaders, Pyotr, she starts to feel at home. But gradually she begins to realise the extent of Pyotr's links with the city's drug-running Mafyosi, and how far she is out of her depth. In this compelling debut, the anarchic underbelly of modern Russia is captured in a tense and moving tale.

'An assured and well-crafted first novel'
The Times

'An atmosphere of chaos in post-Communist Russia is brilliantly created as Natalie slowly realises she's way out of her depth'
Company

'A rich portrayal of contemporary life in Russia'
Scotland on Sunday

'A stunning debut'
Northern Woman

SCEPTRE